Simon Berington

The adventures of Sig. Gaudentio di Lucca

Simon Berington

The adventures of Sig. Gaudentio di Lucca

ISBN/EAN: 9783337137960

Printed in Europe, USA, Canada, Australia, Japan

Cover: Foto ©Andreas Hilbeck / pixelio.de

More available books at **www.hansebooks.com**

THE

PUBLISHER

TO THE

READER.

IT is very natural to think the reader would willingly be apprifed of two things relating to thefe Memoirs: Firft, how this curious manufcript came to light, confidering the dark and deep fecrecy with which all things are tranfacted in the inquifition. Secondly, how it came into the tranflator's hands. To fatisfy fuch a commendable curiofity, he is to be informed, That the manufcript was fent by the fecretary of the inquifition at Bologna to the learned Sig. Rhedi, keeper of the library of S. Mark at Venice, his intimate friend and correfpondent, with the whole account how the author was taken up, and fecured in the inquifition, as the letter of the fecretary to the fame Signor Rhedi will fhew: which letter, as it contains a great many curious particulars in the examination of the criminal, (for he was taken up as fuch, though nothing very material was proved againft him; for which reafon, he

A 2 received

received a more favorable treatment than
is generally believed to be cuftomary in
that dreadful tribunal) ; fo it difcovers no
indirect practices of the inquifition, but,
on the contrary, fhews they proceed with
a great deal of circumfpection within their
walls, though all things are involved in
impenetrable darknefs to thofe without.
Befide, the fucceffion of new popes, and,
generally fpeaking, the change of other
officers attending it, might make them be
lefs upon their guard, as the fecretary
feems to hint in his letter. Neither is
there any thing that might do him any
harm, in cafe he were difcovered ; efpecially writing to a friend of his own com-
munion, and a prieft, as Signor Rhedi was;
which is likewife feen by the letter.

As to the fecond quære, the manufcript
came into the publifher's hands, by the
means of the fame Signor Rhedi, who
is an honor to his church, profeffion, and
country, and one of the moft learned and
polite men in the world. He is not fo bigotted to his religion or profeffion, as to
fhun the company of the *heretical tramontani*, a title the Indians generally give us ;
but loves and efteems a learned man,
though of a different perfuafion. One reafon for this may be, that he breathes a
freer air at Venice, than they do in the
other parts of Italy. The inquifition has
                                    nothing

nothing to do in the Venetian territories. Though they are Roman Catholics, the state admits of no tribunal independant of itself. Besides, as they are a trading people, their commerce obliges them to be civil to persons of all persuasions, especially strangers. But of all others they seem to have the greatest respect for the English; whether it be on account of their power at sea, or their frankness in spending their money, so many of the English nobility and gentry travelling that way; or from the candour and sincerity of our nature, so opposite to the Italians, and therefore the more valued by them: be that as it will, the publisher, who had several, times made the tour of Italy, was not only intimately acquainted, but had contracted a particular friendship with Signor Rhedi, as well on account of their mutual inclinations for learning and anti-quity, as for several reciprocal obligations passing between them. The last time he was at Venice, which was in company of a person of the first rank, who liked the place as well as he did, he staid there upwards of fifteen months; during which time he had the opportunity of enjoying the conversation of his learned friend, with as much liberty, as if he had been of the same persuasion. But the present of a gold repeating watch, with some other of

A 3   ques

our Englifh curiofities, fo won his heart,
that one day being together in the great
library, he unlocks a little grate where he
kept his rarities, and turning to me with a
fmile, Signor Inglefe, fays he, holding a
manufcript in his hand, here is fuch a curiofity, as I am fure, you never faw, and
perhaps never heard of : it is the life of a
perfon who is now in the inquifition at Bologna, taken from his own confeffion before the inquifitors ; with the account of
a country in the heart of the vaft deferts of
Africa, whofe inhabitants have lived unknown to all the world upwards of 3000
years, and inacceffible to all the world,
but by the way he was carried thither.
The inquifitors are fo far perfuaded of the
truth of it, that they have promifed him
his liberty, if he will undertake to conduct fome miffionaries the fame way, to
preach the gofpel to a numerous people,
who by his account have the greateft knowledge of natural religion and polity of any
Heathen nation yet known, even beyond
the Chinefe. For my own part, I could
fcarce have believed it, had not the fecretary of the fame inquifition, who, you
may be fure, by his poft, is not a man to
be impofed upon, affured me of the
truth of it : nay, that he himfelf was
prefent at his feizure and examination, and
fent me a copy of his life, which he was
ordered

ordered to give in by the inquifitors; with
the whole account of the occafion and
manner of his feizure. It feems he had lived fome time in Bologna in quality of a
phyfician, under the name of *Signor Gau-*
dentio di Lucca, which he fays is his true
name, and confirms it by the place of his
birth, the names of his parents, time of
his captivity, &c. He had dropped fome
words of feveral ftrange fecrets he was mafter of, with mutterings of an unknown
nation, religion, and cuftoms, quite new
to the Italian ears; for which reafon the
inquifition thought fit to feize him, and,
by ways and means made ufe of in that tribunal, obliged him to give. an account of
his whole life, which is the moft furprifing
I ever read. Here is the fecretary's letter,
giving a fuccinct account of the whole affair. I have added, continued he, fome
critical remarks in proper places, to fhew
that this account is not fo incredible as it
may appear at firft fight, and that it agrees
with fome hints left us in the remains of
ancient hiftory. Befides, the man ftands
to the truth of it with a ftedfaftnefs that is
furprifing. He is a perfon of a very handfome prefence, well read, good fenfe, and,
as it appears to the inquifitors, (who are
nice judges), of feemingly good morals.
He profeffes himfelf a zealous Roman Catholic, and that he always was fo: for
which

which reafon, the inquifitors are more civil
to him than ordinary.   He gives fuch a rational and circumftantial account of his adventures, that I am of the fecretary's opinion, as to the truth of it. But, added he, I
wont foreftal the fatisfaction you will find in
the perufal: fo delivered the manufcript
and the fecretary's letter into the publifher's hands, who running his eyes over it
for fome time, was fo ftruck with the novelty of the thing, that he afked Sig. Rhedi, whether he might not take a copy of it.
He was anfwered, he could not permit the
manufcript to be taken out of the library ;
nor could he, with fafety to himfelf, allow
a ftranger, and of a different religion too,
the liberty of ftaying fo long in the library
by himfelf, as the tranfcribing would take
up.   The publifher faid, he might put what
guards upon him he pleafed, provided he
might but tranfcribe it. No, fays he,
that is inconvenient too ; but I will order
one of my under librarians I can confide
in, to write you out an exact copy, with
the fecretary's letter, and my own remarks,
if you think them worth your notice;
which he did moft faithfully ; generoufly
commanding the tranfcriber, at the fame
time, not to take any thing of me for his
pains.   Thus this curious manufcript came
to hand, to the infinite fatisfaction of the
publifher, and he hopes it will prove no
                                                lefs

less to the readers, in the perusal of it. The character of Signor Gaudentio cannot be called in question ; nor is the publisher a person so little versed in the nature and ways of the Italians, as to be imposed upon. The translation from the Italian is as exact as possible. This is the previous account the publisher thought proper to give of this affair.

N. B. Great part of the matters treated of in these memoirs, being transmitted in a Roman-Catholic country, and among Roman Catholics, the reader must not wonder, if they speak of their religion, as if it were the only true one in the world.

It will not be improper to admonish the reader, not to discredit immediately some of the relations contained in these Memoirs; but to suspend his judgement, 'till he has read Signor Rhedi's remarks ; particularly when he comes to the origin and antiquity of the people the author speaks of. The learned will find in them such a vast knowledge in history, and the most intricate remains of antiquity, as will render them very well worth their notice. The same Signor Rhedi told the publisher, he had inquired into what happened at Venice ; particularly what the author mentions of Monsieur Godart, one of the most improbable parts of his adventures, and found the whole to be just as he relates it.

The

The publisher is satisfied the reader will be extremely sorry, as well as himself, for the loss of some sheets belonging to the middle part of this history. How they came to be lost, he cannot tell ; but he suppoſes, by the incivility of the cuſtomhouſe-officers at Marſeilles ; for they tumbled over his effects at a very rude rate, and while he had an eye on other matters, they either took ſome of the looſe ſheets, or they dropped out in the tumbling ; he was very much troubled, when he came to miſs them in the courſe of the tranſlation.

INTRO-

INTRODUCTION.

Giving an account of the caufes and manner of the feizure of Signor GAUDENTIO DI LUCCA, *and the firft part of his examination.*

In a letter from the Secretary of the INQUISI-TION, *to Signor* RHEDI.

* *S I R*,

T HE prefent turn of † affairs which fills the heads of other people with intrigues of ftate, gives me an opportunity of returning my beft thanks, for the rich prefent you were pleafed to fend to a per-fon who was yours before by the ftricteft ties of gratitude.—The cabinet, with the other curiofities, came fafe to hand, and fhews, that whoever is fo happy, as to ob-lige Signor Rhedi, fows a feed which re-turns a hundred fold.—The poverty of our ‡ profeffion hinders me from being capable

---

* The Italian titles of Illuftriffimo, &c, are left out, as not ufed in our language.

† He either means the death of fome pope, or fome extraordinary crifis in the Romifh œconomy.

‡ The fecretary was a Dominican friar; the Dominicans being maf-ters of the inquifition.

of

of making a fuitable return for your magnificent prefent ; but nothing ought to take from me the defire of exprefling my acknowledgements. In teftimony of it, and to fhew that poverty itfelf may be grateful, I fend you, by the bearer, the account of a man whofe life has filled our inquifitors with wonder and aftonifhment. He has been in the inquifition at this place about two years : we have employed all our engines to find out the truth of what he is, and can find nothing material againft him, unlefs it be the unheard-of account he gives of himfelf. Our firft inquifitor has obliged him to write his own life, with all the particulars, as fuccinctly as poffible, adding threats withal, that, if we find him in a falfe ftory, it fhall be worfe with him. He tells us ftrange ftories of one of the moft beautiful countries in the world, in the very heart of the vaft deferts of Africa, inacceffible to all the world but by one way, which feems as extraordinary as the country it leads to. As you are a perfon of univerfal knowledge in antiquity, and an admirer of curiofities of this nature, I fend you a copy of the manufcript to have your opinion of it ; and to give you as clear a notion of the man as I can, you muft know, that about three years before he was taken up by the inquifition, he took a neat houfe at Bologna in quality of a phyfician, paffing

fing through fome flight examination for
form's fake, and paying his fee as is cuftomary with ftrangers. His name, as he
fays, is *Gaudentjo di Lucca*, originally of
Lucca*, but born in Ragufa†; he is a tall,
handfome, clean-built man, as you fhall
fee in a thoufand, of a very polite addrefs,
and fomething fo very engaging in his af-
pect, as befpeaks your favor at firft fight.
He feems to be near fifty; he is a man of
good fenfe and fine difcourfe, though his
accent is not pure Italian, from his living,
as he fays, fo long in foreign countries.
He fpeaks almoft all the oriental languages,
and has a very competent fhare of other
parts of learning, as well as that of his profeffion. We fent to Ragufa and Lucca to
inquire about him, but could not get the
leaft information of his being known in
thofe places. The reafon of which he has
given in his life, as you will fee; only at
Ragufa, fome people remembered there
had been a merchant of that name, about
five and twenty or thirty years ago, who
was either loft, or taken by pirates, and
never heard of more.

The inquifition, as you know, fir, has
eyes every where, efpecially on ftrangers;
we kept an eye upon him from his firft fettling at Bologna: but as we proceed with

* A little republic in Italy.
† A republic in Dalmatia, and tributary to the Turks.

B   juftice

juflice as well as caution, wc could not difcover any fufficient reafon to take him up.
His life was as regular as that of others of
his profeffion, which he did not follow very
clofely, but only for form's fake, being chiefly confulted at his own houfe, on account
of fome extraordinary fecrets he pretended
to be mafter of, without making any vifits
but to ladies, with whom he grew in prodigious requeft. They faid he had a fweetnefs and eafe in converfation, that was almoft bewitching. This unaccountable fondnefs of the ladies gave us the firft fufpicion,
leaft he fhould inftill fome ill notions into
that fex, fo credulous where they are fond,
and fo incredulous where they diflike. He
profeffed himfelf a Roman Catholic ; feemed to have a competent knowledge, and
even veneration, confidering he was a phyfician, for our holy myfteries : fo we had
nothing againft him on that account. We
could not find that he wanted for money,
though he lived rather genteelly than magnificently : we found on feveral occafions,
that money, the idol of other people, was
the leaft of his care ; and that he had fome
fecret fprings we could not fathom. His
houfe was but decently, though completely,
furnifhed for one of his rank ; he kept two
fervants in livery and a valet de chambre ;
who, being of his town, knew no more of
him than we did. There was an elderly lady

dy we thought had been his wife, but it
proved fhe was not; a foreigner, for whom
he feemed to have a great refpect, and her
maid a foreigner alfo; and an elderly maid
fervant of the town. We have them all fecured in the inquifition, though he does
not know it. The lady has the remains of
a wonderful fine face, and an air of quality ;
fhe fpeaks a broken Italian, fo that we can
get very little out of her, but what agrees
with his account. I am confident you will
rather be pleafed with thefe particulars than
think them tedious. There is fomething fo
extraordinary in the man, I ought not to
omit the leaft circumftance. We had feveral
confultations about him in our inquifition,
as well as our Leiger intelligences, but could
difcover nothing of moment. We examined what intercourfe he had in other parts,
by ordering the poftmafter to fend us all his
letters, which we could eafily open, and feal
up again with the greateft nicety. But we
found he had only two correfpondents, one
poffeffed of a moderate income of about
four thoufand crowns in the bank of Genoa; the other a lady of your city of Venice, whom we difcovered to be a celebrated courtezan, who fubfcribes herfelf *Favilla*. We find by her laft letter, that he had
given her very good advice, and perfuaded
her to become a penitent: you will oblige
us if you will inquire what fhe is. Amorous

intrigues

intrigues not falling under our cognifance,
we let him alone for fome time, having a
perfon under our examination on fufpicion
of being a Jew in mafquerade, and a fpy
from the Grand Signor, who kept us employed for fome time. Befides, the good advice he gave the courtezan, and he being
paft his prime, made us lefs fufpicious of the
ladies ; we fuppofed they had recourfe to
him, on account of fome female infirmities. Though the young ladies were moft
fond of him, his behaviour to them was
more an endearing fweetnefs and courtefy,
than love, with very little figns, at leaft he
had the addrefs to conceal them, of more
kindnefs for one than another. In fine, perfons of the beft rank, of both fexes, began
to have a prodigious liking for his company; he ftole upon them infenfibly. As he
increafed in this good opinion, he opened
himfelf with greater freedom ; he made no
fhew at all at firft, more than a fine prefence and a polite addrefs : but, after further acquaintance, they difcovered he was
mafter of moft fciences, and fhewed a fuperior genius in any thing they could difcourfe of. We employed proper perfons to
infinuate themfelves into his good liking,
and confult him as a friend on feveral nice
points ; but he had fuch a prefence of mind,
yet appeared, fo unconftrained in his difcourfe, that they owned themfelves novices

in

in comparifon to him. If they talked of
politics, he faid very judicioufly, it was not
for men of his rank, to meddle with affairs
of ftate, or examine what perfons did in
the cabinet. If of religion, he feemed to
underftand it very well for one of his profeffion ; fo that nothing came from him but
what was confonant to the Catholic faith ;
exprefling on all occafions a great deference
for the authority of the church. But ftill
the more fagacious were perfuaded, fomething more than ordinary lay hid under
that fpecious cover. At length, talking one
day with fome of our fpies about the cuftoms of foreign countries, he faid, he
had met with a nation in one of the re-
moteft parts of the world, who, though
they were Heathens, had more knowledge
of the law of nature, and common morality, than the moft civilifed Chriftians. This
was immediately carried to us, and explained as a reflection on the Chriftian religion.
Another time, as he had a great knowledge
in phylofophy, he dropt fome words as if
he had fome fkill in judiciary aftrology ;
which you know, fir, is a capital crime
with us. We were as good as refolved to
feize him, when we were determined to it
by the following accident. Two of the
moft beautiful women in all Bologna had
fallen in love with him, either on account
of the handfomenefs of his perfon, or, by

a.

a whimficalnefs peculiar to fome women, becaufe he was a ftranger, or thinking he might keep their fecrets better under the cloak of being a phyfician ; or, in fine, drawn in by fome love potion or other, we cannot tell ; but the matter grew to fuch a height, that on his fhewing more diftin-guifhing favor to one of them, as it is natural for our women to be violent in their jealoufy, as well as love, the other, to be revenged, faid he had bewitched her ; which fhe was fure of for that, fince the very firft time fhe faw him, fhe thought there was fomething more in him, than ever fhe faw in any man in her life. Befides, fhe faid, fhe had often found him drawing circles and figures on paper, which to her looked like conjuration. Her friends immediately informed our fathers of it ; fo we refolved to feize him, if it were but to find out his fecrets, and fee what the man was. There was another reafon induced us to it, which the world will hardly believe, though it is matter of fact : that is, we were afraid, the man would be affaffinated by fome fecret means or other, for being fo great with our ladies ; fo, to fave his life, and not lofe the difcoveries we expect from him, it was determined he fhould be feized immediately. Accordingly, I was deputed, with three under-officers, to do the bufinefs, but with all
. the

the caution and fecrecy ufual in fuch cafes.
It was done about midnight, when we had
watched one of the two ladies he favored
moft, into his houfe. We went in a clofe
coach, and myfelf and one of the officers-
ftopping at the door, as foon as the fervant
opened it, ftepped in, telling him what we
were, and charging him, at his peril, not
to make the leaft noife. The fervants being Italians, and knowing the confequence
of the leaft refiftance, ftood as mute as fifh-
es. We immediately went into the inner
parlour, and, contrary to our expectation,
found our gentleman, the young lady
with her governante, and the elderly lady
that belonged to him, fitting very decently
at an elegant collation of fruits and fweet-
meats, brought, as we fuppofed, by the fair
lady as a prefent. At our firft appearance,
he feemed more furprifed than terrified ; as
we make no ceremonies in thofe cafes, we
told him our errand, and commanded him
to come along with us without the leaft refiftance; or elfe it fhould be worfe for him.
Then we turned to the young lady, whofe
friends and perfon we knew, and told her
we wondered to find her in fuch company
at fuch unfeafonable hours ; but, on account
of her friends, would not meddle with her,
but bid her for her own fake, as fhe ten-
dered her life and honor, never to take the
leaft notice of the affair. She trembling,
and

and ready to faint away, after fome hefita-
tion, was able to fay, that fhe was come to
confult about her health ; that fhe brought
her governante along with her to take off
all fufpicion, and as fhe was miftrefs of herfelf and fortune, it was not unufal for perfons of her rank to be out at that time,
confidering the heat of the feafon. She had
fcarce pronounced thefe words, when fhe
fell directly into a fwoon. Her governante
having things proper for fuch occafions, revived and comforted her as well as fhe could.
But when we were going to take the gentleman along with us, the elderly lady, to
whom we fuppofe he had told his misfortune, inftead of falling into fits, flew at us
like a tygrefs, with a fury I never faw in
any human creature in my life ; tearing at
us with her nails and teeth, as if fhe had
been in the moft raging madnefs. We, not
accuftomed to refiftance, confidering our
character and cloth, and fhe a woman,
were almoft motionlefs, when the fervants
at the noife came up. We commanded
them, in the name of the inquifition, to
feize her : the gentleman interpofed in our
favour, faying fome words to her in an unknown language, which he affured us,
were to beg her to be pacified, as fhe ten-
dered his life as well as her own ; then the
violence of her paffion turned another way,
and threw her into the ftrongeft convul-
fions

fions I ever faw. By this time the other two officers were come up, wondering at our delay, and to find refiftance againft the officers of the inquifition. The gentleman, with a becoming fubmiffion, rather than fear, yielded himfelf a prifoner, and begged us to pardon the fudden tranfports of a perfon unacquainted with our cuftoms; whofe life in fome manner depended on his. That fhe was a Perfian lady of quality, brought into this country by great misfortunes, who had once faved his life, as he had been afterwards inftrumental in faving hers. That fhe was difpofed to turn Chriftian, with intention after fome time to end her days in a convent. That for his own part, relying on his innocence, he readily fubmitted to our authority, and offered himfelf to be carried where ever we pleafed; he uttered all this with an air of conftancy that was furprifing. We immediately took him into the coach, leaving two of the officers with the elderly lady, and commanding them and the gentleman's fervants not to ftir out of the room till further orders. As foon as we arrived at the inquifition, we lodged him in a handfome ftrong room; not fo much like a criminal, as like a perfon for whom we had fome refpect. There we left him to his own thoughts, and returned to his houfe to feize the elderly lady and his papers,

having

having difmiffed the young lady and her governante before. I forgot to tell you, that Signor Gaudentio, by our permiffion, had fpoke to the elderly lady coming out of her fits in Italian, (for we would not let him fpeak to her in the unknown language, for fear of a combination), and with much pains made her underftand, that he begged her, by all that was dear, to fubmit to whatever we fhould injoin her ; affuring her by that means all would be well for her fafety and his own : which laft words feemed to give fome calm to her tempeftuous fpirits. You may believe, fir, we were much furprifed at the novelty of the thing, and the account he gave of her quality. But as we often meet with falfe ftories in our employment, that did not hinder us from doing our duty. So I took her by the hand with a great deal of refpect, and put her into the coach between myfelf and my companion ; not without apprehenfions of fome extravagant follies, confidering the violence of her temper. But fhe continued pretty fedate, only feemed to be overwhelmed with grief ; we brought her to the inquifition, and lodged her in a very handfome apartment feparate from the convent, on account of her fex ; with two waiting women to attend her with all refpect, till we were better apprifed of the truth of her quality. This obliged me to

tak

take another journey to Signor Gaudentio's houfe, to fecure his papers, with
whatever elfe might contribute to further
our difcovery. I found all things in the
fame order I left them; but being extremely fatigued, I fat down to the elegant
collation that was left, and, after a fmall
repaft, went to bed in his houfe, to have
the morning before us for fecuring his effects. I fealed up all the papers I could
find, to examine them at more leifure,
took an inventory of all the moveables,
that they might be reftored to him in cafe
he were found innocent; and fent for a
proper officer to remain in the houfe, who
was to be refponfible for every thing.
There were two little cabinets of curious
workmanfhip; one of them, as it appeared, belonged to him, the other to the
ftrange lady; but being full of intricate
drawers or tills, we took them both along
with us. Thefe and the papers we delivered to the head inquifitors, not being
willing to proceed in either of their exami-
nations, till we had got all the light we
could, to find out the truth, for that was
all our aim; then we could tell what
courfe to take with them. We placed two
cunning lay brothers, in the nature of fervants, for Signor Gaudentio, who were to
infinuate themfelves into his favour by
their kind offices, compaffionating his mif-
fortunes,

fortunes, and adviſing him to diſcover the whole truth, in the account of his life, quality, profeſſion, opinions, and, in fine, whatever articles he was to be interrogated on, to confeſs ingeniouſly what he knew : as that was the only way to find favour at the hands of the inquiſitors ; that they pardoned almoſt all faults on a ſincere confeſſion, and an aſſurance of amendment. I viſited him myſelf ſeveral times before his examination, and gave him the ſame advice and aſſurance ; he promiſed me faithfully he would, and ſeemed ſo ſteady and confirmed in his own innocence, with ſuch an agreeable, yet ſincere way in his diſcourſe, as really ſurpriſed me, and cauſed me already to be prejudiced in his favour ; adding with a ſmile, that the hiſtory of his life would adminiſter more cauſe of wonder than indignation. Not to be too particular, the chief of the inquiſition, with myſelf along with them, ſet to the ſcrutiny of his papers. We examined them with all the care imaginable, but could find nothing to ground any material accuſation, except ſome imperfect memoirs of the cuſtoms of a country and people unheard of to us, and I believe to all the world beſide, with ſome odd characters, or words, which had no affinity with any language or characters, we ever ſaw. We diſcovered he had a great knowledge in natural philoſophy.

phy, with fome remarks that were very curious. There was a rough draught of a
map of a country, with towns, rivers,
lakes, &c. but no climate marked down.
In fhort, all his papers contained nothing
but fome fmall fketches of philofophy and
phyfic, with fome pieces of poetry of an
uncommon tafte. Neither could we find
any footfteps of judiciary aftrology, or cal-
culations of nativities, of which we had
the greateft fufpicion; only a pair of
globes, a fet of mathematical inftruments,
charts of navigation, forms of unknown
trees and plants, and fuch like things, as
all gentlemen who delight in travelling are
curious to have. There were indeed fome
lines, circles, fegments of circles, which
we fuppofed the informing lady meant;
but looked like an attempt to find out the
longitude, rather than any magical fchemes.
His books were of the fame nature; nothing of herefy that we could fee, but fuch
as belonged to a man of learning. There
were feveral common books of devotion,
fuch as are approved by our church, and
feemed pretty well ufed; by which we
judged him to be really a Catholic, and a
perfon of no bad morals. But as nothing
looks fo like an honeft man as a knave,
this did not take away all our fufpicion.
——When we came to open the cabinets,
in the firft of them, which belonged to
C   him,

him, we found in one of the drawers about
four hundred and fifty Roman crowns,
with other small money, and some foreign
coin along with it, as Turkish sequins
and some we knew nothing of. The sum
not being very extraordinary, we could
conclude nothing from thence. In another drawer we found several precious
stones,⁻ some set, some unset, of a very
great value, so far from being counterfeit,
that we never saw any so brilliant. Besides,
several pieces of native gold, of such finenefs, as nothing with us can come up to
it. In a third, we found a small heap of
medals, most of gold, but of an unknown
stamp and antiquity. There were outland-
ish stones of odd figures enough, which to
others might look like talismans, but we
took them for some out-of-the-way curiofities. In a private drawer in the centre of the
cabinet, there was something wrapt up in a
piece of green silk of wonderful finenefs,
all embroidered with hearts and hands joined together, wrought in gold with prodigious art, and intermixed with different
flowers, unknown in our part of the
world ; in the midst of it was an azure
stone, as large as the palm of one's hand,
set round with rubies of very great value,
on which was most artfully painted in miniature, a woman at length, holding a
little boy in her left hand, the most beautiful

tiful creature that ever eyes beheld; clad
likewife in green filk fpangled with golden
funs: their complexion was fomething
darker than that of our Italian ladies; but
the features, efpecially the woman's, fo
uncommonly beautiful as if fhe had been of
another fpecies. Underneath was ingrav-
ed with a diamond in a modern hand,
Quefto folo. You may be fure, fir, this
raifed our ideas of the man; at firft, we
thought he had the fecret of the philofo-
pher's ftone : but in all his inventory we
could find no implements of that art.
Then we thought he muft have been fome
famous pirate; or one who had robbed the
cabinet of fome great prince, and was come
to live at Bologna in that private manner,
under the difguife of a phyfician. But having been three years in town, if it had
been any European prince, the world
would have had an account of it before
now : fo we concluded that either what he
faid of that unknown country was true, or
that he had robbed fome of the eaftern
princes, and got off clear with his prize.
But the picture of the woman made us in-
cline to think, he had married fome out-
landifh queen, and on her death had retired with his effects. The reft of the drawers were full of natural curiofities of foreign plants, roots, bones of animals,
birds, infects, &c. from whence very like-

ly

ly he took his phyſical ſecrets. The other
cabinet, which belonged to the elderly lady, was very rich, but nothing equal to
the firſt ; there were a great many ſmall
jewels, and ſome very fine pearls, with
bracelets, pendants, and other curious ornaments belonging to women ; and a little
picture of a very handſome man about thirty, nothing like our gentleman, in a warlike dreſs, with a Turkiſh ſcymitar by his
ſide, who by his mien ſeemed to be a man
of note. But we could find nothing that
could give us any knowledge what they
were : ſo that we were at a loſs with all
our ſagacity what to think of the matter,
or to find any juſt cauſe to keep them in
the inquiſition : for though we don't diſcover our motives to other people, we never proceed againſt any one but on very
ſtrong ſuſpicions. On which account we
were reſolved to make his confinement as
eaſy as poſſible, till we could ſee further into the affair. We had thoughts of examining the woman firſt, to get what we
could from her for to interrogate him upon ; but ſhe not underſtanding Italian
enough, we ſent to Venice with our accuſtomed privacy, for ſome of your people,
that trade to the levant, to be our interpre-
ters. In the mean time we reſolved to try
what we could get out of him by his own
confeſſion ; ſo we ſent for him before us.

He

He came into the room with a modeſt un-
concernedneſs, that rather argued wonder
than fear : we had the cabinet and jewels all
before us, ſhewed them to him all together,
with the inventory of his goods, aſſuring
him they ſhould be forthcoming, in caſe
we were appriſed of his innocence; but
withal adviſing him, as well as commanding him to confeſs the truth, and then not
a hair of his head ſhould be touched. But
if ever we caught him in a falſe ſtory, all
ſhould be confiſcated, and he never ſee ſun
or moon more. He aſſured us with great
reſpect, he would own the truth to every
thing we ſhould interrogate him about, in
an accent that would have perſuaded any
one of his ſincerity, humbly deſiring to
know what accuſations we had againſt him.
We anſwered, that was not the method of
the inquiſition ; but that he ſhould anſwer
directly to our interrogatories. As the holy office chiefly concerns itſelf about religion, we aſked him firſt, what religion he
was of. The reaſon of this was, becauſe,
though he profeſſed himſelf a Catholic, we
were to keep up the forms : neither did
we know but that he might be ſome Jew
or Turkiſh ſpy in maſquerade : then his
name; place of his birth ; where he was
educated ; how he came by thoſe jewels ;
what was the occaſion of his ſettling at Bologna ; who that elderly lady was ; in fine,

every thing in general and particular we
could think of at firft, the better to compare his anfwers afterwards. He told us,
he was a Catholic bred and born; always
profeffed himfelf fuch; and in that faith
would live and die, let what would happen
to him. He explained himfelf on the chief
heads, to fhew that he was well inftructed
in his religion : he appealed to all the inquiries we could make, whether he had
not behaved as a Catholic on all occafions;
naming a Capuchin in the town, who was
his father confeffor; to whom, he faid, he
gave leave to declare all he knew on that
head. As to his name, he faid, his true
name was *Gaudentio di Lucca*, though born
at Ragufa. That his father was a merchant
trading to the Levant; which employment
he defigned to follow himfelf; but in his
firft voyage was taken by an Algerine pirate, who carried him a flave to Grand Cairo, and fold him to a merchant, of what
country nobody knew; which merchant
took him along with him, through the vaft
deferts of Africa, by a way he would defcribe to us if we required it, till he came
to a country, perhaps the moft civilized
and polite in the whole univerfe. In that
country he lived near five and twenty
years, till on the death of his wife, and his
only furviving fon, whofe pictures were in
that cabinet, the melancholy difafter made
him

him induce his father-in-law, who was the
merchant that had first bought him, to
take another journey to Grand Cairo, from
whence he might be able to return to his
native country. This the merchant (for
he paffed for fuch, though he was a great
ruler in his own country) complied with :
but happening to come thither when the
plague raged in the city, his father-in-law
and feveral of his attendants died of it ;
leaving him heir to moft of his effects, and
part of the jewels we faw before us. That
being now entirely at liberty, he returned
in a French fhip trading from Marfeilles to
the Levant, the mafter's name *Francois Xa-
vier Godart*, who by agreement was to land
him at Venice; but touching at Candy,
they accidentally faved the life of that elderly lady, and brought her off along with
them, for which they were perfued by two
Turkifh veffels, and carried prifoners to
Conftantinople, but releafed by the order of
the Sultanefs mother. That Monfieur Godart was well known at Venice; particularly by Signor Corridani, an eminent merchant there, who could affure us of the
truth of what he faid. That, in fine, having ftaid fome time at Venice, to fee the
curiofities and the carnival, an affair relating to the young lady we faw with him,
when he was feized, and the love he had
for learning, Bologna being a famous univerfity,

verfity, induced him to fettle there, where
he prefumed we had been very well informed of his behaviour ever fince.   This, faid
he, is the moft fuccinct account I can
give to your Reverences, on the interrogatories you have propofed to me ; though
my life has been chequered with fuch a variety of incidents, as would take a great
deal of time to defcend to particulars.
We looked at one another with fome furprife at this ftrange account, which he delivered with fuch an air of fteadinefs, as
fcarce left any room to doubt of the truth
of it.   However, our fuperior turning to
him, faid, Signor Gaudentio; we neither
believe nor difbelieve what you tell us ;
as we condemn no man without a full con-
viction of his crime, fo we are not to be
impofed upon by the accounts people may
give of themfelves. What is here before
us, fhews there is fomething extraordinary
in the cafe. If we find you to be an im-
poftor, you fhall fuffer as fuch ; in the
mean time, till we can be better informed, we injoin you to give in your whole
life, with all occurrences, except your private fins, if you have any, in writing ;
which you fhall read to us, and be crofs-
examined, as we think proper. It will
concern you therefore to be very exact, for
nothing will pafs here but innocence, or a
fincere repentance.

                                This,

This, fir, is the manufcript I fend you, given in by himfelf as ordered ; with the inquifitors interrogatories as we examined it, article by article. Which interrogatories I have inferted as they were propofed, with a further account at the end, for the better clearing of the whole. We beg you to inform yourfelf of the facts, which his memoirs fay happened to him at Venice, particularly about Monfieur Godart. Befides, fir, you that can trace all the branches of ancient hiftory to the fountainhead, are able to form a better judgment of the probability of his relation. He is ftill in the inquifition, and offers himfelf to conduct fome of our miffionaries, to preach the gofpel to thofe unknown people. The length of this only gives me leave to affure you, that I am, with the greateft efteem imaginable.

SIR, &c.

F. ALISIO DE ST IVORIO.

Bologna, July 29, 1721.

T H E

THE

ADVENTURES

OF

SIG. GAUDENTIO DI LUCCA.

I Should be infenfible, Reverend Fathers, if I were not highly concerned to find myfelf under any accufation before this holy tribunal, which I revere with all the powers of my foul : but efpecially if your Reverences fhould harbour any finifter opinion of my religion ; for I was born and bred up in the bofom of the moft holy Catholic church, as well as my parents before me ; in the defence of which my anceftors fpent part of their blood, againft the infidels, and enemies of our faith ; and for which faith I am ready to lay down my life. But I am as yet a ftranger to your Reverences, and on feveral accounts may be liable to fufpicion. Wherefore I blame not the juftice of your proceedings, but rather extol your goodnefs in allowing me the liberty to clear myfelf, by a true and fincere declaration of my whole life, wherein, I own, have happened feveral

aftonifhing

aftonifhing and almoft incredible occurrences; all which I fhall lay before your Reverences, acording to the commands impofed
on me, with the utmoft candour and fincerity.

My name is *Gaudentio di Lucca:* I was
fo called, becaufe my ancefters were faid to
be originally of that place; though they
had been fettled for fome time at Ragufa,
where I was born : both which places are
not fo far off, but they may be very well
known to your Reverences. My father's
name was *Gafparino di Lucca,* heretofore
a merchant of fome note in thofe parts ;
my mother was a Corfican lady, reported to
be defcended from thofe who had been the
chief perfonages in that ifland. My grand-
father was likewife a merchant: but my
great-grandfather, Bernandino di Lucca,
was a foldier, and captain of the great Venerio's own galley*, who was general for
the Venetians in the famous battle of Lepanto againft the Turks. We had a tradition in our family, that he was Venerio's
fon by a Grecian lady of great quality,
fome fay defcended from the Paleologi, who
had been emperors of Conftantinople. But
fhe dying in childbed, and they having been
only privately married, Venerio bred him
up as the fon of a friend of his who was

* This part of the account is certainly true; there was fuch a captain in the lift of the officers in that famous battle.

killed

killed in the wars.   That famous battle, in
which the Chriftians and Venerio got fo
great renown againft the Turks, inftead
- of raifing my great-grandfather's fortune,
was the occafion of his retiring from the
wars, and turning merchant.   The reafon
was this : Venerio the Venetian admiral had
caufed a Spanifh captain to be hung up at
the yard-arm for mutiny*; which fevere
difcipline fo difpleafed Don John of Auftria, generaliffimo of the whole fleet, that,
after the battle, the Venetians, to appeafe
Don John, and not to be deprived of the
fuccours of the Spaniards againft the Turks,
were forced to facrifice Venerio's honour
to the refentment of the Spaniards, and
put him out of commiffion†.   After this

* It is likewife true, that there was fuch a quarrel between Don
John of Auftria, the generaliffimo, and Venerio admiral of the Venetian galleys ; which had like to have put the whole Chriftian fleet at
variance together, before the battle, and ruined the hopes of all Chrif
tendom.   The occafion was as he relates it: Don John, as generaliffimo, viewing the whole fleet before the fight, and finding the Venetian
galleys too thinly manned, ordered four thoufand Spaniards to be put on
board the faid galleys.   But one Mutio Tortona, a Spanifh captain, proving mutinous, after a great many injurious words, came to blows with
the captain of the Venetian galley where he was ; upon which the
whole fleet fell to it.   Venerio, hearing the uproar, fent his own captain
to fee what was the matter ; but the proud Spaniards treated him no
better than they did the reft ; fo that Venerio himfelf was forced to
come to appeafe them ; but feeing the Spanifh captain perfift in his mutinous temper, and the affront he had put upon his captain, who was
reported to be his fon, ordered Tortona and his enfign to be hung at the
yard-arm.   At this all the Spaniards in the fleet were up in arms, and
threatened to cut the Venetians to pieces ; but, by the interpofition of
the other generals, the matter was made up till after the fight : when
Venerio, who had behaved with incomparable valour, and, according to
Don John's own confeffion, was the chief occafion of the victory, to
appeafe the haughty Spaniard, had his commiffion taken from him, and
was recalled by the fenate.
† It was Fufcarini, who was made general of the Venetians in Venerio's ftead.

difgrace,

· diſgrace, Vénerio retired ; and my great-grandfather, whoſe fortune depended on his having been bred up to the ſea, turned merchant, or rather privateer againſt the Moors ; and, with the knights of Malta, not only did great ſervice againſt them, but made a conſiderable fortune in the world.

But to return to myſelf : My father, having a plentiful fortune, took particular care of the education of his children : he had only two ſons, of whom I was the youngeſt, and a daughter, who died young. Finding I had a great inclination to learning, he promoted it, by providing me with the beſt maſters, till I was fit to go to the univerſity. The knowledge of languages being of great uſe as well as ornament to young gentlemen, he himſelf, by way of recreation, taught me that mixed language called *Lingua Franca,* ſo neceſſary in eaſtern countries. It is made up of Italian,

Every one who is the leaſt acquainted with hiſtory, knows that the battle of Lepanto was the greateſt ſea-fight that ever was fought between the Chriſtians and Turks; and the victory on the Chriſtians ſide the moſt ſignal. The Spaniſh galleys were commanded by Don John of Auſtria, generaliſſimo : the Pope's galleys, by the famous Colonna : the Genoeſe by old Dorio, who had gained ſo much renown againſt the Turks and French, under Charles Vth, the Venetians by the great Venerio, one of the braveſt ſoldiers of his time. Haly the Turk, great baſſa of the ſea, was ſlain, and almoſt all the Turkiſh commanding officers killed or taken. Among the priſoners, were Haly's two ſons, nephews to the Grand Signor. Of the common ſoldiers of the Turks, were ſlain two and thirty thouſand : a hundred and forty-one of the enemy's galleys were taken, forty ſank or burnt ; of galliots and other ſmall veſſels were taken about ſixty. Vide the Turkiſh hiſtory, and other accounts of this famous battle, and the whole affair as is there related. The battle, was fought on the 7th of October, 1571.

' Turkiſh,

Turkiſh, Perſian, and Arabian, or rather a jargon of all languages together. He ſcarce ever ſpoke to us but in that language, ſay-
· ing, we might learn Latin from our maſters, and our mother-tongue from our playfel- lows. The ſame reaſon induced him to ſend me to the famous univerſity of Paris, to learn French at the ſame time with my other ſtudies. I lived in the college des Quatre Nations, and maintained my theſes of univerſal philoſophy under the celebrated Monſieur Du Hamel, who was one of the firſt in the univerſity, who decried Ariſto-tle's philoſophy, and leaned towards the opinions of Deſcartes.

[*Secretary.* Here the inquiſitors muttered a little, fearing he was inclined to the Copernican ſyſtem, which has been condemned at Rome. But, ſince it re-garded philoſophical matters only, they paſſed it over.]

I was entering into my nineteenth year, and had ſome thoughts of taking to the church, when my brother wrote me the melancholy account of my father and mo-ther's death, and the unfortunate occaſion of it ; which in ſhort was, that having loſt his richeſt ſhip, with all his effects, by pi-rates, and his chief factor at Smyrna being gone off, his other correſpondents came upon him thick ; and not being in a con-dition to anſwer their calls, it threw him
and

and my mother into a deep melancholy, which shortened their days, both dying in three weeks of one another. My brother told me he was not able to maintain me longer at the univerſity, as before; but acquainted me, he had made a ſhift to fit out a ſmall veſſel, wherein he had put his all; and invited me to join the ſmall portion that fell to my ſhare along with him, with which, he ſaid, we could make a pretty good bottom; and ſo retrieve the ſhattered fortune of our family. Not to be too prolix, I followed his advice: he ſold his houſe and gardens to pay his father's creditors, and put what was left, together with my little ſtock, into that unfortunate bottom. We ſet ſail from Raguſa the 3d of March, *anno Dom.* 1688, very inauſpiciouſly for my dear brother, as will appear by the ſequel. We touched at Smyrna, to ſee if we could hear any thing of my father's factor: and were told, that he was turned Turk, and gone off, very magnificently dreſſed up in borrowed feathers, to ſettle at Conſtantinople; however we picked up ſomething of ſome honeſt Chriſtian merchants, with whom he had lodged a part of his effects. This encouraged us to proceed to Cyprus and Alexandria; but, as we were purſuing our voyage one morning, in a prodigious fog as if the ſea was fatal to our family, we ſpied on a ſudden two Algerine rovers bearing down upon us, 'one on each fide. We had fcarce time to clear our little veffel, when they fired upon us, and called to us to ftrike, or we were dead men. My brother and I, confidering that our all was at ftake, and that we had better die honorably than be made flaves by thofe unbelieving mifcreants, called up our men, who were but twenty-three in all, of whom five were young gentlemen who had engaged to try their fortune along with us. We were armed only with fwords, and piftols under our girdles. After a fhort confultation, it was agreed to fight it out to the laft man; and we turned back to back to make head againft both fides, my brother in the middle of one rank, and myfelf in the other. The enemy boarded us in great numbers, looking on us as madmen to pretend to make any refiftance; but they were foon made to leap back, at leaft all that were able; for being clofe up with them, and they crouded together, we fired our piftols fo luckily, that fcarce one miffed doing execution. Seeing them in this confufion we made a pufh at them on each fide, ftill keeping our ranks, and drove the remainder headlong off the deck. This we did twice before any of our men dropt. We were grappled fo clofe, they had no ufe of their cannon or mufkets, and fcarce thought of firing their piftols at us, expecting we fhould yield immediately,

mediately, or to have borne us down with
their weight. I am more particular in de-
fcribing this petty fight, fince there are
but few examples, where a handful of men
made fuch a long refiftance. The arch-pirate, who was a ftout, well-built young
man, raged like a lion, calling his men a
thoufand cowards, fo loud that his voice
was heard above all the cries of the foldiers.
The edge of their fury was a little abated
after the dropping of fo many men ; and
they began to fire at fome diftance ; which
did us more harm than their moft furious
attacks. My brother, feeing his men begin to drop in their turn, ordered me to
face the one fhip, while he with his rank
leaped in amongft the enemies in the other.
He did it with fuch a noble intrepidity,
that he made a gap among the thickeft of
them immediately. But their numbers
clofing together, their very weight drove
him back in fpite of all he could do, and he
loft feveral of his men before he could re-
cover his poft.. The enemy would neither
board us, nor leave us ; but firing at us
continually, ftill killed fome of our men.
There were now only eleven of us left ; and
no hopes of victory, or of quarter after
fuch obftinate refiftance. They durft not
come to a clofe engagement with us for all
this ; when my brother, to die as honora--
bly as he could, once more leaped into the
    D 3,   pirate's

pirate's fhip, and feeing their captain in
the midft of them, made at him with all
his might, calling on the few he had left to
fecond him. He foon cut his way through;
but juft as he was coming up to him, a cow-
ardly Turk clapt a piftol juft below his two
fhoulder-blades, and, I believe, fhot him
quite through the heart, for he dropped
down dead on the fpot. The Turk that
fhot him was run through the body by one
of our men, and he himfelf with the others
that were left, being quite overpowered,
were all cut in pieces. I had yet four men
left on my fide againft the lefs fhip, and
had till then kept off the enemy from boarding ; but the pirates giving a great fhout
at my brother's fall, the captain of the fhip
I was engaged with, who was the arch-pirate's brother, cried out to his crew, that
it was a fhame to ftand all day firing at five
men ; and leaping on my deck, made at
me like a man of honor, with his piftol
fteadily poifed in his hand : I met him with
equal refolution. He came boldly up within fword's length, and firing his piftol directly at my face; he aimed his fhot fo well,
that one of the balls went through my hair,
and the other grazed the fide of my neck.
But before he could fecond his fhot, I gave
him fuch a ftroke with my broad fword, between the temple and the left ear, that it
cut through part of his fcull, his cheek-bone,
and

and going crofs his mouth, almoft fevered
the lower part of his face from the upper.
I had juft the fatisfaction to fee him fall,
when a mufket-ball went through the braw-
ny part of my right arm, and, at the fame
time, a Turk hit me juft in the nape of the
neck with the butt end of his mufket, that
I fell down flat on my face, on the body of
my flain enemy. My companions, all but
one, who died of his wounds foon after,
fell honorably by my fide. The Turks
poured in from both fhips like wolves upon
their prey. After their barbarous fhouts and
yelling for the victory, they fell to ftrip-
ping the dead bodies, and threw them into
the fea without any further ceremony. All
our crew, befide myfelf, were flain, or
gafping, with threefcore and fifteen of the
enemy. The reafon why we fought fo defperately was, that we knew very well, having killed fo many at the firft attacks, we
were to expect no quarter ; fo we were refolved to fell our lives as dear as we could.
When they came to ftrip me like the reft,
I was juft come to myfelf, being only ftun-
ned by the ftroke of the mufket. They
found by my cloaths, that I was one of
the moft confiderable perfons of the crew.
I was got upon my knees, endeavouring to
rife, and reaching for my fword to defend
myfelf to the laft gafp ; I found I could not
hold it in my hand, by reafon of the wound

in

in my arm, though if I could, it had been
needlefs ; for three of them fell down upon me ; and preffed me to the deck, while
others brought cords and tied my hands,
to carry me to the captain. He was dreffing
a flight wound he had in his leg with a pif-
tol-fhot ; and four women in Perfian habits were ftanding by ; three of whom
feemed to be attendants to the fourth, who
was a perfon of the largeft fize, about five
or fix and twenty, a moft exquifite beauty,
except that fhe had an Amazonian kind of
fiercenefs in her looks. When I was
brought thus bound to the captain, they affured him I was the man that had flain his
brother, and done the moft harm of any.
Upon which, ftarting up in the greateft fury a barbarian was capable of, and calling
for a new fcymitar he had in his cabin, he
faid, " Let me cleave, if I can, the head of
" this Chriftian dog, as he did my poor
" brother's ; and then do you chop him
" into a thoufand pieces." With that he
drew the fcymitar, and was going to ftrike,
when, to the aftonifhment of the very barbarians, the ftrange lady cried out, " O
" fave the brave young man !" and immediately falling on her knees by me, catched
me in her arms, and clafping me clofe to
her bofom, covered my body with hers,
and cried out, " Strike, cruel man, but
" ftrike through me, for otherwife a hair
of

" of his head fhall not be hurt." The barbarians that ftood round us were ftruck dumb
with amazement ; and the pirate himfelf lifting up his eyes towards heaven, faid,
with a groan enough to break his heart,
"How, cruel woman ! fhall this ftranger in
" a moment obtain more than I can with
" all my fighs and tears ! Is this your para-
" mour that robs me of what I have fought
" for with the danger of life ? No, this
" Chriftian dog fhall be no longer my curf-
" ed rival ;" and lifting up his hand,
was again going to ftrike, when, covering
me more clofely with her delicate body, fhe
cried out again, " Hold, Hamet ! this is no
" rival ; I never faw his face before, nor
" ever will again, if you will but fpare his
" life : grant me this, and you fhall obtain
" more from me, than all your fervices
" could ever do." Here he began to paufe
a little. For my part, I was as much in
amaze as he was. After a little paufe,
" Cruel woman," faid he, " what is the
" meaning of this ?" Says fhe, " There is
" fomething in this young man (for I was
" but turned of nineteen) that he muft not
" die. But if you will engage and fwear
" by the moft holy Alcoran, that you will
" do him no harm, I not only promife to
" be your wife, but, to take off all umbrage
" of jealoufy, I give you leave to fell him to
" fome honorable perfon for a flave ; and
                                        " will

" will never fee him more." Nor would
fhe part from me, till he had fworn in that
folemn manner, never to do me any hurt
directly or indirectly ; and, for greater fecurity, fhe ordered one of her own fervants
to attend me conftantly. So I was unbound ;
and the lady, without fo much as looking
at me, or ftaying to receive my thanks, retired with her woman into the cabin. The
pirate, who had fomething very noble in
his looks for a Turk, confirmed again to
me in the hearing of her officer, that I
fhould receive no harm ; and then ordered
me to be carried under deck to the other
end of the fhip ; commanding his men to
fteer back for Alexandria, in order, as I
fuppofed, to difpofe of me the firft opportunity, that he might be rid as he thought,
of fo formidable a rival*.

[*Secretary.* Here the fuperior of the inquifition receiving a meffage on fome
other bufinefs, we told him we would
confider further of the account he had
given us, which, we faid, might be
true, though the adventure was extraordinary ; and that we would hear the
remaining narrative of his life another
time. He affured us with the moft na-

---

* This is an odd adventure enough ; but the circumftances are pretty
well connected together. There happen very ftrange accidents among
thofe lawlefs eaftern people, and the wild Arabs, who obferve no rules
but what the lions and tigers, could they fpeak, would make for their
own prefervation. I fear there are fome who profefs themfelves Chriftians would do the fame.

tural

tural air, that the whole, let it feem
never fo extraordinary, was real fact.
Whether it were true or falfe, it did
not much concern the holy office, only
fo far as we might catch him tripping
in his ftory : however, fome of the
inquifitors afked him the following
queftions.

1*ft inquifitor*. Why did you not yield at
firft, confidering the prodigious inequality of your ftrength and numbers,
when you might have been ranfomed
afterwards ; and not, like madmen,
expofe yourfelves to be cut in pieces,
as they all really were, except yourfelf?

Gaudentio. I told your Reverences, we
had put our all in that bottom ; which
once loft, we had nothing to ranfom
ourfelves with, but in all likelihood
muft have remained in miferable flavery all our life. We were moft of us
rafh young men, of more courage than
prudence ; we did not doubt but we
could keep them off from boarding us,
as we did ; and thought, by their
warm reception, they would have been
forced to fheer off ; befides, fighting
againft Turks and infidels, though for
our lives and fortunes, we judged me-
ritorious at the fame time, and that it
might be looked upon as laying down
our lives for our holy religion.

2d *inquifitor*. You faid that the ftrange lady cried out, " There is fomething " in that young man, that tells me *he muft not die :*" I hope you do not pretend to the fcience of phyfiognomy; which is one of the branches of divination ; or that an infidel or Heathen woman could have the fpirit of prophecy ?

Gaudentio. I cannot tell what was her motive for faying fo ; I only relate matter of fact. As for phyfiognomy, I do not think there can be any certainty in it. Not but that a perfon of penetration, who has obferved the humours and paffions of men, and confidering the little care the generality of the world take to conceal them ; I fay, fuch a perfon may give a great guefs, *a pofteriori*, how they are inclined; though reafon and virtue may indeed overcome the moft violent. But I entirely fubmit my opinion to your better judgments.

Secretary. I cannot fay, we were diffatisfied with thefe anfwers : we faw he has a very noble prefence ; and muft have been extremely handfome in his youth : therefore no wonder a Barbarian woman fhould fall in love with him, and make ufe of that turn to fave his life. However, for the prefent, we remanded him back to his apartment.

Some days after he was called again to profecute his ftory.]

While I was under deck in confinement with the pirates, feveral of them were tole-rably civil to me; knowing the afcendant the lady had over their captain, and being witneffes, how fhe had faved my life. But yet fhe would not confent to marry him, till fhe was affured I was fafe out of his hands. The arch-pirate never came to fee me himfelf, not being willing to truft his paffion ; or elfe to watch all favourable op-portunities of waiting on his miftrefs. One day, being indifpofed for want of air, I beg-ged to be carried upon deck to breathe a little ; when I came up, I faw the lady, with her women, ftanding at the other end of the fhip on the fame account. I made her a very refpectful bow at a diftance ; but as foon as ever fhe caft her eye on me, fhe went down into the cabin, I fuppofe, to keep her promife with the captain, and not to adminifter any caufe of jealoufy. I defired to be carried down again, not to hinder my benefactrefs from taking her di-verfion. I cannot fay I found in myfelf the leaft inclination or emotion of love, only a fenfe of gratitude for fo great a benefit; not without fome admiration of the odd-nefs of the adventure. When I was below, I afked the moft fenfible and civilized of the pirates, who their captain was, and who

E   was

was my fair deliverer. How long, and by what means she came to be among them ; because she seemed to be a person of much higher rank. He told me his captain's name was *Hamet*, son to the Dey of Algiers ; who had forsaken his father's house on account of his young mother-in-law's falling in love with him. For which reason his father had contrived to have him assassinated, believing him to be in the fault. But his younger brother by the same mother, discovered the design. So gathering together a band of stout young men like themselves, they seized two of their father's best ships, and resolved to follow the profession they were now of, till they heard of their father's death. That as for the lady who had saved his life, she was the late wife of a petty prince of the Curdi*, tributary to the king of Persia, whose husband had been lately killed by treachery, or in an ambuscade of the wild Arabs. That, as far as he had been informed, the prince her husband had been sent by the king his master to Alexandria† ; who, apprehend-

* The Curdi, or people of Curdistan, are a warlike nation, paying a small tribute to the Persians, and sometimes to the Turks ; their very women are martial, and handle the sword and pike. The country runs from the Aliduli, a mountainous people, made tributary to the Turks by Selim I. father of Solomon the Magnificent, and reaches as far as Armenia.

† Alexandria is a sea-port, at the further end of the Mediterranean, belonging to the Turks, but much frequented by Arabian merchants, both by land and sea. One point of Curdistan is not far from this port.

ing

ing an infurrection among his fubjects*, had ordered him to treat for fome troops of Arabian horfe†. That he went there with a very handfome equipage, and took his beautiful wife along with him. Our cap-tain, continued he, happened to be there at the fame time to fell his prizes, and had not only fold feveral things of great value to the Curdifh lord and lady, but had con-tracted a particular friendfhip with him, though, as we found fince, it was more on account of his fair wife than any thing elfe. Nothing in the world could be more obfe-quious than our captain. He attended them, and offered his fervice on all occa-fions : you fee, he is a very handfome man, and daring by his profeffion. We could not imagine of a long while, why he made fuch a ftay at that town, contrary to his cu-ftom ; living at a very high rate, as men of our calling generally do. At length the Curdifh lord having executed his commif-fion, was upon the return, when we per-ceived our captain to grow extremely pen-

* This infurrection he fpeaks of, might be the feeds, or the firft plot-ting of the grand rebellion of Merowits, which begin about the date of this account, and caufed fuch a terrible revolution in the Perfian empire ; which no one who underftands any thing can be ignorant of.

† The Arabian horfes are the beft in the world, though not very large. The horfemen are very dexterous in the eaftern way of fighting. On which account, one cannot wonder, if the king of Perfia, and his rebel-lious fubjects, made it their intereft to procure as many auxiliaries, as they could. It is very likely the little parties would always be on watch, to furprife one another when they could find an opportunity. And this petty Curdian prince being zealous for the fervice of his king, might be taken off by the rebels that way,

five

five and melancholy, but could not tell
what was the caufe of it. He called his
brother, who loft his life by your hand, and
me to him, and told us in private, he had
obferved fome of the Arabian ftrangers
muttering together, as if they were hatching fome plot or other, whether againft
himfelf, or the Curd, he could not tell;
but bid us be fure to attend him well armed where ever he went. The event proved he had reafon for his fufpicions; for
one evening, as the Curd and his wife were
taking the air, with our captain, who was
always of the party, paffing through a little grove about a league out of town, fix
Arabian horfemen, exceedingly well moun-
ed, came full gallop up to us; and without
faying a word, two of them fired their piftols directly at the Curdifh lord, who was
the foremoft, but by good fortune miffed
us all. The Curd, as all that nation are naturally brave, drew his fcymitar, and rufhing in among them, cut off the foremoft
man's head, as clean as if it had been a
poppy; but advancing too far unarmed
as he was, one of them turned fhort, and
fhot him in the flank, that he dropped
down dead immediately. Our captain feeing him fall, rufhed in like lightning, his
brother and myfelf falling on them at the
fame time: but the affaffins, as if they
wanted nothing but the death of the Curd,

or

or faw by our countenance their ftaying
would coft them dear, immediately turned
their horfes, and fled fo fwiftly on their
jennets, that they were out of fight in an
inftant.   We conducted the poor difconfo-
late lady and her dead hufband back to the
town, where thofe people made no more of
it (being accuftomed to fuch things) than
if it had been a common accident. · When
her grief was a little abated, our captain
told the lady, that it was not fafe for her to
return home the fame way fhe came ; that,
in all probability, thofe who killed her hufband were in confederacy with the difaf-
fected party, and would waylay her, either
for his papers, or her goods.   That he had
two fhips well-manned at her fervice, and
would conduct her fafe by fea to fome part
of the Perfian empire, from whence fhe
might get into her own country. She confented at laft, having feen how gallantly my
mafter had behaved in her defence. So fhe
came aboard with her attendants and effects,
in order to be tranfported into her own
country. · Our captain, you may be fure,
was in no hafte to carry her home, being
fallen moft defperately in love with her : fo
that inftead of carrying her to any of the
Perfian dominions, he directed his courfe
for Algiers, hearing his father was dead ;
but meeting with you, it has made him al-
ter his meafures for the prefent. · He has

tried all ways to gain her love, but she
would not give him the leaft encouragement, till this late accident, by which she
faved your life.———When he had ended
his relation, I reflected on it a good while,
and confidering the natue of thofe pirates,
I thought I faw a piece of treachery in the
affair, much more black than what he defcribed, and could not forbear compaffionating the poor lady, both for her difafter,
and the company fhe was fallen into. However, I kept my thoughts to myfelf.   Not
long after we arrived at Alexandria, where
the pirate fold all our effects, that is, the
merchandife he had taken aboard our fhip,
except fome particular things that belonged
to my brother and myfelf, as books, pa-
rs, maps and fea-charts, pictures, and
the like.   He determined to carry me to
Grand Cairo*, the firft opportunity, to
fell me, or even give me away to a ftrange
merchant he had an acquaintance with,
where I fhould never be heard of more.

Nothing remarkable happened during
our ftay at Alexandaia ; they told me the
captain had been in an extraordinary good
humour, ever fince the lady's promife to
marry him.   But fhe, to be fure he fhould
not deceive her by doing me any injury
when I was out of the fhip, ordered her of-

* Grand Cairo is the place of refidence of the great Baffa of Egypt,
higher up the country, on the river Nile.

fice

ficer to attend me where-ever I was carried, till I was put in safe hands, and entirely out of the pirates power. When we were arrived at Grand Cairo, I was carried to the place where the merchants meet to ex-, change their commodities; there were persons of almost all the Eastern and Indian nations. The lady's officer, according to his miftrefs's order, never ftirred an inch from me to witnefs the performance of the articles. At length, the pirate and a ftrange merchant fpied one another almost at the inftant, and advancing the fame way, faluted each other in the Turkifh language, which I underftood tolerably well. After fome mutual compliments, the pirate told him he had met with fuch a perfon he had promifed to procure for him two years before, meaning myfelf; only I was not an eunuch, but that it was in his power to make me fo, if he pleafed. Your Reverences cannot doubt but I was a little ftartled at fuch a fpeech, and was going to reply, that I would lofe my life a thoufand times, before I would fuffer fuch an injury. But the lady's officer turned to the pirate, and faid, he had engaged to his lady I fhould receive no harm; and that he muft never expect to obtain her for his wife, if fhe had the leaft fufpicion of fuch a thing. But the merchant foon put us out of doubt, by affuring us, that it was againft their laws to do fuch an injury to any

any one of their own fpecies ; but if it were
done before, they could not help it. Then
turning to me, he faid in very good *Lingua
Franca*, " Young man, if I buy you, I fhall
foon convince you, you need not apprehend any fuch ufage from me." He eyed
me from top to toe, with the moft pene-
trating look I ever faw in my life ; yet
feemed pleafed at the fame time. He was
very richly clad, attended with two young
men in the fame kind of drefs, though not
rich, who feemed rather fons than fervants.
His age did not appear to me to be above
forty, yet he had the moft ferene and almoft venerable look imaginable. His complexion was rather browner than that of
the Egyptians, but it feemed to be more
the effect of travelling, than natural. In
fhort, he had an air fo uncommon, that I
was amazed, and began to have as great an
opinion of him, as he feemed to have of
me. He afked the pirate, what he muft
give for me ; he told him, I had coft him
very dear, and with that recounted to him
all the circumftances of the fight wherein I
was taken ; and, to give him his due, reprefented it nowife to my difadvantage.
However, thefe were not the qualifications
the merchant defired ; what he wanted was
a perfon who was a fcholar, and could give
him an account of the arts and fciences,
laws, cuftoms, &c. of the Chriftians. This
the

the pirate affured him I could do : that I
was an European Chriftian, and a fcholar,
as he gueffed by my books and writings ;
that I underftood navigation, geography,
aftronomy, and feveral other fciences. I
was out of countenance to hear him talk fo ;
for though I had as much knowledge of
thofe fciences, as could be expected from
one of my years, yet my age would not
permit me to be mafter of them, but only
to have the firft principles, by which I
might improve myfelf afterwards.

[*Secretary.* The inquifitors demurred a
little at this, fearing he might be addicted to judicial aftrology ; but confidering he had gone through a courfe
of philofophy, and was defigned for
the fea, they knew he was obliged to
have fome knowledge in thofe fciences.]

The pirate told him, I had fome fkill in
mufic and painting, having feen fome inftruments and books of thofe arts among
my effects, and afked me if it were not fo.
I told him, all young gentlemen of liberal
education in my country learned thefe arts,
and that I had a competent knowledge and
genius that way. This determined the
merchant to purchafe me. When they
came to the price, the pirate demanded
forty ounces of native gold, and three of
thofe filk carpets he faw there with him, to
make

make a prefent to the Grand Signor. The merchant agreed with him at the firſt word ; only demanded all the books globes, mathematical inſtruments, and, in fine, whatever remained of my effects, into the bargain. The pirate agreed to this, as eaſily as the other did to the price ; ſo, upon performance of articles on both ſides, I was delivered to him. As ſoon as I was put into his power, he embraced me with a great deal of tenderneſs, ſaying, I ſhould not repent my change of life. His attendants came up to me, and embraced me in the ſame manner, calling me brother, and expreſſing a great deal of joy for having me of their company. The merchant bid them take me down to the caravanſera or inn, that I might refreſh myſelf, and change my habit to the ſame as they wore. I was very much ſurpriſed at ſuch unexpected civilities from ſtrangers. But, before I went, I turned to the pirate, and ſaid to him with an air that made the merchant put on a very thoughtful look, that I thanked him for keeping his promiſe in ſaving my life ; but added, that though the fortune of war had put it in his power to ſell me like a beaſt in the market, it might be in mine ſome time or other to render the like kindneſs. Then turning to the lady's officer, who had been my guardian ſo faithfully, and embracing him with all imaginable tenderneſs, I begged

ged him to pay my beſt reſpects to my fair deliverer; and aſſure her, that I ſhould eſteem it the greateſt happineſs to be one day able to make a return for ſo unparallelled a favour, though it were at the expenſe of that life ſhe had ſo generouſly ſaved. So we parted, the pirate grumbling a little within himſelf; and I in an amazing ſuſpenſe, to know what was likely to become of me. As they were conducting me to the caravaniera where they lodged, I was full of the ſorrowful reflection, that I was ſtill a ſlave, though I had changed my maſter: but my companions, who were ſome of the handſomeſt young men I ever ſaw in life, comforted me with the moſt endearing words, telling me that I need fear nothing; that I ſhould eſteem myſelf one of the happieſt men in the world, when they were arrived ſafe in their own country, which they hoped would be before long; that I ſhould then be as free as they were, and follow what employment of life my inclinations led me to, without any reſtraint whatſoever. In fine, their diſcourſe filled me with freſh amazement, and gave me at the ſame time an eager longing to ſee the event. I perceived they did not keep any ſtrict guard on me; that I verily believed I could eaſily have given them the ſlip; and might have gotten ſome Armenian Chriſtian to conceal me, till I ſhould find an opportunity

portunity of returning into my own country.   But, having loft all my effects, I
thought I could fcarce be in a worfe condition, and was refolved to run all hazards.
When I came to the houfe, I was ftruck
with wonder at the magnificence of it, efpecially at the richnefs of the furniture. It
was one of the beft in all Grand Cairo,
though built low according to the cuftom
of the country.   It feems they always ftaid
a year before they returned into their own,
country, and fpared no coft to make their
banifhment, as they called it, as eafy as they
could.   I was entertained with all the rarities of Egypt; the moft delicious fruits,
and the richeft Greek and Afiatic wines
that could be tafted ; by which I faw they
were not Mahometants.   Not knowing
what to make of them, I afked them who
they were; of what country, what fect
and profeffion, and the like.   They fmiled
at my queftions, and told me they were
children of the Sun, and were called *Mezoranians;* which was as unintelligible to me
as all the reft.   But their country, they
told me, I fhould fee in a few months, and
bid me afk no further queftions.   Prefently my mafter came in, and embracing me,
once more bid me welcome, with fuch an
engaging affability, as removed almoft all
my fears.   But what followed, filled me
with the utmoft furprife.   " Young man,"
                                                faid'

faid he, " by the laws-of this country you
are mine ; I have bought you at a very
high price, and would give twice as much
for you, if it were to be done again : but
(continued he, with a more ferious air) I
know no juft laws in the univerfe, that can
make a free-born man become a flave to
one of his own fpecies. If you will voluntarily go along with us, you fhall enjoy as
much freedom as I do myfelf: you fhall be
exempt from all the barbarous laws of thefe
inhuman countries, whofe brutal cuftoms
are a reproach to the dignity of a rational
creature, and with whom we have no commerce, but to inquire after arts and fciences,
which may contribute to the common benefit of our people. We are blefled with
the moft opulent country in the world ;
we leave it to your choice to go along with
us, or not ; if the latter, I here give you
your liberty, and reftore to you all that remains of your effects, with what affiftance
you want to carry you back again into your
own country. Only, this I muft tell you,
if you go with us, it is likely you will never come back again, or perhaps defire it."
Here he ftopped, and obferved my countenance with a great deal of attention. I
was ftruck with fuch admiration of his ge-
nerofity, together with the fentiments of
joy for my unexpected liberty, and gratitude to my benefactor, coming into my

F   mind

mind all at once, that I had as much difficulty to believe what I heard, as your Reverences may now have at the relation of it, till the sequel informs you of the reasons for such unheard of proceedings. On the one hand, the natural desire of liberty prompted me to accept my freedom ; on the other, I considerd my shattered fortune ; that I was left in a strange country so far from home, among Turks and infidels ; the ardour of youth excited me to push my fortune. The account of so glorious, though unknown country, stirred up my curiosity ; I saw gold was the least part of the riches of these people, who appeared to me the most civilized I ever saw in my life ; but, above all, the sense of what I owed to so noble a benefactor, who I saw desired it, and had me as much in his power now, as he could have afterwards. These considerations almost determined me to go along with him. I had continued longer thus irresolute, and fluctuating between so many different thoughts, if he had not brought me to myself, by saying, what say you, young man, to my proposal ? I started out of my reveries, as if I had awaked from a real dream ; and making a most profound reverence, My Lord, said I, or rather my father and deliverer, I am yours by all the ties of gratitude a human heart is capable of ; I resign myself to your conduct;

and

and will follow you to the end of the world. This I faid with fuch emotion of fpirit, that I believe he faw into my very foul ; for embracing me once more with a moft inex-preffible tendernefs, I adopt you, faid he, for my fon ; and thefe are your brothers, pointing to his two young companions ; all I require of you is, that you live as fuch. Here, Reverend Fathers, I muft confefs one of the greateft faults I ever did in my life : I never confidered whether thefe men were Chriftians or Heathens : I engaged myfelf with a people, where I could never have the exercife of my religion, although I al-ways preferved it in my heart. But what could be expected from a daring young man, juft in the heat of his youth, who had loft all his fortune, and had fuch a glorious profpect offered him for retrieving it ?——— Soon after this, he gave orders to his at-tendants to withdraw, as if he intended to fay fomething to me in private ; they obey-ed immediately with a filial refpect, as if they had indeed been his fons, but they were not ; I only mention it to fhew the nature of the people I was engaged with : then taking me by the hand he made me fit down by him, and afked me if it were really true, as the pirate informed him, that I was an European Chriftian ? though, added he, be what you will, I do not re-pent my buying of you. I told him I was,

and

and in that belief would live and die. So
you may, faid he, (feeming pleafed at my
anfwer). But I have not yet met with any
of that part of the world, who feemed to
have the difpofitions of mind I think I fee
in you, looking at the lineaments of my
face with a great deal of earneftnefs. I
have been informed, continued he, that
your laws are not like barbarous Turks,
whofe government is made up of tyranny
and force, and making flaves of all who
fall under their power. Whereas the European Chriftians, as I am told, are governed by a divine law, that teaches them
to do good to all, injury to none ; particularly not to kill and deftroy their own fpecies : nor to fteal, cheat, over-reach, or de-
fraud any one of their juft due ; but to do
in all things juft as they would be done by ;
looking on all men as common brothers of
the fame flock, and behaving with juftice
and equity in all their actions public and
private, as if they were to give an account
to the univerfal Lord and Father of all. I
told him our law did really teach and command us to do fo ; but that very few lived
up to this law ; that we were obliged to
have recourfe to coercive laws and penalties,
to enforce what we acknowledged otherwife to be a duty : that if it were not for
the fear of fuch punifhments, the greateft
part of them would be worfe than the very

Turks

Turks he mentioned. He seemed strange-
ly surprised at this. What, says he, can
any one do in private, what his own reason
and solemn profession condemns? Then ad-
dressing himself to me in a more particular
manner: Do you profess this just and holy
law you mentioned? I told him, I did:
then, said he, do but live up to your own
law, and we require no more of you*. Here
he made a little noise with his staff, at which
two of his attendants came in : he asked
them if my effects were come from the pirate. Being answered, they were ; he ordered them to be brought in, and examined them very nicely. There were among
them

* If it appear incredible to any one, that Heathens, as these people
were, should have such strict ideas of morality and justice, when they see
such horrid injustice, frauds, and oppressions among Christians, let them
consider, first, that the law and light of nature will never be entirely ex-
tinguished in any who do not shut their eyes against it; but that they
would esteem the injuries they do to others, without any scruple, to be
very great hardships if done to themselves : they have therefore the
ideas of justice and equity imprinted in their minds however obscured
by their wicked lives ---2dly, Let them read the celebrated Bishop of
Meau's universal history, pr. lii. of the morals and equity of the ancient
Egyptians under their great king Sesostris, or about that time.----3dly,
Not only the lives and maxims of the first Heathen philosophers, afford
us very just rules of morality, but there are also fragments of ancient
history, from the earliest times, of whole Heathen nations, whose lives
would make Christians blush at their own immoralities, if they were not
hardened in them. The people of Colchos, whom the great Bochart, in
his Phaleg, proves to have been a colony of ancient Egyptians, as will
be seen in the sequel of these memoirs, or the ancient inhabitants of
Pontus, who come from them, were according to Homer the most just of
men.

Milk-eaters the most just of men. Hom. Il. K.

Chœrilus in Xerxis Diabasi apud Bochart, speaking of the Scythians
on the Euxine sea, says, they were a colony of the Nomades, a just people.

Strabo says, that Anacharsis and Abaris, both Scythians, esteemed by
the ancient Greeks, for their peculiar and national affability, probity
and justice; And Nicholaus Damascenus, of the Galactophagi, they are
the most just of men. Vide Bochart, lib. iii. c. 9.

them some pictures of my own drawing, a
repeating watch, two compass boxes, one
of them very curiously wrought in ivory
and gold, which had been my great-grandfather's, given him by Venerio ; a set of
mathematical instruments, draughts of sta-
tuary and architecture by the best masters ;
with all which he seemed extremely pleased.   After he had examined them with a
great deal of admiration, he ordered one
of his attendants to reach him a cabinet full
of gold ; he opened it to me, and said,
young man, I not only restore all your effects here present, having no right to any
thing that belongs to another man, but
once more offer you your liberty, and as
much of this gold, as you think sufficient to
carry you home, and make you live easy
all your life.   I was a little out of countenance, imagining what I said of the illmor-
als of the Christians, had made him afraid
to take me along with him.   I told him, I
valued nothing now so much as his company, and begged him not only to let me go
along with him, but that he would be
pleased to accept whatever he saw of mine
there before him : adding, that I esteemed
it the greatest happiness, to be able to make
some small recompense for the obligations
I owed him.   I do accept of it, says he; and
take you solemnly into my care : go along
with these young men, and enjoy your liberty

berty in effect, which I have hitherto only
given you in words. Here fome of his elder companions coming in, as if they were
to confult about bufinefs; the young men
and myfelf went to walk the town for our
diverfion. Your Reverences may be fure,
I obferved all the actions of thefe new people, with the greateft attention my age was
capable of. They feemed not only to have
a horror of the barbarous manners and
vices of the Turks, but even a contempt of
all the pleafures and diverfions of the country. Their whole bufinefs was to inform
themfelves of what they thought might be
an improvement in their own country, particularly in arts and trades, and whatever
curiofities were brought from foreign parts;
fetting down their obfervations of every
thing of moment. They had mafters of
the country at fet hours to teach them the
Turkifh and Perfian languages, in which I
endeavoured to perfect myfelf along with
them. Though they feemed to be the moft
moral men in the world, I could obferve
no figns of religion in them, till a certain
occafion that happened to us in our voyage,
of which I fhall fpeak to your Reverences
in its proper place. This was the only
point they were fhy in; they gave me the
reafons for it afterwards; but their behaviour was the moft candid and fincere in
other matters that can be imagined. We
lived

lived thus in the moſt perfect union all the time we ſtaid at Grand Cairo ; and I enjoyed the ſame liberty that I could have had in Italy. All I remarked in them was an uneaſineſs they expreſſed to be ſo long out of their own country ; but they comforted themſelves with the thought it would not be long. I cannot omit one obſervation I made of theſe young mens conduct while we ſtaid in Egypt. They were all about my own age, ſtrong and vigorous, and the handſomeſt race of people, perhaps, the world ever produced : we were in the moſt voluptuous and lewd town in the whole eaſtern empire ; the young women ſeemed ready to devour us as we paſſed along the ſtreets. Yet I never could perceive in the young men the leaſt propenſity to lewdneſs. I imputed it at firſt to the apprehenſion of my being in their company, and a ſtranger ; but I ſoon found they acted by principle. As young men are apt to encourage, or rather corrupt one another; I own I could not forbear expreſſing my wonder at it. They ſeemed ſurpriſed at the thought ; but the reaſons they gave were as much out of our common way of thinking, as their behaviour. They told me, for the firſt reaſon, that all the women they ſaw were either married ; or particular mens daughters ; or common. As to married women, they ſaid, it was ſuch a heinous piece of
injuſtice

injuſtice to violate the marriage bed, 'that every man living would look upon it as the greateſt injury done to himſelf : how could they therefore in reaſon do it to another ? If they were daughters of particular men, bred up with ſo much care and ſolicitude of their parents, what a terrible afflicſtion muſt it be to them, or to ourſelves, to ſee our daughters or ſiſters violated and corrupted, after all our care to the contrary ; and this too, perhaps, by thoſe we had cheriſhed in our own boſoms ? If common ſtrumpets, what rational man could look on them otherwiſe than brute beaſts, to proſtitute themſelves to every ſtranger for hire ? Beſides, their abandoned lewdneſs generally defeats the great deſign of nature to propagate the ſpecies ; or, by their impure embraces, ſuch diſorders may be contracſt-ed, as to make us hereafter, at beſt, but fathers of a weak and ſickly offspring. And if we ſhould have children by them, what would become of our fathers grandchil-dren ? But what man who had the leaſt ſenſe of the dignity of his own birth, would ſtain his race, and give birth to ſuch a wretched breed, and then leave them expoſed to want and infamy ? This they ſaid chiefly with reference to the vaſt ideas they had of their own nation, valuing themſelves above all other people ; though the conſideration holds good with all men. I own,

own, I was mute at these reasons, and
could not say but they were very just,
though the warmth of my youth had hindered me from reflecting on them before.
These reflections appeared so extraordinary
in young men, and even Heathens, that I
shall never forget them.—Sometime after,
I found by ther diligence in settling their
affairs, and the chearfullness of their countenances, that they expected to leave Egypt
very soon ; they seemed to wait for nothing but orders from their governor. In
the mean time there happened an accident
to me, scarce fit indeed for your Reverences to hear ; nor should I ever have tho't
of relating it, had you not laid your commands on me to give an exact account of
my whole life. Besides, that it is interwoven with some of the chief occurrences
of my life in the latter part of it. Our governor whom they called *Pophar*, which in
their language signifies Father of his people, and by which name I shall always call
him hereafter, looking at his ephemeris,
which he did very frequently, found by
computation, that he had still some time
left to stay in the country, and resolved to
go down once more to Alexandria, to see
if he could meet with any more European
curiosities, brought by the merchant-ships
that are perpetually coming at that season
into the port. He took only two of the
young

young men and me along with him, to
fhew me, as he faid, that I was entirely at
my liberty, fince I might eafily find fome
fhip or other to carry me into my own
country ; and I, on the other hand, to con.
vince him of the fincerity of my intentions,
generally kept in his company, The affair
I am going to fpeak of, foon gave him full
proof of my fincerity.

While we were walking in the public
places to view the feveral goods and curiofities, that were brought from different parts
of the world, it happened that the Baffa of
Grand Cairo, with all his family, was come
to Alexandria on the fame account, as well
as to buy fome young female flaves. His
wife and daughter were then both with
him : the wife was one of the Grand Signior's fifters, feemingly about thirty, and
a wonderful fine woman. The daughter
was about fixteen, of fuch exquifite beauty,
and lovely features, as were fufficient to
charm the greateft prince in the world*.
When he perceived them, the Pophar, who
naturally abhorred the Turks, kept off, as
if he were treating privately with fome
merchants. But I, being young and in-
confiderate, ftood gazing, though at a refpectful diftance, at the Baffa's beautiful

---

* N. B. The Baffa of Grand Cairo is one of the greateft officers in
the Turkifh empire, and the moft independent of any fubject in Turky ;
it is cuftomary for the Sultans to give their daughters in marriage to
fuch perfons ; but they are often difliked by their hufbands, on account
of their imperious behaviour.

daughter,

daughter, from no other motive but mere
curiofity. She had her eyes fixed on my
companions and me at the fame time, and,
as I fuppofed, on the fame account. Her
drefs was fo magnificent, and her perfon
fo charming, that I thought her the moft
beautiful creature I had ever feen in my life.
If I could have forefeen the troubles which
that fhort interview was to coft both the
Pophar and myfelf, I fhould have chofen
rather to have looked on the moft hideous
monfter. I obferved, that the young lady,
with a particular fort of emotion, wifpered
fomething to an elderly woman that attended her, and that this laft did the fame to a
page, who immediately went to two natives
of the place, whom the Pophar ufed to hire
to carry his things: this was to enquire of
them who we were. They, as appeared by
the event, told them, that I was a young
flave lately bought by the Pophar. After
a while, the Baffa with his train went away,
and I, for my part, thought no more of the
matter. The next day, as the Pophar and
we were walking in one of the public gar
dens; a little elderly man, like an eunuch,
with a moft beautiful youth along with
him, having dogged us to a private part
of the walks, came up to us, and addreff-
ing themfelves to the Pophar, afked him
what he would take for his young flave,
pointing at me, becaufe the Baffa defired

to buy him. The Pophar feemed to be more furprifed at this unexpected queftion, than I ever obferved him at any thing before, which confirmed me more and more in the opinion of the kindnefs he had for me. But foon coming to himfelf, as he was a man of great prefence of mind, he faid very calmly, that I was no flave; nor a perfon to be fold for any price, fince I was as free as he was. Taking this for a pretext to enhance the price, they produced fome oriental pearls with other jewels of immenfe value; and bid him name what he would have, and it fhould be paid immediately: adding, that I was to be the companion of the Baffa's fon, where I might make my fortune for ever, if I would go along with them. The Pophar perfifted in his firft anfwer, and faid he had no power over me: they alledged, I had been bought as a flave, but a little before, in the Grand Signior's dominions, and they would have me. Here I interpofed, and anfwered brifkly, that though I had been taken prifoner by the chance of war, I was no flave, nor would I part with my liberty but at the price of my life. The Baffa's fon, for fo he now declared himfelf to be, inftead of being angery at my refolute anfwer, replied with a moft agreeable fmile, that I fhould be as free as he was; making at the fame time the moft folemn proteftations by his

G   holy

holy Alcoran, that our lives and deaths
should be inseparable. Though there was
something in his words the most persuasive
I ever felt; yet considering the obligations
I owed to the Pophar, I was resolved not to
go; but answered with a most respectful
bow, that though I was free by nature, I
had indispensable obligations not to go with
him, and hoped he would take it for a de-
terminate answer. I pronounced this with
such a resolute air, as made him see there
was no hopes. Whether his desire was
more inflamed by my denial, or whether
they took us for persons of greater note
than we appeared to be I cannot tell; but I
observed he put on a very languishing air,
with tears stealing down his cheeks, which
moved me to a degree I cannot express. I
was scarce capable of speaking, but cast
down my eyes, and stood as immoveable
as a statue. This seemed to revive his
hopes; and recovering himself a little, with
a trembling voice he replied; Suppose it be
the Baffa's daughter, you saw yesterday,
that desires to have you for her attendant,
what will you say then? I started at this,
and casting my eyes on him more attentively, I saw him swimming in tears, with
a tenderness enough to pierce the hardest
heart. I looked at the Pophar, who I saw
was trembling for me; and feared it was
the daughter herself that asked me the question

tion. I was soon put out of doubt ; for
she, finding she had gone too far to go
back, discovered herself, and said, I must
go along with her, or one of us must die*.

—I

* Love adventures are not the design of these memoirs, as will appear by the rest of his life; otherwise, this account of the Bassa's daughter
had like to have made me lay down my pen, without troubling myself to write any further remark. But, when I considered, the man is
no fool, let him be what he will, nor could design to embellish his history by this extraordinary adventure, so like the former, and just upon
the back of it, I am inclined to believe he wrote the matter of fact
just as it happened. More unaccountable accidents than this have
happened to some men.

The amorous temper of the Turkish ladies, especially at Grand Cairo
where the women are the most voluptuous in the world, and the sur-
prising beauty of this young man, who, the secretary says, has the noblest
presence he ever saw, even at that age, might easily charm a wanton
giddy girl at the first sight. Besides, she was informed he was alive, and
might think she could have purchased him for her private gallant: or
might be encouraged in it by the lustful elderly woman that attended
her. Such things have been done before now ; but when she came nearer to the tempting object, and found him to be something more noble
than she expected, her passion might thereby grow to the highest pitch.

Extraordinary beauty, in either sex, is oftentimes a great misfortune;
since it frequently leads them into very great follies, and even disasters
What will not heedless youth do, when fired with flattery or charms?
It is no new thing for women to fall in love at first sight, as well as men
and on as unequal terms; in spite of all reasons and considerations to
the contrary. I believe there may be men in the world, as charming in
the eyes of women, as ever the fair Helen appeared to the men. The
almost incredible catastrophes caused by her beauty, are so far from being fabulous, that, besides the account Homer gives of her, there is ex-
tant an oration of the famous Isocrates De laudibus Helenæ, before Al-
exander the Great's time, which gives a more amazing account of the
effects of her beauty, than Homer does. He says, she was ravished for
her beauty by the great and wise Theseus, when she was but a girl. She
was afterwards courted by all the Grecian princes; and. after her
marriage, was carried from Europe into Asia by the beautiful Paris;
which kindled the first war that is recorded in history to have been made
in those parts of the world. Yet, notwithstanding that false and fatal
step, her beauty reconciled her to her husband. The sight of some men
may have as violent effects on women.

It is possible the young lady would have been very angry
with any one who should have persuaded Signior Gaudentio
to do as he did ; yet in effect it was the greatest kindness : for this very
lady, some time after, became mistress of the whole Ottoman empire.
Whereas if she had run away with him, as the violence of her passion
suggested, they had both of them been inevitably miserable. Notwithstanding all these reasons, I should not have believed this story, if I had
not examined some other facts, which, he said, happened to him at Venice, as incredible as this, and found them to be really true.

—I hope your Reverences will excufe this account I give of myfelf, which nothing fhould have drawn from me, though it is literally true, but your exprefs commands to tell the whole hiftory of my life. The perplexity I was in cannot be imagined. I confidered fhe was a Turk, and I a Chriftian ; that my death muft certainly be the confequence of fuch a rafh affair, were I to engage in it ; that whether fhe concealed me in her father's court, or attempted to go off with me, it was ten thoufand to one, we fhould both be facrificed : neither could the violence of fuch a fudden paffion ever be concealed from the Baffa's fpies. In a word, I was refolved not to go : but how to get off, was the difficulty. I faw the moft beautiful creature in the world all in tears before me, after a declaration of love, that exceeded the moft romantic tales ; youth, love, and beauty, and even an inclination on my fide, pleaded her caufe. But at length the confideration of the endlefs miferies I was likely to draw on the young lady, fhould I comply with what fhe defired, prevailed above all other. I was refolved to refufe, for her fake more than my own, and was juft going to tell her fo on my knees, with all the arguments my reafon could fuggeft to appeafe her ; when an attendant came running in hafte to the other perfon, who was alfo a woman, and
told

told her the Bassa was coming that way.
She was roused out of her lethargy at this.—
The other woman immediately snatched
her away, as the Pophar did me; and she
had only time to call out with a threat.
Think better on it, or die. I was no sooner out of her sight, but I found a thousand reasons for what I did, more than I
could think of before, while the inchant-
ing object was before my eyes. I saw the
madness of that passion which forced the
most charming person of the Ottoman empire, capable by her beauty to conquer the
Grand Signior himself, to make a declaration of love, so contrary to the nature and
modesty of her sex, as well as her quality
and dignity, and ready to sacrifice her reputation, the duty she owed her parents,
her liberty, perhaps her life, for an unknown person who had been a slave but
some time before. I saw on the other hand,
that had I complied with the fair charm-
ers proposal, I must have run the risk of
loosing my religion or life, or rather both,
with a dreadful chain of hidden misfortunes, likely to accompany such a rash adventure. While I was taken up with these
thoughts, the wife Pophar, after reflecting
a little upon what had happened, told me,
this unfortunate affair would not end so,
but that it might cost us both our lives,
and something else that was more dear to

him,

him.   He feared fo violent a paffion would
draw on other extremes : efpecially confidering the wickednefs of the people, and
the brutal tyranny of their government :
however, he was refolved not to give me
up but with his lite, if I would but ftand
to it myfelf : adding, that we muft make
off as faft as we could ; and having fo many fpies upon us, ufe policy as well as expedition.   Accordingly he went down directly to the port, and hired a fhip in the
moft public manner to go for Cyprus, paid
the whole freight on the fpot, and told
them they muft neceffarily fail that evening.   We fhould actually have done fo, had
not our companions and effects obliged us
to return to Grand Cairo ; but inftead of
imbarking for Cyprus, he called afide the
mafter of the veffel, who was of his acquaintance, and, for a good round fum
privately agreed with him to fail out of
the port, as if we were really on board,
while the Pophar hired a boat for us at the
other end of the town, in which we went
that night directly for Grand Cairo.   As
foon as we were arrived there, we inquired
how long it would be before the Baffa returned to that city.   They told us it would
be about a fortnight at fooneft ; this gave
the Pophar time to pay off his houfe, pack
up his effects, and get all things ready for
his great voyage ; but he ftill had greater
apprehenfions

apprehenfions in his looks than ever I remarked in him. However, he hoped the
affair would end well. In five days time
all things were in readinefs for our departure. We fet out a little before funfet, as
is cuftomary in thofe countries, and marched but a flow pace whilft we were near the
town, to avoid any fufpicion of flight. After we had travelled thus about a league
up by the fide of the river Nile, the Pophar
leading the van, and the reft following in a
pretty long ftring after him, we met five
or fix men coming down the river-fide
on horfeback, whofe fine turbans and habits fhewed they were pages, or attendants
of fome great perfon. The Pophar turned
off from the river, as if it were to give
them way : and they paffed on very civil-
ly without feeming to take any further notice of us. I was the hindmoft but one of
our train, having ftaid to give our dromedaries fome water. Soon after thefe, came
two ladies riding on little Arabian jennets,
with prodigious rich furniture, by which
I gueffed them to be perfons of quality, and
the others gone before to be their attendants. They were not quite over-againft
where I was, when the jennet of the younger of the two ladies began to fnort and
ftart at our dromedaries, and became fo
unruly, that I apprehended fhe could fcarce
fit him. At that inftant, one of the led
                                    dromedaries

dromedaries coming pretty near, that and
the ru'tling of its loading fo frighted the
jennet, that he gave a bound all on a fud.
den, and being on the infide of us towards
the river, he ran full fpeed towards the
edge of the bank, where not being able to
ftop his career, he flew directly off the pre-
cipice into the river, with the lady ftill fitting him; but the violence of the leap
threw her off two or three yards into the
water. It happened very luckily that there
was a little iHand juft by where fhe fell,
and her cloaths keeping her up for fome mi-
nutes, the ftream carried her againft fome
ftakes that ftood juft above the water, which
catched hold of her clothes, and held her
there. The fhrieks of the other lady bro't
the nigheft attendants up to us; but thofe
fearful wretches durft not venture into the
river to her affiftance. I jumped off my
dromedary with indignation, and throwing
off my loofe garment and fandals, fwam to
her, and with much difficulty getting hold
of her hand, and loofing her garments from
the ftakes, I made a fhift to draw her acrofs
the ftream, till I brought her to land. She
was quite fenfelefs for fome time; I held
down her head, which I had not yet looked
at, to make her difgorge the water fhe had
fwallowed; but I was foon ftruck with a
double furprife, when I looked at her face,
to find it was the Baffa's daughter, and to
fee

see her in that place, whom I thought I had left at Alexandria. After some time, she came to herself, and looking fixed on me a good while, her senses not being entirely recovered, at last she cried out, " O Mahomet, must I owe my life to this man!" and fainted away. The other lady, who was her confident, with a great deal of pains brought her to herself again ; we raised her up, and endeavoured to comfort her as well as we could : No, says she, throw me into the river once more ; let me not be obliged to a barbarian for whom I have done too much already. I told her in the most respectful terms I could think of, that providence had ordered it so, that I might make some recompense for the undeserved obligations she had laid on me ; that I had two great value for her merit, ever to make her miserable, by loving a slave, such as I was, a stranger, a Christian, and one who had indispensable, obligations to act as I did. She startled a little at what I said ; but after a short recollection answered, whether you are a slave, an infidel, or whatever you please, you are one of the most generous men in the world. I suppose your obligations are on account of some more happy woman than myself ; but since I owe my life to you, I am resolved not to make you unhappy, any more than you do me. I not only pardon you, but

am

am convinced my pretenfions are both un-
juft, and againſt my own honor. She faid
this with an air becoming her quality : ſhe
was much more at eafe, when I affured her
I was engaged to no woman in the world ;
but that her memory fhould be ever dear
to me, and imprinted in my heart till my
laſt breath. Here ten or a dozen armed
Turks came upon us full fpeed from the
town, and feeing the Pophar and his companions, they cried out, Stop villains, we
arreſt you in the name of the Baſſa. At
this we ſtarted up to fee what was the matter, when the lady who knew them, bid
me not be afraid : that ſhe had ordered
thefe men to purfue me, when ſhe left Alexandria. That hearing we were fled off by
fea, ſhe pretended ficknefs, and afked leave
of her father to return to Cairo, there to
bemoan her misfortune with her confident:
and was in thofe melancholy fentiments,
when the late accident happened to her.
That ſhe fuppofed thefe men had difcovered the trick we had played them in not
going by fea, and on better information
had purfued us this way. So ſhe difmiffed
them immediately. I was all this while in
one of the greateſt agonies that can be expreffed, both for fear of my own refolutions
and hers : fo I begged her to retire, leſt
her wet cloaths fhouid endangar her health.
I fhould not have been able to pronounce
thefe

thefe words, if the Pophar had not caft a look at me, which pierced me through and made me fee the danger I was in by my delay. Her refolutions now feemed to be ftronger than mine. She pulled off this jewel your Reverences fee on my finger, and juft faid, with tears trickling down her beautiful cheeks, take this, and adieu! She then pulled her companion away, and never looked at me more. I ftood amazed, almoft without life or motion in me; and cannot tell how long I might have continued fo, if the Pophar had not come and congratulated me for my deliverance. I told him, I did not know what he meant by deliverance, for I did not know whether I was alive or dead, and that I was afraid he would repent his buying of me, if I procured him any more of thefe adventures. If we meet with no worfe than thefe, says he, we are well enough; no victory can be gained without fome lofs. So he awakened me out of my lethargy, and commanded us to make the beft of our way.

Though the Pophar was uneafy to be out of the reach of the fair lady and her faithlefs Turks, yet he was not in any great hafte in the main, the proper time for his great voyage not being yet come. There appeared a gaiety in his countenance, that feemed to promife us a profperous journey.

For

For my own part, though I was glad I had escaped my dangerous inchantrels, there was a heavinels lay on my spirits, which I could give no account of ; but the thoughts of such an unknown voyage, and variety of places, dissipated it by degrees. We were eleven in number, five elderly men, and five young ones, myself being a super-, numerary person. We were all mounted upon dromedaries, which were very fine for that sort of creature : they are some-thing like camels, but less, and much swift-er ; they live a great while without water, as the camels do, which was the reason they made use of them, for the barren sands they were to pass over ; though they have the finest horses that can be seen in their own country. They had five spare ones to car-ry provisions, or to change, in case any one of their own should tire by the way. It was upon one of these five that I rode. We went up the Nile, leaving it on our left hand all the way, steering our course di-rectly for the Upper Egypt. I presume your Reverences know, that the river Nile divides Egypt into two parts length-wise, descending from Abyssinia with such an immense course, that the Ethiopians said it had no head, and running through the hither Ethiopa, pours down upon Egypt, as the Rhine does through the Spanish Ne-therlands, making it one of the richest
.countries

countries in the univerſe. We viſited all
the towns on that famous river upwards,
under pretence of merchandiſing; but the
true reaſon of our delay was, becauſe the
Pophar's critical time for his great voyage
was not yet come. He looked at his ephemeris and notes almoſt every hour, the reſt
of them attending his nod in the moſt minute circumſtances. As we approached the
upper parts of Egypt, as nigh as I could
gueſs, over againſt the deſerts of Barca, they
began to buy proviſions, proper for their
purpoſe: but particularly rice, dried fruits,
and a ſort of dried paſte that ſerved us for
bread. They bought their proviſions at
different places, to avoid ſuſpicion; and I
obſerved they laid up a conſiderable quantity, both for their dromedaries and themſelves: by which I found we had a long
journey to make. When we came over-
againſt the middle coaſt of the vaſt deſert
of Barca, we met with a delicate clear rivulet, breaking out of a riſing part of the
ſands, and making towards the Nile. Here
we alighted, drank ourſelves, and gave our
dromedaries to drink as much as they
would; then we filled all our veſſels, made
on purpoſe for carriage, and took in a
much greater proportion of water than we
had done proviſions.—I forgot to tell your
Reverences, that, at ſeveral places as we
paſſed, they diſmounted, and kiſſed the

H   ground

ground with a very superstitious devotion, and scraped some of the dust, which they put into golden urns. which they had brought with them on purpose, letting me do what I pleased all the while. This sort of devotion I then only guessed, but found to be true afterwards, was the chief occasion of their coming into those parts, though carried on under the pretence of merchandising. They did the same in this place; and when all were ready, the Pophar looking on his papers and needle, cried *Gaulo benim*, which, I was informed, was as much as to say, *Now children for our lives;* and immediately as he had steered south all along before, he turned short on his right hand due west, cross the vast desert of Barca, as fast as his dromedary could well go. We had nothing but sands and sky before us, and in a few hours were almost out of danger of any one's attempting to follow us.

Being thus imbarked, if I may say so, on this vast ocean of sand, a thousand perplexing thoughts came into my mind, which I did not reflect on before. Behold me in the midst of the inhospitable deserts of Africa, where whole armies* had often perished.

* Ancient histories give us several instances of a great number of persons, and even whole armies, who have been lost in the sands of Africa. Herodotus in Thalia, says that Cambyses the son of Cyrus the Great, in his expedition against the Ethiopians, was brought to such straits in those vast deserts, that they were forced to eat every tenth man before they could get back again. The other army, which he sent

rifhed. The further we advanced, the more our danger increafed. I was with men, who were not only ftrangers to myfelf, but to all the world befide : ten againft one : but this was not all ; I was perfuaded now they were Heathens and idolaters: for, befide their fuperftitious kiffing the earth in feveral places, I obferved they looked up towards the fun, and feemed to addrefs their oraifons to that planet, glorious indeed, but a planet and a creature neverthelefs : then I reflected on what the Pophar faid when he bought me, that I was not likely to return. It is poffible, thought I, I am deftined for a human facrifice to fome Heathen god in the midft of this vaft defert. But not feeing any arms they had, either offenfive or defenfive, except their fhort goads to prick on their dromedaries, I was a little eafy : I had privately provided myfelf with two pocket-piftols, and was refolved to defend myfelf till the laft gafp. But when I confidered that unparallelled juftice and humanity I had experienced in their treatment of me, I was a little comforted. As for the difficulty of paffing the deferts, I reflected that their own lives

were

to deftroy the temple of Jupiter Ammon, was entirely overwhelmed and loft in the fands. Herodot. Thalia. The idolaters imputed it as a punifhment for his impiety againft Jupiter, but it was for want of knowing the danger.——I fuppofe very few are ignorant of the contrivance of Marius the Roman general, to get over the fands to Capfa, to feize Jugurtha's treafure, which he thought fecure. Salluft. de bello Jugurthin.

were as much in danger as mine ; that they muft have fome unknown ways of paffing them over, otherwife they would never expofe themfelves to fuch evident danger.

I fhould have told your Reverences, that we fet out a little before fun-fet to avoid the heats, June the 9th, 1688 ; the moon was about the firft quarter, and carried on the light till nigh dawn of day ; the glittering of the fands, or rather pebbly gravel, in which there were abundance of fhining ftones like jewels or cryftal, increafed the light, that we could fee to fteer our courfe by the needle very well, We went on at a vaft rate, the dromedaries being very fwift creatures ; their pace is more running than gallopping, much like that of a mule ; that I verily believe, from fix o'clock in the evening till about ten the next day, we ran almoft a hundred and twenty Italian miles : we had neither ftop nor let, but fteered our courfe in a direct line, like a fhip under fail.   The heats were not nigh fo infufferable as I expected ; for though we faw nothing we could call a mountain in thofe immenfe Bares, yet the fands, or at leaft the way we fteered, was very high ground : that as foon as we were out of the breath of the habitable countries, we . had a perpetual breeze blowing full in our aces ; yet fo uniform, that it fcarce raifed
any

any duſt; partly becauſe, where we paſſed, the ſands were not of that ſmall duſty kind, as in ſome parts of Africa, which fly in clouds with the wind overwhelming all before them, but of a more gravelly kind; & partly from an imperceptible dew, which, though not ſo thick as a fog, moiſtened the ſurface of the ground pretty much. A little after nine next morning we came to ſome clumps of ſhrubby trees, with a little moſs on the ground inſtead of graſs: here the wind fell, and the heats became very violent. The Pophar ordered us to alight, and pitch our tents, to ſhelter both ourſelves and dromedaries from the heats. Their tents were made of the fineſt ſort of oiled cloth I ever ſaw, prodigious light and portable; yet capable of keeping out both rain and ſun. Here we refreſhed ourſelves and beaſts till a little after ſix; when we ſet out again, ſteering ſtill directly weſt as nigh as I could gueſs. We went on thus for three days and nights without any conconſiderable accident; only I obſerved the ground ſeemed to riſe inſenſibly higher, and the breezes not only ſtronger, but the air itſelf much cooler. About ten, the third day, we ſaw ſome more clumps of trees on our right hand, which looke! greener and thicker than the former, as if they were the beginning of ſome habitable vale, as in effect they were. The Pophar

II 3   ordered!

ordered us to turn that way, which was the only turning out of our way we had yet made. By the chearfulnefs of their countenances, I thought this might be the beginning of their country; but I was very much miftaken; we had a far longer and more dangerous way to go, than what we had paffed hitherto. However, this was a very remarkable ftation of our voyage, as your Reverences will find by the fequel. As we advanced, we found it to open and defcend gradually; till at length we faw a moft beautiful vale, full of palms, dates, oranges, and other fruit-trees, entirely unknown in thefe parts, with fuch a refrefhing fmell from the odoriferous fhrubs, as filled the whole air with perfumes*. We rode into the thickeft of it as faft as we could to enjoy the inviting fhade. We eafed our dromedaries, and took the firft care of them; for on them all our fafeties depended. After we had refrefhed ourfelves, the Pophar ordered every one to go to fleep as foon as he could, fince we were like to have but little the three following days. I fhould have told your Reverences, that as foon as they alighted they fell down flat on their faces, and kiffed the earth, with a great deal of

seeming

* The prodigious fertility of Africa, in the vales between the deferts and the fkirts of it for a great breadth towards the two feas, is recorded by the beft hiftorians; though the ridge of it, over which our author was conducted, and other particular tracts, are all covered with fands.

feeming joy and ardour, which I took to
be a congratulation for their happy arrival
at fo hofpitable a place, but it was on a
quite different account. I was the firft who
awoke after our refrefhment ; my thoughts
and fears, though much calmer than they
had been, would not fuffer me to be fo fedate as the reft. Finding the hour for de-
parting was not yet come, I got up, and
walked in that delicious grove, which was
fo much the more delightful, as the deferts
we had paffed on, defcending towards the
centre of the vale, not doubting but, by
the greennefs and fragrancy of the place, I
fhould find a fpring of water. I had not
gone far, before I faw a moft delicate rill,
bubbling out from under a rock, forming
a little natural bafon, from whence it ran
gliding down the centre of the vale, increafing as it went, till in all appearance it
might form a confiderable rivulet, unlefs it
were fwallow up again in the fands. At
that place the vale ran upon a pretty deep
defcent, fo that I could fee over the trees
and fhrubs below me, almoft as far as my
eyes could reach ; increafing or decreafing
in breadth as the hills of fands, for now
they appeared to be hills, would give it
leave. Here I had the moft delightful profpect that the moft lively imagination can
form to itfelf ; the fun-burnt hills of fand
on each fide, made the greens look ftill
more

more charming ; but the finging of innu‧
merable unknown bids, with.the different
fruits and perfumes exhaling from the aromatic fhrubs, rendered the place delicious
beyond expreffion. After I had drank my
fill, and delighted myfelf with thofe native
‧rarieties, I faw a large lion come out of the
grove, about two hundred paces below me,
going very quietly to the fpring to lap‧
When he had drank, he wifked his tail two
or three times, and began to tumble on
the green grafs. I took the opportunity to
flip away back to my companions, very
glad I had efcaped fo : they were all awake
when I came up, and had been in great
concern for my abfence. The Pophar feem‧
ed more difpleafed that I had left them,
than ever I faw him ; he mildly chid me
for expofing myfelf to be devoured by wild
beafts : but when I told them of the water
and the lion, they were in a greater fur‧
prife, looking at one another with a fort
of fear in their looks, which I interpreted
to be for the danger I had efcaped ; but it.
was on another account. After fome words
in their own language, the Pophar fpoke
aloud in *lingua Franca*, I think, fays he,
we may let this young man fee all our ceremonies, efpecially fince he will foon be out
of danger of difcovering them, if he fhould
have a mind to do it. At this they pulled
out of their ftores, fome of their choiceft
fruits, .

fruits, a cruife of rich wine, fome bread, a burning glafs, a thurible*, perfumes, and other inftruments commonly ufed in the Heathen facrifices. I looked aghaft at this ftrange fight ; which was fuch as I had never obferved in them before, and began to apprehend that I was now really defign-ed for a human facrifice† to fome infernal god or other ; but when I compared the Pophar's late words with what I faw, I fcarce doubted of it, and was contriving with myfelf to fell my life as dear as I could. The Pophar ordered us to bring the dro-medaries, and every thing along with us, for fear, as he faid, they fhould be devour-ed by wild beafts. We defcended towards the centre of the vale, where I faw the foun-tain. They went on a great way lower into the vale, till it began to be very fteep ; but we found a narrow way made by art, and not feeming to have been very long unfrequented, which was more furprifing, becaufe I took the place to be uninhabited, and even inacceffible to all but thefe peo-ple. We were forced to defcend one by

one,

---

* An inftrument to hold incenfe.

† Our author's fears were not vain, confidering the preparatives he faw, and other circumftances. Befides, it is well known, the ancient Africans, particularly the Getulians and Libyans, and even the Cartha-genians, made ufe of human facrifices to appeafe their deities. Bochart, in the fecond part of his Geographia Sacra, proves beyond queftion, that the Carthagenians were part of the people of Canaan driven out by Jofhua, who ufed to facrifice their children to Moloch, &c. Even in Hannibal's time, when they were grown more polite, they fent privately, children to Tyre for a facrifice to Hercules.

one, leading our dromedaries in our hands :
I took particular care to be the hindmoft,
keeping at a little diftance from the reft,
for fear of a furprife. They marched down
in a mournful kind of proceflion, obferving
a moft profound filence all the while. At
length we came into the fineft natural amphitheatre that is poffible to defcribe. There
was nothing but odoriferous greens and
fky to be feen ; except downwards right
before us, where we had a moft delicious
profpect over that glorious vale, winding
a little to the right, till it was intercepted
by the collateral hills. At the upper part
of the amphitheatre, where the break of
the hill made that agreeable efplanade, there
ftood an ancient pyramid, juft after the
manner of thofe in Egypt, but nothing
near fo big as the leaft of them. In the
front of it that faced the vale, the fteps
were cut out in the form of an altar, on
which was erected a ftatue of a venerable
old man, done to the life, of the fineft polifhed marble, or rather fome unknown
ftone of infinite more value. Here I had
not the leaft doubt, but that I was to be
facrificed to this idol. The Pophar feeing
me at a diftance called to me, to come and
fee their ceremonies. Then I thought it
was time to fpeak or never. Father, faid
I, fince you give me leave to call you fo, I
am willing to perform all your commands,
                                        where

where the honor of the fupreme God is not called in queftion ; but I am ready to die a thoufand deaths, rather than give his honor to another. I am a Chriftian, and believe one only God, the fupreme being of all beings, and Lord of the univerfe; for which reafon I cannot join with you in your idolatrous worfhip. If you are refolved to put me to death on that account, I here offer my life freely! if I am to be made a part of your infernal facrifice, I will defend myfelf to the laft drop of my blood, before I will fubmit to it. He anfwered me with a fmile, rather than with any indignation, and told me, when I came to be better acquainted with them, I fhould find they were not fo inhuman as to put people to death, becaufe they were of a different opinion from their own. That this was only a religious ceremony they performed to their deceafed anceftors*, and if I had not a mind to affift at it, I might fit down at what diftance I pleafed.

[*Secretary.* The inquifitors were extremely pleafed with the firft part of
his

---

* The earlieft accounts of Egypt, from whence the'e peop'e came, tell us that they had a great veneration for their deceafed anceftors - See the third part of the Bifhop of Meaux's Univerfal hiftory, quoted above. Diodorus Siculus, who lived in the beginning of Auguftus's re gn. fays of the Egyptians, they were particularly diligent about their fepulchres, or in the worfhip of their dead. The fame fuperftition reigns ftill among the Chinefe, whom I fhall fhew afterwards to have been a colony of Egyptians, notwithftanding that China and Egypt are fo far diftant from each other.

his difcourfe, wherein he fhewed fuch courage in defence of his religion, and refolution to die rather than join in their idolatrous worfhip ; but all had liked to have been dafhed again by the fecond part, which made one of the inquifitors interrupt his narration, and afk him the following queftion.

Inquifitor. I hope you do nôt think it unlawful to perfecute, or even to put to death, obftinate heretics, who would deftroy the religion of our forefathers, and lead others into the fame damnation with themfelves. If treafon againft one's prince may be punifhed with death, why may not treafon againft the king of heaven be punifhed with the like penalty? Have a care you do not caft reflections on the holy inquifition.

Gaudentio. Reverend Fathers! I only relate bare matter of fact, as it was fpoke by the mouth of a Heathen, ignorant of our holy myfteries. I have all the reafon in the world, to extol the juftice of the holy inquifition : nor do I think, but, in fuch cafes mentioned by your Reverences, it may be lawful to ufe the utmoft feverities to prevent greater evils. But it argued a wonderful moderation in the Pophar, which I found to

be

be his real sentiments, not unbe-
coming a Chriftian in fuch circumftances, where it did not tend to the
deftruction of the whole.—But in
this, as in all other matters, I fubmit
to your decifions.

Secretary. I interpofed in his favour,
and put the inquifitors in mind, that
there was nothing but what was juft
in his anfwers : and we ourfelves
only ufed thofe rigours in the laft
extremity, to prevent greater mif-
chiefs. So they bid him read on.]

When the Pophar had faid this, he and
the reft of them fell down on their faces,
and kiffed the earth : then with the burn-
ing-glafs they kindled fome odoriferous
woods; put the coals in the thurible with
the incenfe, and incenfed the idol or ftatue :
that done, they poured the wine on the
altar ; fet bread on the one fide, and fruits
on the other : and having lighted two
little pyramids of moft delicious perfumes
at each end of the great pyramid, they
fat them down round the fountain, which
I fuppofe was conveyed by art under the
pyramid*, and iffued out in the middle of

I the

* The ancient Egyptians had a ftrange fondnefs for building pyramids; whether they were for the fame end as the tower of Babel,
that is, to make themfelves a name, or for other ends, we cannot
tell.——The great pyramid is more ancient than all the reft, infomuch
that the beft authors do not know when to fix its date, fome laying

the amphitheatre. There they refreshed themselves, and gathered the fruits which hung round us in the grove, eating of them very heartily, and inviting me to do the like. I made some difficulty at first, fearing it might be part of the sacrifice; but they assuring me all was but a civil ceremony, I joined them, and did as they did. The Pophar turned to me, and said, My son, we worship one most high God, as you do: what we did just now, was not that we believe any deity in that statue, or adored it as a God; but only respect it as a memorial, and in remembrance of our great ancestor, who heretofore conducted our forefathers to this place, and was buried in this pyramid*. The rest of our forefa- thers, who died before they were forced to leave this valley, are buried all around us. That is the reason we kissed the ground, not thinking it lawful to stir the bones of the dead. We did the same in Egypt, be- cause we were originally of that land: our particular ancestors lived in that part, which was afterwards called *Thebes*†. The time will

---

it was built by Mœris their first king, others by Cecrops Lesser. But if the account the Pophar gives of their origin, at the next station, be true, it was built before there was any king in Egypt. The river Nile was conveyed by art under the great pyramid.

* One of the ends of building the pyramids, was certainly for burying-places for some great men.

† Thebes once the most famous city of Egypt, having a hundred gates, &c. was the No-Amon, or Diaspolis of the ancients, Bochart. Phaleg. lib. 4. Tacitus says, that, in the time of Germanicus, there was

will not permit me to acquaint you at prefent, how we were driven out of our native
country to this place, and afterwards from
this place to the land we are now going to,
but you fhall know all hereafter. The
bread, fruits, and wine we laid on the al-
ter*, as they are the chief fupport of our
being ; fo we leave them there as a teftimony, that the venerable old man, whofe
ftatue you fee, was, under God, the author
and father of our nation. This faid, he
told us it was time to make the beft of our
way ; fo they all got up, and having kiffed
the ground once more, the five elderly men
fcraped a little of the earth, and put it in
fine golden veffels, with a great deal of care
and refpect. After refreshing ourfelves a-
gain, we made our provifion of fruits and
water, and leading our dromedaries up the
way we came down, mounted, and fet out
for the remainder of our journey.

We were now paft the tropic of Can-
cer†, as I found by our fhadows going
I 2 fouthward ;

was remaining an infcription in the Egyptian language, fignifying
Habitaffe quondam (Thebis) feptingenta milia hominum ætate militari :
That there were once feven hundred thoufand inhabitants in Thebes
fit to bear arms. Tacit. Annal. lib. 2.

* This is rank idolatry, notwithftanding the Pophar calls it but a
civil ceremony. Thus the worfhip the Chinefe pay to their dead, and
allowed by the Jefuits, was faid by them to be but a pious civil ceremony, though it was like this, or rather more fuperftitious. See the
condemnation of it by Pope Clement XI.

† When perfons are beyond that tropic, at mid-day the fhadows of
things are towards the fouth, becaufe the fun is then north of us ;

Miranturque umbras tranfire finiftras.

They might have paffed the tropt before, fince it runs over part of the

southward; and went on thus a little, bending towards the west again, almost parallel to the tropic, the breezes increasing rather stronger than before, so that about midnight it was really cold. We gave our dromedaries water about sun-rising, and refreshed ourselves a little : then set out with new vigour at a prodigious rate : still the breezes fell between nine and ten ; however we made shift to go on, because they came again about noon : between three and four was the hottest time of all. Besides, going now parallel to the tropic, we travelled on the hot sands, a very little descending ; whereas, when we pointed southwards towards the line, we found the ground to be insensibly rising upon us* ; but as we went on these almost flats, if it had not been that we were almost on the ridge of Africa, which made it cooler than one can well believe, it had been impossible to bear the heats. When we rested, we not only pitched our tents for ourselves, and dromedaries, but the sands were so hot, that we were

forced

---

desert of Barca, not much southward of Egypt ; but it seems they steered westward for some time.

  * His observations are just, since all the new philosophers allow the earth to be spheroidal and gibbous towards the equator. Whoever therefore goes by land, either from the north or south towards the equator, must ascend. This seems to be a very natural reason, why those immense Bares are not so excessive hot. The highest mountains are considerably nigher the sun than the low lands, yet excessive cold in the hottest climates ; in the vales the rays of the sun are cooped in, and doubled and trebled by refraction and reflection, &c. The same air put in a turbulent motion will be hot, and in a direct one cold.

forced to lay things under our feet to preferve them from burning. Thus we travelled through thofe difmal deferts for four
days, without fight of any living creature
but ourfelves. Sands and fky were all that
prefented itfelf to our view. The fatigue
was the greateft I ever underwent in my
life. The fourth day about eight in the
morning, by good fortune for us, or elfe
by the prudent forecaft of the Pophar, who
knew all his ftations, we faw another vale
towards the right hand, with fome ftrag-
gling trees here and there, but not feeming
nigh fo pleafant as the firft, we made to it
with all our fpeed, and had much ado to
bear the heats till we came to it. We a-
lighted immediately, and led our dromedaries down the gentle defcent, till we
could find a thicker part of it. The firft
trees were thin and old, as if they had juft
moifture enough to keep them alive : the
ground was but juft covered over with a
little fun burnt mofs, without any fign of
water, but our ftock was not yet gone.
At length, as we defcended, the grove increafed every way, the trees were large,
with fome dates here and there, but not fo
good as in the other. We refted a little,
and then continued to defcend for fome
time, till we came into a very cool and
thick fhade. Here, the Pophar told us,
we muft ftay two or three days, perhaps

longer, till he faw his ufual figns for proceeding on his journey ; and bid us be
fparing of our water, for fear of accidents.
We fettled our dromedaries as before : for
ourfelves, we could fcarce take any thing,
we were fo fatigued, wanting reft more
than meat and drink. The Pophar, ordering us fome cordial wines they had along
with them for that purpofe, told us, we
might fleep as long as we would ; only bid
us be fure to cover ourfelves well ; for the
nights were long, and even cold about
midnight. We were all foon afleep, and
did not wake till four the next morning.
The Pophar, folicitous for all our fafeties as
well as his own, (for this was the critical
time of our journey), was awake the firft
of us. When we were up, and had refreshed ourfelves, which we did with a very
good appetite, he told us we muft go upon the fands again to obferve the figns.
We took our dromedaries along with us,
for fear of wild beafts, though we faw
none, walking gently up the fands, till we
came to a very high ground. We had but
a dreary profpect, as far as our eyes could
carry us, of fun-burnt plains, without grafs,
ftick, or fhrub, except when we turned
our backs to look at the vale below us,
which running lower became a rivulet ; but
that, either by an earthquake, or fome
flood of fand, it was quite choaked up,
                                    running

running under ground, without any one's knowing whether it broke out again, or was entirely fwallowed up*. He faid alfo, that, by the moft ancient accounts of his forefathers, the fands were not in their times fo dangerous to pafs as they are now, or of fuch vaft extent†, but had fruitful vales much nearer one another than at prefent. He added, that he wifhed earneftly to fee the figns he wanted for proceeding on our way; fince there was no ftirring till they appeared : and that, according to his ephemeris and notes, they fhould appear about this time, unlefs fomething very extraordinary happened. This was about eight in the morning, the 9th day after we fet out for the deferts. He was every now and then looking fouthward, or fouthweft, with great folicitude in his looks, as if he wondered he faw nothing. At length he cried out with great emotions of joy, it is coming! Look yonder, fays he, towards the

* Geographers agree, that rivers, and even great lakes in Africa fink under ground, and are quite loft without any vifible outlets. The vaft depth of the ftrata of fand feems more proper to fwallow them up there, than in other parts of the word.

† There feems to be a natural reafon for what he fays ; for thofe vaft fands, or hills of gravel, were undoubtedly left by the general deluge, as probably all the leffer ftrata or beds of gravel were. Yet great part of them muft have been covered with flime or mud for feveral years after the deluge, fome thinner, fome thicker, and confequently more moift and productive accordingly. Neverthelefs, the violent rays of the fun ftill render them more dry and barren. and, in all probability, thefe deferts will increafe more and more, where the country is not cultivated.

the fouthweft, as far as your eyes can carry you, and fee what you can difcover. We
told him, we faw nothing but· fome clouds
of fand, carried round here and there like
whirlwinds. That is the fign I want, continued he ; but mark well which way it
drives. We faid it drove directly eaftward,
as nigh as we could guefs. It does,
fays he ; then turning his face weftwards,
with a little point of the fouth. All
thofe vaft deferts, fays he, are now in
fuch a commotion of ftorms· and whirlwinds, that man and beaft will foon be
overwhelmed in the rolling waves of fands.
He had fcarce faid this, but we faw, at a
vaft diftance, ten thoufand little whirl-fpouts
of fand, rifing and falling with a prodigious tumult and velocity*eaftward, with vaft
thick clouds of fand and duft following them.
Come, fays he, let us return to our refting-place ; for there we muft ftay, till we
fee further how matters go. As this appeared newer to me than any of the reft,
and being poffeffed with a great idea of the
knowledge

* Though in the vaft occean between the tropics, where promontories
do not intervene, the winds are generally eafterly, yet there is a perpetual weft wind blows into Guinea —There are vaft rains at the fol-
ftices between the tropics, as the accounts of thofe parts declare ;
though at that time of the year, more beyond the line than on this fide
of it. It is not to be queftioned, but in fuch violent changes, particularly before thofe rains, there muft be furious hurricanes of wind and
fand, enorgh to overwhelm whole armies and countries.——The moft
incredible part of this narration, is, how they could travel at all under
the tropic, in the fummer-folftice, only, as he fays, the ground being
very high and open, it muft draw air.

knowledge of the man, I made bold to afk
him, what was the caufe of this fudden
phænomenon: he told me, that, about that
full moon, there always fell prodigious
rains*, coming from the weftern part of
Africa, on this fide the equator, and driving
a little fouth-weft for fome time at firft,
but afterwards turning almoft fouth, and
croffing the line till they came to the fource
of the Nile; in which parts they fell for
three weeks or a month together, which was
the occafion of the overflowing of that river †: but that, on this fide the equator, it
only rained about fifteen days, preceded by
thofe whirlwinds and clouds of fand, which
rendered all that tract impaffable, till the
rains had laid them again.—By this time we
were come down to our refting-place, and
though we did not want fleep or refreshment, yet we took both; to have the cool
of the evening to recreate ourfelves after fo
much

* Naturalifts agree, that beyond the line there are great rains at
that feafon. It is poffible, they may begin on this fide, being driven
by the perpetual weft winds into Guinea, and then, by natural caufes,
turn towards the line and fouthern tropic.

† The caufes of the overflowing of the river Nile, unknown to moft
of the ancients, are now allowed to be the great rains falling in June
and July about the line, and the fouthern tropic, and the melting of the
fnow on the mountains of the moon lying in that tract. None can
wonder there fhould be fnow in thofe hot climates, who have heard of
the Andes or Cordilleras bordering on Peru. Our Italy is very hot, yet
the Alps and Apennines are three parts of the year covered with
fnow.———The Nile overflows in Auguft, which feem to be a proper
diftance of time for the waters to come down to Egypt, fuch a vaft
way off from the caufe of it. There is a river in Cochinchina, and
elfewhere, that overflows in the fame manner.

much fatigue, not being likely to move till
the next evening at fooneſt.

At five in the evening, the pophar called
us up to go with him once more to the
higheſt part of the defert, faying he wanted
one fign yet, which he hoped to have that
evening, or elfe it would go hard with us
for want of water, our proviſion of it being
almoſt fpent; and there were no fprings in
the deferts that we were to pafs over, till
we came within a long days journey of the
end of our voyage. However, he fcarce
doubted but we ſhould fee the certain fign
he wanted this evening ; on which account,
there did not appear fuch a folicitude in his
countenance as before : for though he was
our governor, or captain, and had the refpectful deference paid to him ; yet he governed us in all refpects, as if we were
his children, with all the tendernefs of a
father, as his name imported; though none
of the company were his real children. If
there were any figns of partiality, it was in
my favour, always expreſſing the moſt endearing tendernefs for me, which the other
young men, inſtead of taking any diſlike
at, were really pleafed with. No brothers
in the world could be more loving to one
another than we were. The elderly men
took delight in feeing our youthful gambols
with one another : it is true their nature is,
of the two, a little more inclined to gravity

ty than that of the Italians, who are no light nation ; yet their gravity is accompanied with all the ferenity and cheerfulnefs imaginable, and I then thought at our firft acquaintance, that I had never feen fuch an air of a free-born people in my life ; as if they knew no other fubjection but what was merely filial. When we came to the high ground, we could fee the hurricanes play ftill ; but, what was more wonderful, very few effects of that aerial tumult came our way, but drove on almoft parallel to the equator : the air looked like a brown dirty fog, towards the eaft and fouth-eaft ; all the whirlwinds tending towards thofe parts ; it began after fome time to look a little more lightfome towards the weft; but fo, as if it were occafioned by a more ftrong and fettled wind. At length we perceived, at the fartheft horrizon, the edge of a prodigious black cloud, extending itfelf to the fouth-weft and weftern points, rifing with a difcernable motion, though not very faft. We faw plain enough, by the blacknefs and thicknefs of it, that it prognofticated a great deal of rain.——Here they all fell proftrate on the earth : then raifing up their hands and eyes towards the fun, they feemed to pay their adorations to that great luminary. The Pophar, with an audible voice, pronounced fome unknown words, as if he were returning thanks to that planet for

what

what he faw. At this I ftepped back, and
kept myfelf at a diftance; not fo much
for fear of my life, as before, as not to
join with them in their idolatrous worfhip.
For I could not be ignorant now, that
they had a wrong notion of God, and if
they acknowledged any, it was the fun:
which in effect is the leaft, irrational idolatry people can be guilty of*. When they
had done their oraifons, the Pophar turned
to me, and faid, I fee you won't join with
us in any of our religious ceremonies; but
I muft tell you, continued he, that cloud
is the faving of all our lives: and as that
great fun, pointing to the luminary, is the
inftrument that draws it up, as indeed he
is the preferver of all our beings, we think
ourfelves obliged to return our thanks to
him.

* All idolatry being a worfhip of creatures inftead of the one fu
preme God, muft be irrational. But it is certain, and wel. attefted by
ancient hiftory, that the eaftern nations worfhipped the fun: probably
it was the firft idolatrous worfhip that was in the world. The great
benefits all nature receives from his influence; the glorious brightnefs
of his rays; the variety, yet conftant tenor of his motions, might induce
ignorant people to believe him to be of a fuperior nature to other
creatures, though it is evidently certain, he is limited in his perfections,
and confequently no God. It is true, the ancient Egyptians, from
whom thefe people fprung, is will be feen afterwards, worfhipped the
fun in the moft early times. There was a prieft of the fun in the
patriarch Jofeph's time. And the Egyptians were fome of the firft
aftronomers in the world, contending for antiquity with the Chaldeans.
Though both the Chaldeans and Egyptians had their knowledge from
the defcendents of Sem, or his father Noah, who, by the admirable
ftructure of the ark, appears to have been mafter of very great fciences.
I fay, the Egyptians being fo much addicted to aftronomy, it is probable
that glorious luminary was the chief object of their worfhip. They
did not worfhip idols and beafts till long afterwards. See the learned Bochart's Phaleg, in Mifraim.

him. Here he stopped, as if he had a mind to hear what I could say for myself. I was not willing to enter into disputes, well knowing that religious quarrels are the most provoking of any : yet I thought myself obliged to make profession of my belief in the supreme God, now I was called upon to the professed worship of a false deity. I answered with the most modest respect I was capable of, that that glorious planet was one of the physical causes of the preservation of our beings, and of the production of all things ; but that he was produced himself by the most high God, the first cause and author of all things in heaven and earth ; the sun only moving by his order, as an inanimate being, incapable of hearing our prayers, and only operating by his direction. However, I offered to join with him, in returning my best thanks to the most high God, for creating the sun, capable by his heat to raise that cloud for the saving our lives. Thus I adapted my answer as nigh to his discourse as I could, yet not so as to deny my faith. For I could not entirely tell what to make of them as yet ; since I observed, they were more mysterious in their religious ceremonies, than in any thing else* ; or rather, this was the only

K   thing

* This agrees with all ancient accounts of the first people of Egypt ; witness their emblems, hieroglyphics, &c. Most of the ancient fables, under which so many mysteries were couched, did not first spring from the Greeks, though improved by them ; but from the Egyptians and Chaldeans.

thing they were referved in.   He ponder-
ed a good while on what I faid, but at
length he added, You are not much out
of the way : you and I will talk this matter over another time ; fo turned off the
difcourfe ; I fuppofed it to be becaufe of the
young men ftanding by us; whom he had
not a mind fhould receive any other notions of religion, but what they had been
taught.   It was fun-fet by the time we
came down to the grove.   We had fome
fmall flights of fand, caufed by an odd
commotion in the air, attended with little
whirlwinds, which put us in fome fmall
apprehenfions of a fand-fhower ; but he
bid us take courage, fince he could not find
in all his accounts, that the hurricanes or
rains ever came, in any great quantity, as
far as we were, the nature of them being
to drive more parellel to the equator : but
he was fure we fhould have fome: and ordered us to pitch our tents as firm as we
could, and draw out all our water-veffels,
to catch the rain againft all accidents. When
this was done, and we had eat our fuppers,
we recreated ourfelves in the grove, wandering about here and there, and difcourf-
ing of the nature of thefe phænomena.
We did not care to go to reft fo foon, having

Chaldeans, who at firft held a communication of fciences with one another, but grew to emulofity afterwards. The wonderful things the
Egyptian Magi did, in imitation of the miracles wrought by Mofes, fhew
they were great artifts.

ing repofed ourfelves fo well that day, and
having all the following night and the next
day to ftay in that place.   The grove grew
much pleafanter as we advanced into it ;
there were a great many dates and other
fruits, the natural produce of Africa ; but
not quite fo rich as in the firft grove.   I
made bold to afk the Pophar, how far that
grove extended, or whether there were
any inhabitants. He told me, he could not
tell any thing of either.   That it was poffible the grove might enlarge itfelf different ways, among the winding hills : fince
his accounts told him, there had been a rivulet of water, though now fwallowed up ;
but he believed there were no inhabitants,
fince there was no mention made of them
in his papers.   Nor did he believe any other
people in the world, befide themfelves,
knew the way, or would venture fo far into thofe horrid inhofpitable deferts.   Having a mind to learn whether he had any
certain knowledge of the longitude, which
creates fuch difficulties to the Europeans, I
afked how he was fure that was the place ;
or by what rule he could know how far he
was come, or where he was to turn to
right or left.   He ftopped a little at my
queftions ; then, without any apparent he-
fitation, Why, faid he, we know by the
needle, how far we vary from the north or
fouth point, at leaft till we come to the

tropic* ; if not, we can take the meridi-
an and height of the fun, and knowing the
time of the year, we can tell how near we
approach to, or are off the equator. Yes,
faid I : but as there are different meridians
every ftep you take, how can you tell how
far you go eaft or weft, when you run either
way in parallel linest to the tropics, or the
equator ? Here he ftopped again, and either
could not make any certain difcovery, or
had not a mind to let me into the fecret.
The firft was moft likely ; however, he anfwered readily enough, and faid, You
pleafe me with your curious queftions, fince
I find you are fenfible of the difficulty.
Why, continued he, all the method we
have, is, to obferve exactly how far our
dromedaries go in an hour, or any other
fpace of time : you fee we go much about
the fame pace : we have no ftops in our
way, but what we know of, to refrefh ourfelves or fo, for which we generally allow

fo

---

* Experimental phylofopy tells us, that the needle is of little ufe in
navigation, when under the line ; but lies fluctuating without turning to
any point of itfelf ; becaufe, as fome fuppofe, the current of the magnetic
effluvia, fluxing from pole to pole, has there its longeft axis, as the diameter
of the equator is larger than the axis of the world. But whether this has
the fame effect on the needle by land, which is the cafe, as it has by fea, we
muft have more certain experiments to know, tho' it is probable it may.

† Where-ever we ftand, we are on the fummit of the globe with refpect to us. Whoever therefore thinks to go due weft, parallel to the
equator or eaft, will not do fo, but will cut the line at longrun, becaufe
he makes a greater circle. Thefe men therefore, when they thought
they went due weft, were approaching to the line, more than they were
aware of, and fuppofing the ftructure of the earth to be fpheroidical,
went up hill all the way, bating fome fmall inequalities.

so much time*. When we set out from Egypt, we went due west; our beasts gain so many miles an hour; we know by that, how far we are more west than we were†. If we decline to the north or the south, we know likewise, how many miles we have advanced in so many hours, and compute how much the declination takes off from our going due west. And though we cannot tell to a demonstrative exactness, we can tell pretty nigh. This was all I could get out of him at that time, which did not satisfy the difficulty. I afterwards asked him, how they came to find out this way, or to venture to seek out a habitation unknown to all the world beside. He answered, " For liberty, and the preservation of our laws." I was afraid of asking any further, seeing he gave such general answers. By this time it was prodigious dark, though full moon‡. We had some sudden gusts of wind that startled us a little; and it lightened at such a rate, as I never saw in my life. And although it was towards the horizon, and drove sidewise of us,

K 3

* This must be understood according to the foregoing remark,

† At first sight, it seems to be easier to find out the longitude by land than by sea, because we may be more certain how far we advance. At sea there are currents, and tides, and settings in of the sea which make the ship to go aslant more or less insensibly. As yet there has been no certain rule found to tell us, how far we advance due east or west well. The elevation of the pole, or the height of the sun, shews us how far we decline to the north or south; but we have no certain rule for the east or west.

‡ The full moon about the summer-solstice generally brings rain, and the overflowing of the Nile is now known to be caused by the vast rains in the regions near the equator,

us, yet it was really terrible to fee ; the flaſhes were ſo thick, that the ſky was al-moſt in a light fire. We made up to our tents as faſt as we could ; and though we had only the ſkirts of the clouds over us, it rained ſo very hard, that we had our veſſels ſoon ſupplied with water, and got ſafe into our ſhelter. The thunder was at a vaſt diſtance, but juſt audible, and, for our comfort, drove ſtill to the eaſtward. I do not know in what diſpoſitions the elder-ly men might be, being accuſtomed to the nature of it ; but I am ſure I was in ſome ap-prehenſion, fully perſuaded, if it had come directly over us, nothing could withſtand its impetuoſity. I had very little inclina-tion to reſt, whatever my companions had ; but pondering with myſelf, both the na-ture of the thing, and the prodigious ſkill theſe men muſt have in the laws of the uni-verſe, I ſtaid with impatience waiting the event.

I was muſing with myſelf on what I had heard and ſeen, not being able yet to gueſs with any ſatisfaction what theſe people were, when an unexpected accident was the cauſe of a diſcovery, which made me ſee they were not greater ſtrangers to me, than I was to myſelf. The weather was ſtifling hot, ſo that we had thrown off our garments to our ſhirts, and bared our breaſts for coolneſs ſake ; when there came

a prodigious flafh, or rather blaze of lightning, which ftruck full againft the breaft
of one of the young men oppofite to me,
and difcovered a bright gold medal hanging down from his neck, with the figure of
the fun engraved on it, furrounded with
unknown characters ; the very fame in all
appearance I had feen my deceafed mother
always wear about her neck, and fince her
death I carried with me for her fake. I
afked the meaning of that medal, fince I
had one about me, as it appeared, of the
very fame make. If the Pophar had been
ftruck with lightning, he could not have
been in a greater furprife, than he was
at thefe words : You one of thefe medals !
faid he ; how, in the name of wonder, did
you come by it ? I told him my mother
wore it about her neck, from a little child ;
and with that pulled it out of my pocket.
He fnatched it out of my hands with a prodigious eagernefs, and held it againft the
lightning perpetually flafhing in upon us.
As foon as he faw it was the fame with the
other, he cried out, Great fun, what can
this mean ? Then afked me again, where
I had it ? how my mother came by it ? who
my mother was ? what age fhe was of
when fhe died ? As foon as the violence of
his ecftafy would give me leave, I told him
my mother had it ever fince fhe was a little
child : that fhe was the adopted daughter
of

of a noble merchant in Corfica, who had given her all his affects when my father married her : that fhe was married at thir-teen ; and I being nineteen, and the fecond fon, I guefled fhe was towards forty when fhe died. It muft be Ifiphena, cried he, with the utmoft ecftafy, it muft be fhe. Then he caught me in his arms, and faid, You are now really one of us, being the fon of my father's daughter, my dear fif-ter Ifiphena. The remembrance of whom made the tears run down the old man's cheeks very plentifully. She was loft at Grand Cairo about the time you mention, together with a twin-fifter who I fear is never to be heard of. Then I reflected I had heard mother fay, fhe had been in-formed, the gentleman who adopted her for his daughter, had bought her when fhe was a little girl of a Turkifh woman of that place ; that being charmed with the early figns of beauty in her, and having no children, he adopted her for his own. Yes, faid the Pophar, it muft be fhe ; but what is become of the other fifter ? For, faid he, my dear fifter brought two at one unfortunate birth, which coft her her life. I told him I never heard any thing of the other. Then he acquainted me that his fifter's hufband was the perfon who con-ducted the reft to vifit the tombs of their anceftors, as he did now : that the laft voy-age,

age, he took his wife with him, who out of her great fondnefs had teafed him and importuned him fo much to go along with him, that, though it was contrary to their laws, he contrived to carry her difguifed in man's cloths, like one of the young men he chofe to accompany him in the expedition : that ftaying at Grand Cairo till the next feafon for his return, fhe proved with child of twins ; and, to his unfpeakable grief, died in childbed. That when they carried her up to Thebes to be interred with her anceftors, of which I fhould have a more exact information by and by, they were obliged to leave the children with a nurfe of the country, with fome Egyptian fervants to take care of the houfe and effects ; but before they came back, the nurfe with her accomplices ran away with the children, and, as was fuppofed, murdered them, rifled the houfe of all the jewels and other valuable things, and were never heard of afterwards. But it feems they thought it more for their advantage to fell the children, as we find they did, by your mother ; but what part of the world the other fifter is in, or whether fhe be at all, is known only to the great author of our being. However, continued he, we rejoice in finding thefe hopeful remains of your dear mother, whofe refemblance you carry along with you. It was that gave me fuch a kindnefs

for

for your perfon the firft time I faw you, methought, perceiving fomething I had never obferved in any other race of people,   But, faid he, I deprive my companions and children here of the happinefs of embracing their own flefh and blood; fince we all fprung from one common father, the author of our nation, with whom you are going to be incorporated once more. Here we embraced one another with a joy that is inexpreffible. Now all my former fears were entirely vanifhed : though I had loft the country where I was born, I had found another, of which I could nowife be afhamed, where the people were the moft humane and civilized I ever faw, and the foil the fineft, as I had reafon to hope, in the world. The only check to my happinefs was, that they were infidels. However, I was refolved not to let any confideration blot out of my mind that I was a Chriftian. On which account, when the Pophar would have tied the medal about my neck, as a badge of my race, I had fome difficulty in that point, for fear it fhould be an emblem of idolatry, feeing them to be extremely fuperftitious. So I afked him, what was the meaning of the figure of the fun, with thofe unknown charaĉters round about it ? He told me the charaĉters were to be pronounced *Omabim*, i. e. *The fun is the author of our being*, or
more

more literally, *The sun is our father. Om* or *On* signifies the sun [This will be explained in another place]. *Ab* signifies *Father, Im* or *Mim, Us.* This made me remember, they had told me in Egypt that they were children of the sun ; and gave me some uneasiness at their idolatrous notions. I therefore told him, I would keep it as a cognisance of my country ; but could not acknowledge any but God to be the supreme author of my being. As to the supreme author, said he, your opinion is little different from ours*. But let us leave these religious matters till another time : we'll close this happy day with thanksgiving to the supreme being for this discovery : to-morrow morning, since you are now really one of us, I will acquaint you with your origin, and how we came to hide ourselves in these inhospitable deserts.—

[*The reader is desired not to censure or disbelieve the following account of the origin and transmigration of these people, till he has perused the learned remarks of Signor Rhedi.*]

The next morning the Pophar calling me to him, Son, said he, to fulfil my promise which

---

* These people are something like the Chinese, who worship the material heaven or sky, which some missionaries could think compatible with Christianity.

which I made you laſt night, and that you
may not be like the reſt of the ignorant
world, who know not who their forefathers and anceſtors were*; whether they
ſprung from brutes or barbarians, is all
alike to them, provided they can but gro-
vel on the earth, as they do : you muſt
know therefore, as I ſuppoſe you remember what I told you at our firſt ſtation,
that we came originally from Egypt. When
you aſked me, how we came to venture
through theſe inhoſpitable deſerts, I told
you, it was for liberty, and the preſerva-
tion of our laws; but as you are now found
to be one of us, I deſign to give you a
more particular account of your origin.
Our anceſtors did originally come from
Egypt, once the happieſt place in the
world; though the name of *Egypt*, and
Egyptians, has been given to that country,
long ſince we came out of it; the original
name

* It would certainly be a great ſatisfaction to moſt nations to know
from what race of people, country, or family, they ſprung originally.
This ignorance is owing chiefly to the Barbari Tramontani†, and other
nothern nations, who have from time to time over-run the face of Europe, leaving a mixture of their ſpawn in all parts of it; ſo that no one
knows, whether he came originally from Scythia or Aſia, from a civilized nation, or from the greateſt brutes; and though wars and invaſions
have deſtroyed, or interchanged the inhabitants of moſt countries : yet
this man's obſervation is a juſt cenſure of the neglect of moſt people,
with reſpect to their genealogy and knowledge of their anceſtors, where
they have been ſettled in a country for ſeveral ages. But there are
matters of greater moment in this man's relation, true or falſe, which
lead us into ſome curious remains of ancient hiſtory.
† Signor Rhedi being an Italian, one cannot wonder he ſpeaks ſo con-
temptibly of the nothern people; the Italians call them all Barbari.

name of it was *Mezzoraim**, from the first man that peopled it, the father of our nation ; and we call ourselves *Mezzoranians* from him. We have a tradition delivered down to us from our first ancestors, that when the earth first rose out of the water†, six persons, three men and three women, rose along with it : either sent by the supreme deity to inhabit it, or produced by the sun‡. That Mezzoraim our first founder was one of those six : who increasing in number, made choice of the country

L   now

---

* The original name of Egypt was Misraim ; from Misraim, or Mezoraim, as the learned Bochart explains it, lib. 4. of Geograph. Sacra in Misraim. M. Du Pin's history of the Old Test. c. 6. and others. All ancient authors agree, that it was once the richest and happiest country in the world ; flourishing with plenty, and even learning, before the patriarch Abraham's time. There is a very remarkable fragment of Eupolemus an ancient Heathen writer, taken from the Babylonian monuments, preserved by Eusebius, lib. 9. The whole fragment, in our mother tongue, signifies, that, according to the Babylonians, the first was Belus, the same with Kronos or Saturn : from him came Ham or Cham, the father af Canon, brother to Mesraim, father of the Egyptians.

† This is an obscure notion of Noah's flood, known to all nations, at least the eastern, as appears by the oldest remains ; of which see Bochart on that article, lib. 1. " The earth rose out of the water," or the waters sunk from the earth. These people might mistake something of that undoubted and ancient tradition. But Misraim could not be ignorant of the flood, his father Ham having been in the ark, whether ignorance or other motives made his posterity vary in the account ; but it is evident the ancients had a notion of the general deluge, as may easily be proved by the remains of Heathen authors bearing testimony to the scripture-account of it.

‡ The ancient Egyptians thought men, as well as insects, were produced out of the slime of the Nile, by the heat of the sun, and called themselves Aborigines, as several other nations did. Though it is wise man is inclined to think they were created by God ; as it is evident and certain they were ; for since we see one single insect cannot be produced without a cause, it is nonsense, as well as impossible, to imagine an infinite series of men and animals could be produced without a separate cause ; on which account Atheism is one of the most foolish and absurd notions in the world.

now called *Egypt**, for the place of his habitation, where he settled with sixty of his children and grandchildren, all of whom he brought along with him, governing them as a real father and instructing them to live with one another, as brothers of one and the same family†. He was a peaceable man, abhorring the shedding of blood‡, which he said would be punished by the supreme ruler of the world; extremely given to the search of sciences, and contemplation

* Herodotus tell us, the Egyptians pretended to be the first inhabitants of the earth; though the Ethiopians contended with them for antiquity. I must quote the words in Latin, out of Laurenzo Valla's translation, because I have him not in Greek. Omnium hominum priores se extitisse arbitrabantur. They esteemed themselves, says he, to have been the first of all men. Herodot lib. 2. Euterpe,

† It is certain from Bochart, and other learned authors, that the Egyptian government, as well as that of most nations, was at first patriarchal: till Nimrod founded the first kingdom or empire in the world; whose example others followed, according to their power. However, the patriarchal government was soon broke in upon in Egypt, since they had kings in Abraham and Isaac's time, as we learn from the Old Testament. See Bochart's Geographia Sacra.

‡ The celebrated Bishop of Meaux, in part 3. of his Univ-Hist. gives us a wonderful description of the justice and piety of the first Egyptians, who had such a horror of shedding men's blood, that they punished their criminals after they were dead; which was as much in terrorem, considering their superstitious reverence for their deceased friends and parents, as if they had been punished when alive. The reason why the ancient moral Heathens abhorred the shedding of blood, might be, that Noah's sons having lived before the deluge, knew that the wickedness of the world was the cause of that dreadful judgment; and shedding of blood being the first crime punished by God, they might take warning by such terrible examples thorgh the impiety of some nations soon obscured this innate light of nature, particularly the descendents of Ham; all but this Misraim; who with his family, by all accounts, first peopled Egypt; and they were noted for justice and knowledge. It will be made evident in the subsequent remarks, that these Hicksoes were the descendents of wicked Canaan, or Cush, who destroyed the peaceable state of the first Egyptians, and introduced idolatry among them; which made great numbers of them fly into other parts of the world to save themselves.

templation of the heavens*. It was he who was the firſt inventor of all our arts, and whatever is uſeful for the government of life, ſprung from him. Though his grandſon Thaoth† rather excelled, him, particularly in the more ſublime ſciences. Thus our anceſtors lived four hundred years, increaſing and ſpreading over all the land of Egypt, and abounding with the bleſſings of peace and knowledge ; without guile or deceit, neither doing or fearing harm from any; till the wicked deſcendents of the other men, called *Hickſoes*‡, envying their

L 2   happineſs,

* The ſame learned Biſhop of Meaux, and other hiſtorians, aſſure us, as it is a thing well known to all the learned, that arts and ſciences were brought to very great perfection in the earlieſt times in Egypt. Moſes was inſtructed in the ſciences of the Egyptians. Triptolemus, the founder of agriculture, came out of Egypt. Bacchus, the inventor of wine, according to the ancients. came out of Egypt, or Libya, which borders upon it though it was firſt learned from Noah. Pythagoras, and other learned men, went into Egypt to be inſtructed by the prieſts, &c. Herodotus ſays the ſame of himſelf.

† This Thaoth, the famous philoſopher of the Egyptians, was before Mercury or Triſmegiſtus ; though ſome take him to be the ſame. All allow him to be extremely ancient, but cannot fix the time when he lived. Hiſtorians murder his name at a ſtrange rate. Bochart calls him Taatus, lib. 2. cap. 12 Clemens Alex. lib. 6. Strom. ſays, he wrote forty-two books of aſtrology, geography, phyſic, policy, theology, religion, and government Joſeph Ben-Gorion, de diviſione Gentium, calls him Tutis ; ſome call him Theut, others, Tent, Taut, Thoth, &c. But, according to this man, his name was Thaoth. It is certain, however, that he was the great maſter of the Egyptians ; but derived his learning from Noah, who might have the knowledge of arts and ſciences from the antediluvian world, or from the columns of Seth, which, Joſephus ſays, contain the principles of aſtrology, and were erected before the flood by the nephews of Seth: one of which columns, as he ſays, remained in Syria in his time. Joſeph. Ant. lib. 2.

‡ The ſame Joſephus, lib. 2. contra Appion, ſays, that Hyckſoes, an old Egyptian word, ſignifies king ſhepherds, or kings of beaſts, given them by the native Egyptians, as a name of diſgrace and contempt. It s out of all controverſy that there was a great revolution in Egypt, about

four

happinefs and the richnefs of their country, broke in upon them like a torrent, deſtroying all before them, and taking poſſeſſion of that happy place our anceſtors had rendered ſo flouriſhing. The poor innocent Mezzoranians abhorring, as I ſaid, the ſhedding of blood, and ignorant of all violence, were ſlaughtered like ſheep all over the country ; and their wives and daughters violated before their eyes. Thoſe whom their mercilefs enemy ſpared, were made ſlaves to work and till the earth for their new lords.

Secretary. Here the inquiſitors interrupted him, and aſked him, whether he thought it unlawful in all caſas to reſiſt

four hundred years after the flood, or a little before Abraham's time. Monſieur Du Pin makes the time from the flood to Abraham's birth three hundred and fifty years ; and about four hundred to his being called by God. It is certain alſo, there were kings in Egypt in Abraham's time. It is probable theſe kings were the Hyckſoes, or king ſhepherds, who altered the government of the ancient Egyptians, and continued about five kings reigns. For when the patriarch Joſeph called his father and brethren into Egypt, he bid them aſk the land of Goſhen to inhabit, becauſe, ſaid he, all ſhepherds are an abomination to the Egyptians. By which it appears the ſhepherds were lately driven out. In all likelihood theſe were the kings who introduced idolatry and the adoration of brute beaſts among the Egyptians, for which reaſon they called them in deriſion king-ſhepherds, or king-beaſts.——The great Bochart in his Phaleg, looks upon this revolution in Egypt to have been before Abraham's time, and ſo far from being a fiction, that he ſays in expreſs words, Caſluços et Caphthoræos (whom he proves to be the people of Colchos, for all it is ſo far from Egypt) ex Ægypto migraſſe certum eſt. ante Abrahami tempora. "It is certain," ſays he, "that the Caſluci and the Caphthoræi went out of Egypt before Abraham's time." Bochart Phaleg. lib. 4. c. 31. Herodotus in Euterpe ſays, that the people of Colchos were originally Egyptians ; though ſome ſay they went back ſome ages after, and ſettled in Paleſtine, and were called after that Philiſtines.

fift force by force, or whether the law of nature did not allow the Mezzoranians to refift thofe cruel invaders even to the fhedding of blood ; as alfo to punifh public malefactors with death for the prefervation of the whole. Their intent was, as they are cautious of any new opinions, to know whether he might not be a dogmatizer, and advance fome erroneous notions, either by holding that to be lawful, which was not fo ; or denying things to be lawful, which really may be allowable by the light of nature.

Gaudentio. Doubtlefs they might lawfully have refifted even to the fhedding of blood in that cafe, as public criminals may be put to death. I only acquaint your Reverences with the notions peculiar to thefe people ; as for the punifhment of their criminals, your Reverences will fee, when I come to their laws and cuftoms, that they have other ways and means of punifhing crimes as effectual as putting to death ; though living entirely within themfelves, free from all mixture and commerce with other people, they have preferved their primitive innocence in that refpect to a very great degree. Inquifitor. Go on.

The

The Pophar continuing his relation, added: But what was most intolerable was, that these impious Hickfoes forced them to adore men and beasts, and even insects, for gods; nay, and some to see their children offered in sacrifice to those inhuman deities*. This dreadful inundation fell at first only on the lower parts of Egypt, which was then the most flourishing. As many of the distressed inhabitants as could escape their cruel hands, fled to the upper parts of the country, in hopes to find there some little respite from their misfortunes. But alas! what could they do? they knew no use of arms: neither would their laws suffer them to destroy their own species; so that they expected every hour to be devoured by their cruel enemies. The heads of the families in such distress were divided in their counsels, or rather they had no counsel to follow: some of them fled into the neighbouring deserts, which you have seen are very dismal, on both sides the upper part of that kingdom; they were dispersed like a flock of sheep scattered by the ravenous wolves. The consternation was so great, they were resolved to fly to the farthest parts of the earth, rather than fall in-

to

---

* These Hickfoes being in all appearance the descendents of wicked Cannan or Cush, were so abominably impious as to sacrifice human victims and children to their false gods; and even were the first authors of all impiety and idolatry.

to the hands of thofe unhuman monfters. The greateft part of them agreed to build fhips, and try their fortune by fea. Our great father Mezzoraim had taught them the art of making boats*, to crofs the branches of the great river [Nile]; which fome, faid he, had learned by being prefer-ved in fuch a thing from a terrible flood that overflowed all the land†. Which inftru-ment of their prefervation they fo impro-ved afterwards, that they could crofs the leffer fea‡ without any difficulty. This being refolved on, they could not agree where to go : fome being refolved to go by one fea, fome by the other. However they fet all hands to work ; fo that in a year's time they had built a vaft number of vef-fels ; trying them backwards and forwards along the coafts, mending what was defici-ent, and improving what they imagined might be for their greater fecurity. They thought

---

* It is highly probable the Egyptians had the know'edge of fhipping long before the Greeks, whofe fineft fhip was Argo, built by Jafon to fetch the golden fleece from Colchos. The firft notion of fhipping was undoubtedly taken from the ark; the Egyptians were neceffitated to make ufe of boats, by reafon of the annual overflowing of the river Nile, and to pafs the different branches into which that famous river divides itfelf in the Lower Egypt. The Sidonians, whom Bochart proves to be the defcendents of Canaan, had the ufe of fhipping as he alfo proves, before the children of Ifrae departed out of Egypt.

† In all appearance this muft have been Noah's flood, which it is much S gnor Rhedi paffes over in his remarks.

‡ Egypt is bounded on the one fide by the end of the Mediterranea ; on the other fide by the Red fea, dividing it from Arabia: this he cals the leffer fea, as being much narrower than the Mediterranean.

thought now, or at leaft their eagernefs to avoid their enemies made them think, they could go with fafety all over the main fea. As our anceftors had chiefly given them-felves to the ftudy of arts and fciences, and the knowledge of nature, they were the moft capable of fuch enterprifes of any peo-ple in the world. But the apprehenfion of all that was miferable being juft frefh before their eyes, quickened their induftry to fuch a degree, as none but men in the like circumftances can have a juft idea of. Moft of thefe men were thofe who had fled in clouds from lower Egypt. The natural inhabitants of the upper parts, though they were in very great confternation, and built. fhips as faft as they could, yet their fears were not fo immediate, efpecially feeing the Hickfoes remained yet quiet in their new poffeffions. But news being brought them, that the Hickfoes began to ftir again, more fwarms of their cruel brood ftill flocking into that rich country, they re-folved now to delay the time no longer, but to commit themfelves, wives, and chil-dren, with all that was moft dear and pre-cious, to the mercy of that inconftant ele-ment, rather than truft to the barbarity of their own fpecies. They who came out of the Lower Egypt, were refolved to crofs
the

the great fea*, and with immenfe labour were forced to carry their materials partly by land, till they came to the outermoft branch of the Nile, fince their enemies coming over the ifthmus, though they hindered them from going out of their country by land, unlefs by the deferts, yet had not taken poffeffion of that part of the country. It is needlefs to recount their cries and lamentations at their leaving their dear country. I fhall only tell you, that they ventured into the great fea, which they croffed, and never ftopped till they came to another feat, on the fides of which they

fixed

---

* This great fea, as diftinguifhed from the lefs, muft be the Mediterranean. Thofe who fled by that fea, muft be got who went to Colchos; they could not go by land over the ifthmus, becaufe the Hickoes poured in upon them that way; we muft that they went all the way by fea to Colchos, quite round by the coaft of the Hellefpont. They muft crofs the end of the Mediterranean, and go by land the fhorteft way they could till they came to the borders of the Euxine fea. It is almoft incredible men fhould go fo far to feek an habitation. But Bochart fays, it is certain the people of Colchos came out of Egypt; they muft therefore have been driven out by fome terrible enemies. You will fay, Why may not this firft revolution in Egypt, which Bochart fpeaks of, have been made by the great Semiramis, wife to Ninus, the fon of Nimrod? It is anfwered in the firft place, becaufe Jofephus calls the firft invaders of Egypt, king-fhepherds, which cannot agree with the great heroine Semiramis. 2dly. Becaufe it is not credible, notwithftanding the contrary opinion of moft hiftorians, that Ninus, the hufband of Semiramis, could be fo early as they make him to be, i. e. the fon of Nimrod, but fome other Ninus long after him: for though Semiramis conquered Egypt, and afterwards loft her army againft the Ethiopians; this could not be fo foon after the flood; becaufe hiftorians defcribe that army to confift of three hundred thoufand men inftructed in difcipline after a military manner, armed with warlike chariots, &c. as were the Ethiopians againft her, and even fuperior to her. I fay, it is not credible fuch great armies could be raifed fo foon after the flood, if fhe was daughter-in-law to Nimrod the great hunter, who was the fon of Cufh, and great-grandfon to Noah.

† i. e. the Euxine fea.

fixed their habitation, that they might go off again in cafe they were purfued. This we learned from the account of our ancef, tors who met with fome of them that came to vifit the tombs of their deceafed parents, as we do ; but it is an immenfe time fince, and we never heard any more of them.—— The other part, who were much the great-er number, went down the leffer fea*, having built their fhips on the fea ; they never ftopped or touched on either fide, till they came to a narrow part of it†, which led them into the vaft ocean ; there they turned of to the left into the eaftern fea. But whether they were fwallowed up in the mercilefs abyfs, or carried into fome unknown regions, we cannot tell, for they were never heard of more. Only of late years, we have heard talk at Grand Cairo, of a very numerous and civilized nation in the eaftern parts of the world, whofe laws

and

---

* i. e. the Red fea. There were feveral other revolutions in Egypt as by the Ethiopian, after Semiramis was conquered ; who were ex-pelled again, either by the great Sefoftris, of whom Herodotus relates fuch famous exploits ; or a little before by his predeceffor. The Ca-naanites alfo, who were driven out of Palefline by Jofhua, conquered part of it, as we fhall fee afterwards. Long after that, it was fubdued by Nabuchodonofor, who deftroyed the renowned city of Thebes, with her hundred gates. Bochart in Nineve. Then the Perfians under Camby'es the fon of Cyrus the Great. In fine, the Romans made a province of it in Auguftus's time. Strabo fays, that famous city of Thebes, at prefent is but a poor village.

Atque vetus Thebe centum jacet obruta portis.

Juven. fat. 1.

† This muft be the ftreights of Babelmandel, which let them into the vaft eaftern ocean.

and cuftoms have fome refemblance to ours; but who, and what they are, we cannot tell, fince we have never met with any of them.

The father of our nation, fince we fepa- rated ourfelves from the reft of the world, who was prieft of the fun at No-om*, call- ed afterwards by thofe mifcreants No-Am- mon†, becaufe of the temple of Hammon), was not afleep in this general confternation; but did not as yet think they would come up fo high into the land. However, he thought proper to look out for a place to
fecure

---

* No-om or No-on, fignifies, in the old Mezzoranian, o old Egyptian language, the houfe of the fun. Their words are made up of monofyl- lables put together like the Chinefe, which is another reafon why the Chinefe ought to be looked upon as a colony of the Egyptians. Vide the remarks of the foregoing part of this relation. The patriarch Jo- feph married the daughter of the prieft of On: which, feveral learned men fay, is the fame with Heliopolis, or city of the fun. From No comes the Egyptian nomes, or divifions of the country, which the great Bochart in his Phaleg, ays is an Egyptian, not a Greek word, though dynafty is Greek. Bochart lib, 4. c. 24. Hence very likely came the Nomades and Numidæ, from their wandering and frequently changing their habitation, or names; the firft and moft ancient of all nations lived thus.

† That is, the houfe or temple of Ham, or Hammon; or Chamoon, or Chum, as Bochart varies it. Th & Ham was the Tyrian Jupiter, and in this place was afterwards fituated the great city of Thebes, as has been obferved before, called by the Greeks Diofpolis, or the city of Ju- piter. Cadmus, who was of Thebes in Palefline, being driven out from thence by Jofhua, built it; but was driven out from it, and forced to retire to Tyre, from whence he conducted a colony of Tyrians, or banifhed Canaanites into Bæotia, where he built Thebes alfo, or ra- ther the citadel of Thebes, called Cadmeia. Vide Bochart, in Cadmus and Hermione. Which lift the fame author fays, came originally from mount Hermon in Palefline: and as that word in the Canaanean languages fignifies a ferpent, from hence arofe the fable of the ferpent's teeth turning into men. The temple of Jupiter Ammon, or Ham- mon, in Africa, was built by the Chinani, who fpread themfelves from Egypt into Libya.

secure himself and family in case of need.
He was the descendent, in a direct line
from the great Tha-oth ; and was perfectly
versed in all the learned sciences of his ancestors. He guessed there must certainly
be some habitable country, beyond those
dreadful sands that surrounded him, if he
could but find a way to it, where he might
secure himself and family ; at least, till
those troubles were over : for he did not
at that time think of leaving his native
country for good and all. But, like a true
father of his people, which the name of
Pophar implies, he was resolved to venture
his own life, rather than expose his whole
family to be lost in those dismal deserts. He
had five sons, and five daughters married
to as many sons and daughters of his deceased brother. His two eldest sons had
even grandchildren, but his two youngest
sons as then had no children. He left the
government and care of all to his eldest son,
in case he himself should miscarry ; and
took his two youngest sons, who might best
be spared along with him. Having provided themselves with water for ten days,
with bread and dried fruits, just enough
to subsist on, he was resolved to try five
days journey endwise through these lands;
and if he saw no hopes of making a discovery that time, to return again before his
provisions were spent, and then try the

same

fame method towards another quarter. In short, he fet out with all fecrecy, and pointing his courfe directly weftward, the better to guide himfelf, he came to the firft grove that we arrived at, in a little more time than we took up in coming thither. Having now time enough before him, and feeing there was water and fruits in abundance, he examined the extent of that delicious vale : he found it was large enough to fubfift a great many thoufands, in cafe they fhould increafe, and be forced to ftay there fome generations, as in effect they did. After this they laid in provifions as before, with dates and fruits of the natural produce of the earth, finer than ever were feen in Egypt, to encourage them in their tranfmigration, and fo fet out again for his native country. The time prefixed for his return was elapfed by his ftay in viewing the country ; fo that his people had entirely given him up for loft. But the joy for his unexpected return, with the promifing hopes of fuch a fafe and happy retreat, made them unanimoufly refolve to follow him. Wherefore, on the firft news of the Hickfoes being in motion again, they packed up all their effects and provifions as privately as they could ; but particularly all the monuments of arts and fciences left by their anceftors, with notes and obfervations of

M   every

every part of their dear country, which they were going to leave, but hoped to fee again when the ftorm was over. They arrived without any confiderable difafter, and refolved only to live in tents till they could return to their native homes. As they increafed in number, they defcended further into the vale, which there began to fpread itfelf different ways, and fupplied them with all the neceffaries of life ; fo that they lived in the happieft banifh-ment they could wifh ; never ftirring out of the vale for feveral years, for fear of being difcovered. The Pophar finding himfelf grow old, (having attained almoft two hundred years of age*', though he was hale and ftrong for his years, refolved to vifite his native country once more be-fore he died, and get what intelligence he could for the common intereft. Accord-ingly, he and two more difguifed them-felves, and repaffed the deferts again. They juft ventured at firft into the borders of the

---

* The regular lives of the firft Egyptians, and of thefe people de-fcended from them, together with the climate, their diet of fruits and liqsors, their exemption from violent paffions, without being corrupted by the fpurious fpawn of other nations, and the like, might contribute very much to the length of their lives, and ftrength proportionably. The Macrobii, or long-livers, a people of Ethiopia, and a colony of the ancient Egyptians, lived to a vaft age, and were called Macrobii from their long lives. See Herodotus of the Ethiopians ; and what he fays of their ftrength in the bow, which they fent to Cambyfes, when he had denounced war againft them ; faying, that when he could bend that bow, he might make war againft them ; which bow only Smerdis, Cambyfes's brother, could bend, and for that reafon was afterwards put to death by his brother out of envy.

the country : but, alas! when he came there, he found it all over run by the barbarous Hickfoes. All the poor remains of the Mezzoranians were made flaves ; and thofe barbarians had begun to build habitations, and eftablifh themfelves, as if they defigned never more to depart the country. They had made No-om one of their chief towns*, where they erected a temple to their ram-god†, calling it *No-Hammon‡*, with fuch inhuman laws and cruelties, as drew a flood of tears from his aged eyes§. However, being a man of great prudence and forefight, he eafily imagined, by their tyrannical way of living, they could not continue long in that ftate without fome new revolution. After making what obfervations he could, and vifiting the tombs of his forefathers, he returned to the vale, and died in that place where you faw the pyramid built to his memory. Not many generations after, according as he had forefeen,

M 2

---

* It feems Thebes, though afterwards fuch a prodigious city, was then but the head of the name of that man's family.

† Jupiter Hammon, whom Bochart proves to have been Ham or Cham, the fon of Noah, was reprefented with a ram's head, which was held in fuch abomination by the firft Egyptians, from whence they called thofe firft invaders Hickfoes.

‡ No-Hammon, the houfe of the ram-god.

§ It is likely he means Bufiridis aras, fo infamous in antiquity ; or the cruel Bufiris, who facrificed his guefts. Though hiftorians do not agree about the time when Bufiris lived, which fhews he was very ancient ; yet all agree, he was a monfter of cruelty, and became a proverb on that account. This was a very natural reafon for the Egyptians to difperfe themfelves into fo many colonies as they did, to avoid fuch cruelties.

feen, the natives, made defperate by the tyrannical oppreffions of the Hickfoes, were forced to break in upon their primitive laws, which forbade them to fhed blood ; made a general infurrection, and, calling in their neighbours around them. fell upon the Hickfoes when they leaft expected it, and drove them out of the country. They were headed by a brave man of a mixed race, his mother being a beautiful Mezzoranian, and his father a Sabæan*. After this young conqueror had driven out the Hickfoes, he eftablifhed a new form of government, making himfelf king over his brethren, but not after .yrannical manner of the Hickfoes , and grew very powerful. Our anceftors fent perfons from time to time to inform themfelves how matters went. They found the kingdom in a flourifhing condition, indeed, under the conquering Sofs†, for fo he was called.

He

* Thefe Sabæans were the defcendents of fome of the fons of Chufh or Chufe, a very tall race of men, great negotiators, and more polite than the other Arabians.
The bodies of the inhabitants (the Sabæans) are more majeftie than other men.

† This muft be the great Sefoftris or Sefofis, of whom the learned Bifhop of Meaux, as alfo Herodotus, fays fuch glorious things. Though authors do not fay precifely when he lived, all acknowledge him to have flourifhed in the earlieft times. He extended his conquefts over the greateft part of the eaft, and almoft over the known world, as fome fay. Where his enemies were cowards, and made no refiftance, he fet up ftatues of them refembling women. Herodot. lib. 2. Euterpe. Monf. de Meaux, par. 3. Hift. Univ. This great conqueror's name is very much varied by authors.

He and his fucceffors made it one of
the moft powerful kingdoms of the
earth ; but the laws were different from
what they had been in the time of our anceftors, or even from thofe the great Sofs
had eftablifhed.   Some of his fucceffors began to be very tyrannical ; they made
flaves of their brothers, and invented a
new religion ; fome adoring the fun, fome
the gods of the 'Hickfoes ; fo that our anceftors, as they could not think of altering
their laws, though they might have returned again, chofe rather to continue ftill unknown in that vale, under their patriarchal government. Neverthelefs, in procefs
of time, they increafed fo much, that the
country was not capable of maintaining
them ; fo that they had been obliged to return, had not another revolution in Egypt
forced them to feek out a new habitation.
This change was made by a race of people
called *Cnanim**, as wicked and barbarous in
effect, but more politic, than the Hickfoes ;

M 3.   though

* Thefe in all appearance were the wicked Canaaneans, who being to
be deftroyed, and being driven out of Canaan by Jofhua, difperfed
themfelves, and invaded the greateft part of the countries round about
them.   Bochart in Canaan proves almoft demonftrably, that they
difperfed themfelves over all the iflands and fea-ports of Europe, Afia,
and Africa.   In his preface he quotes a moft curious paffage out of
Procop us de bello Vandelico, of a pillar that was found in Africa, with
a Phœnician or Canaanean infcription, which fignifies in Greek
We are thofe who fled from the face of Jefus, or Jofhua the robber.
the fon of Nave. Eufebius, in Chronico, has much the fame ; and St.
Auftin, in his City of God, fays, that the ancient country-people
about Hippo in Africa, who were the remains of the ancient Carthaginians, if you afked them who they were, would anfwer, We are
or ſadly Canaani, or Canaaneans.

though some said they were originally the
same people, who being driven out of their
own country by others more powerful than
themselves, came pouring in, not only
over all the land of Mezzoraim, but all a-
long the coasts of both seas, destroying all
before them, with greater abominations
than the Hickfoes had ever been guilty of :
in short, a faithless and most perfidious
race of men, that corrupted the innocent
manners* of the whole earth. Our forefathers were in the most dreadful consternation imaginable. There was now no
prospect of ever returning into their ancient country. They were surrounded with
deserts on all sides. The place they were
in began to be too narrow for so many
thousands as they were increased to : nay,
they did not know but the wicked Cnanim, who were at the same time the bold-
est and most enterprising nation under the
sun†, might find them out some time or
other.

* The celebrated Bochart so often quoted, proves that the Phœnicians or Carthaginians, whom he also proves to have been Cinaancans,
were the persons who spread idolatry, with all the tribe of the Heathen gods, and their abominable rites, over the whole world. Bochart
in Canaan. The same author says the Phœnicians or Canaani, invaded
Egypt about that very time. This he proves directly: and that they
had their castra about Memphis: as also that Cadmus and Phœnix ,
whom he makes contemporaries with Joshua, having fled before him ,
came out of Egypt afterwards, and built Thebes in Bœotia. See also
Erodotus in Euterpe.

† Herodotus says, that they sailed (even in those early days) from
the Red sea, round Africa, and came back to Egypt thro' the streights,
and up the Mediterranean. Herodot. Melpomene, and Bochart.
That Hanno the elder, by order of the senate of Carthage, sailed

other.   Being in this diftrefs, they refolved to feek out a new habitation ; and, to
that end, compared all the notes and obfervations on the heavens, the courfe of
the fun, the feafons, and nature of the
climate, and whatever elfe might direct
them what courfe to fteer.   They did not
doubt but that there might be fome habitable countries in the midft of thofe vaft
deferts, perhaps as delicious as the vale
they lived in, if they could but come at
them.   Several perfons were fent out to
make difcoveries, but without fuccefs.
The fands were too vaft to travel over
without water, and they could find no
fprings nor rivers.   At length the moft fagacious of them began to reflect, that the
annual overflowing of the great river Nile,
whofe head could never be found out, muft
proceed from fome prodigious rains which
fell fomewhere fouthward of them about
that time of the year ; which rains, if
they could but luckily time and meet with,
might not only fupply them with water,
but alfo render the country fertile where
they fell.   Accordingly the chief Pophar,
affifted by fome of the wifeft men, generoufly refolved to run all rifks to fave his
people.

pound the greateft part of the world, and after his return delivered to
them an account of his voyage, which is called the Periplus of Hanno.
He affected to be honoured as a god for it, and lived before Solomon's
time.   Bochart in Canaan, lib. 1. c. 37.

people. They computed the precife time
when the Nile overflowed, and allowed for
the time the waters muft take in defcending fo far as Egypt. They thought therefore, if they could but carry water enough
to fupply them till they met with thefe
rains, they would help them to go on further. At length, five of them fet out,
with ten dromedaries, carrying as much
water and provifions as might ferve them
for fifteen days, to bring them back again
in cafe there was no hopes. They fteered
their courfe as we did, though not quite fo
exact the firft time, till they came to the
place, where we are now. Finding here,
as their notes tell us*, a little rivulet, which
is fince fwallowed up by the fands, they
filled their veffels, and went up to take an
obfervation ; as we did : but feeing the
figns of the great hurricanes, which was
our greateft encouragement, it had like to
have driven them into defpair ; for the
Pophar knowing the danger of being overwhelmed in the fands, thought of nothing
but flying back as faft as he could, fearing
to be fwallowed up in thofe ftifling whirl-
pools. This apprehenfion made him lay
afide all thoughts of fucceeding towards
                                          that

---

* Thofe wife ancients kept records of every thing that was memorable and ufful for their people. If this had been the practice of the
Europeans, we fhould not have loft fo many fecrets of nature as
we have.

that climate ; and now his chief care was how to get back again with fafety for him-felf and his people. But finding all conti-nue tolerably ferene where they were, they made a halt in order to make fome farther obfervations. In the mean time, they re-flected that thofe hurricanes muft be fore-runners of tempefts and rain. Then they recollected, that no rain, or what was very inconfiderable, ever fell in Egypt*, or for a great way fouth of it, till they came with-in the tropics , and thence concluded, that the rains muft run parallel with the equa-tor, both under it, and for fome breadth on both fides, till they met the rife of the river Nile, and there caufed thofe vaft in-undations fo hard to be accounted for by other people. That, in fine, thofe rains muft laft a confiderable while, and proba-bly, though beginning with tempefts, might continue in fettled rain, capable of being paffed through. Then he at firft refolved to venture back again to the firft vale : but being a man of great prudence, he prefent-ly

* This is well known by all the defcriptions of that country, the inundation of the Nile fupplying the want of it, and making it one of the moft fertile kingdoms in the world ; every one knows it was, once the granary of the Roman empire. However, fome fmall rain falls fometimes : nor is there any more higher up in the country. The overflowing of the Nile is known to be caufed by vaft rains falling under the line, or about that climate ; and fince thofe dont take Egypt and the adjoining part of Africa in their way; they muft by confequence run parallel with the line ; which was a very natural and philofophical obfervation of thefe wife men.

ly confidered, that as he could not proceed on his way without rains, fo he could not come back again but by the fame help, which coming only at one feafon, muft take up a whole year before he could re- turn. However, he was refolved to ven- ture on, not doubting but if he could find a habitable country, he fhould alfo find fruits enough to fubfift on, till the next feafon. Therefore he ordered two of his companions to return the fame way they came, to tell his people not to expect him till the next year, if Providence fhould bring him back at all; but if he did not return by the time of the overflowing of the Nile, or thereabouts, they might give him over for loft, and muft never attempt that way any more. They took their leaves of one another as if it were the laft adieu, and fet out at the fame time; two of them, for their homes in the firft vale, and the other three for thofe unknown re- gions; being deftitute of all other helps but thofe of a courageous mind. The three came back to this place, where it thundered and lightened as it does now; but the Pophar obferved it ftill tended fidewife, and gueffed, when the firft vio- lence was over, the rains might be more fettled. The next day it fell out as he fore- faw; whereupon, recommending himfelf to the great author of our being, he launch-

ed

ed boldly out into that vaſt ocean of ſands and rain, ſteering his courſe ſouth-weſt, rather inclining towards the ſouth. They went as far; as the heavy ſands and rains would let them, till their dromedaries could hardly go any further. Then they pitched their tents and refreſhed them-ſelves juſt enough to undergo new labour, well knowing all their lives depended on their expedition. They obſerved the ſands to be of a different kind from what they had ſeen hitherto, ſo fine, that any guſt of wind muſt overwhelm man and beaſt, only the rains had clogged and laid them.

Not to prolong your expectation too much : they went on thus for ten days, till the rains began to abate ; then they ſaw their lives or deaths would ſoon be determined. The 11th day the ground began to grow harder in patches, with here and there a little moſs on the ſurface, and now and then a ſmall withered ſhrub. This revived their hopes, that they ſhould find good land in a ſhort time, and in effect, the ſoil changed for the better eve-ry ſtep they took ; and now they began to ſee little hills covered with graſs, and the valleys ſink down as if there might be brooks and rivers. The twelfth and thir-teenth day cleared all their doubts, and brought them into a country, which, though

though not very fertile, had both water and fruits, with a hopeful prospect further on, of hills and dales, all habitable and flourishing. Here they fell prostrate on the earth, adoring the creator of all things, who had conducted them safe through so many dangers, and kissing the ground, which was to be the common nurse for them, and, as they hoped, for all their posterity: when they had reposed themselves for some days, they proceeded further into the country, which they found to mend upon them the more they advanced into it. Not intending to return till next year, they sought the most proper place for their habitation; and setting up marks at every moderate distance not to lose their way back again, they made for the highest hills they could see, from whence they perceived an immense and delicious country every way; but to their greater satisfaction, no inhabitants. They wandered thus at pleasure through those natural gardens, where there was a perpetual spring in some kinds of the produce of the earth, and the ripeness of autumn with the most exquisite fruits in others. They kept the most exact observations possible. Whichever way they went, there were not only springs and fountains in abundance, but, as they guessed, (for they kept the higher ground), the heads of great

rivers

rivers and lakes, fome of which they could perceive ; fo that they were fatisfied there was room enough for whole nations, with-out any danger, as they could find, of be-ing difturbed.   By their obfervation of the fun, they were nigher the equator than they had imagined*, fo that they there paffed the middle fpace between the tropic and the line.   Being come back to their firft ftation, they there waited the proper feafon for their return.   The rains came fomething fooner than the year before, becaufe they were further weftward.   The hurricanes were nothing like what they were in the vaft fands.   As foon as they began to fix in fettled rains, they fet out again as before, and in twenty days time from their laft fetting out. happily arrived at the place where they left their dear friends and relations, whofe joy for their fafe and happy arrival was greater than I can pretend to defcribe.   Thus this im-mortal hero accomplifhed his great under-taking, fo much more glorious than all the victories of the greateft conquerors, as it

N   was

---

* Though we may imagine a leffer circle parallel to the tropics and the equator, which is called maximus parallelorum ; yet whoever tra-vels either by land or fea, parallel, as he thinks, to the equator, does not fo, but will approach to it ; nay and crofs it at laft, (unlefs he goes fpirally), and makes indentures as he goes along: the reafon is, becaufe where-ever we are, we are on the fummit of the globe with refpect to us, and our feet make a perpendicular to the centre ; fo that if we go round the globe, we fhall make a great circle, and by confequence cut the equator.

was projected, formed, and executed by his own wisdom and courage; not by exposing and sacrificing the lives of thousands of his subjects, perhaps greater men than himself, but by exposing his own life for the safety of those that depended on him.

It were too tedious to recount to you all the difficulties and troubles they had, both in resolving to undertake such a hazardous transmigration, as well as those of transporting such a multitude, with their wives and children, and all their most precious effects, over those merciless sands, which they could only pass at one season of the year. But the voyage being at length resolved on, and the good Pophar wisely considering the difficulties, and necessity, the mother of invention, urging him, at the same time, to gain as much time as he could, since the vale where they were at present was sufficient to maintain them till the rains came; got all his people hither in the mean time, to be ready for the season. The new-born children were left with their mothers, and people to take care of them, till they were able to bear the fatigue. Thus, in seven years time going backwards and forwards every season, they all arrived safe, where we ourselves hope to be in ten or twelve days time. This great hero we deservedly honour, as another Misraim, the second founder of our nation, from whose

whose loins you yourself sprung by the surer side, and are going to be incorporated again with the offspring of your first ancestors.

Here he ended his relation, and your Reverences may easily believe, I was in the greatest admiration at this unheard-of account. As it raised the ideas I had of the people, so I could not be sorry to find myself, young and forlorn as I was before, incorporated with, and allied to such a flourishing and civilized nation. My expectation was not disproportionable to my ideas: I was persuaded I was going into a very fine country; but the thoughts of their being Pagans left some little damp on my spirits, and was a drawback to my expected happiness. However, I was resolved to preserve my religion, at the expense of all that was dear to me, and even of life itself.

By this time, the Pophar ordered us to refresh ourselves, and prepare all things for our departure, though the storm of thunder and lightning did not cease till towards morning. At length, all things being ready for our moving, we marched on slowly till we came into the course of the rains. It was the most settled and downright rain (as the saying is) that ever I saw; every thing seemed to be as calm, as the tempest was violent before. Being ac-

customed

cuftomed to it, they had provided open vefſels on each ſide of the dromedaries, to catch enough for their uſe as it fell, and they covered themſelves and their beaſts with that fine oiled cloth I mentioned before. All the ſands were laid, and even beaten hard by the rains, though heavy and cloggy at the ſame time. We made as much way as poſſible, for five days, juſt reſting and refreſhing ourſelves when abſolutely neceſſary. I muſt own, nothing could be more diſmal than thoſe dreary ſolitary deſerts, where we could neither ſee ſun nor moon, but had only a gloomy, malignant light, juſt ſufficient to look at the needle, and take our obſervations. On the ſixth day we thought we ſaw ſomething move ſidewiſe of us, on our right hand, but ſeemingly paſſing by us ; when one of the young men cried, *There they are*, and immediately croſſed down to them. Then we perceived them to be perſons travelling like ourſelves, croſſing in the ſame manner up towards us. I was extremely ſurpriſed to find, that thoſe deſerts were known to any but ourſelves. But the Pophar ſoon put me out of pain, by telling me, they were ſome of their own people. taking the ſame ſeaſon to go for Egypt, and on the ſame account. By this time we were come up to one another. The leader of the other caravan, with all his company, immediately ly got off their dromedaries, and fell proftrate on the earth before our Pophar; at which he ftept back; and cried, *Alas! is our father dead?* They told him, Yes; and that he being the firft of the fecond line, was to be regent of the kingdom, till the young Pophar, who was born when his father was an old man, fhould come to the age of fifty. Then our people got off, and proftrated themfelves before him*, all but myfelf. They took no notice of my neglect, feeing me a fupernumerary perfon, and by confequence a ftranger; but as foon as the ceremonies were over, came and embraced me, and welcomed me into their brotherhood with the moft fincere cordiality, as if I had been one of their nation. The Pophar foon told them what I was, which made them repeat their careffes with new ecftafies of joy peculiar to thefe people. After reiterated inquiries concerning their friends, and affurances that all was well, except what they had juft told him, the Pophar afked them, how they came to direct their courfe fo much on the left hand, expecting to have met them the day before; and they feeming to point as if they were going out of their way. They told us, they were now fenfible of it, and

N 3   were

---

* The eaftern manner of fhewing refpect.

were making. up for the true road as faft
as they could : but that the day before, they
had like to have loft themfelves by the darknefs of the weather, and their too great fecurity ; for beating too much on the left
hand, one of their dromedaries founder-
ed, as if he were got into a quickfand*.
The rider thinking it had been nothing
but fome loofer part of the fand, thought
to go on, but fell deeper the further he
went, till the commander ordered him to
get off immediately, which he did with fo
much hafte, that not minding his dromedary, the poor beaft going on further into
the quickfands, was loft. Then the Pophar told them, there was fuch a place
marked down in their ancient charts,
which, being fo well acquainted with the
roads, they had never minded of late years :
that he fuppofed thofe quickfands to be either the rains, which had funk through the
fands, and meeting with fome ftrata of clay,
ftagnated, and were forming a lake ; or
more

* Perfons may wonder to hear of quickfands in the midft of the fun-
burnt deferts of Africa. But the thing will not feem fo improbable,
when we come to examine the reafons of it. Without doubt, our author does not mean fuch quickfands as are caufed by the coming in of
the tide under the fands ; a man of fenfe would be incapable of fuch a
blunder. But that there fhould be fome ftagnating waters in the low
fwamps of the fands, is fo far from being incredible, that it can be hardly thought to be otherwife. It is very well known, there are vaft
lakes in fome parts of Africa, which have no vifible outlets. There
are rivers alfo that lofe themfelves in the fands, where finking under for
fome time, they may form fandy marfhes, or quickfands, as the author
calls them.

more probably, it was the course of some distant river, rising perhaps out of a habitable country, at an unknown distance, but had lost itself in those immense sands. However, he congratulated them on their escape, and, like a tender father, gently chid them for their too great security in that boundless ocean. Our time not permitting us to stay long, each caravan set out again for their destined course, having but five or six days journey to make, that is, as far as we could travel in so many days and so many nights; for we never stopped but to refresh ourselves. The rains had so tempered the air, that it was rather cold than hot, especially the nights, which grew longer, as we approached the line. Here we steered our course more to the west again, but not so as to leave the ridge of the world. I observed the more we kept to the west, the more moderate the rains were, as indeed they flackened in proportion as we came nigher our journey's end; because coming from the west, or at least with a little point of the south, they began sooner than where we set out. The tenth day of our journey, I mean from the last grove or resting-place, one of our dromedaries failed. We had changed them several times before, to make their labour more equal. They would not let it die, for the good it had done; but too of the

company

company having water enough, and knowing where they were, ftaid behind, to bring
it along with them. We now found the
nature of the fands and foil to begin to
change, as the Pophar had informed me :
the found began to be covered with a little mofs, tending towards a green fward,
more like barren downs than fands ; and I
unexpectedly perceived in fome places, inftead of thofe barren gravelly fands, large
fpaces of tolerable good foil*. At length,
to our expreffible joy and comfort, at leaft
for myfelf, who could not but be in fome
fufpenfe:

---

* It was obferved in fome of the former remarks, that not only the
deferts of Africa, but all the ftrata, or great beds of gravel, which are
found in all parts of the world, probably were caufed by the univerfal deluge. Nor can they be well accounted for otherwife. The deeper the
beds of gravel are, the more they fhew, by the heterogeneous ftuff lodged with them, that they were brought thither, not produced there ab
origine. The vaft falls and gullets which are feen on the fkirts of all
the mountains in the world, evidently fhew they were caufed by fome
violent gitation, which carried the looser earth and fmall ftones along
with it : for which nothing can be more natural, than the fuppofition
of a flood, or agitated fluid, which, by its violence and fhakings, carried
all that was moveable before it for fome time. This gravel was incorporated with the loofe earth before the flood, and was carried to and
fro, while the waters were in their greateft agitation, wafhing and melting the loofe earth from the gravel and ftones. But when the waters
came to their higheft pitch, and began to fubfide, the ftones and gravel
would fink fooer than lighter things, and fo be left almoft in a body in
thofe ftrata they appear in. This might be illuftrated much further, if
there were occafion. The vaft numbers of petrified fhells and fcallops,
which are found in all parts of the world, on the higher grounds, could
never be a mere lufus naturæ, as fome too curious philofophers imagine,
but muft be accounted for by fuch a flood ; and thefe appearing in all
parts of the univerfe, the flood muft have been univerfal. The fudden
change of foils in every region, with the exceeding richnefs of fome
more than others, and that too fometimes all at once, is to be accounted for from the fame caufe: for the fame violence of waters wafhing the
earth from the ftones, muft naturally make an unequal accumulation of
both. As for Africa, all the ancients fpeak of the incredible fertility of
it in fome places, and the extreme barrennefs of the deferts in others.

suspense in such an unknown world, we came to patches of trees, and grass, with slanting falls and heads of vales, which seemed to enlarge themselves beyond our view*. The rains were come to their period; only it looked a little foggy at a great distance before us, which was partly from the exhalations of the country after the rains†; partly from the trees and hills stopping the clouds, by which we found that the weather did not clear up in the habitable countries so soon as in the barren deserts. The Pophar told me, that, if it were not for the haziness of the air, he would shew me the most beautiful prospect that ever my eyes beheld. I was sensibly convinced of it by the perfumes of the spicy shrubs and flowers, which struck our senses with such a reviving fragrancy, as made us almost forget our past fatigue, especially me, who had not felt the like even in the first vale : neither do I believe all the odours of the Happy Arabia could ever come up to it. I was just as if I had risen out of the most delicious repose. Here the Pophar ordered us to stop for refreshment,

* The prodigious height of the sands in Africa, in those parts which lie between the tropics, may not only be the cause of the sands or gravel sinking in greater quantities at the decrease of the flood; but the most extensive vales may have their rise from very small gullets at first.

† It is very natural to think, that those barren sun-burnt deserts send up but few exhalations;

ment, and added, that we muft ftay there till next day. We pitched our tents on the laft defcent of thofe immenfe Bares, by the fide of a little rill that iffued out of the fmall break of the downs, expecting further orders.

The caufe of our ftay here, where we were out of danger, was not only for our companions we had left behind us, but on a ceremonious account, as your Reverences will fee by and by : they were alfo to change their habits, that they might appear in the colours of their refpective tribe or name, which were five, according to the number of the fons of the firft Pophar, who brought them out of Egypt, whofe ftatue we faw at the pyramid. By their laws all the tribes are to be diftinguifhed by their colours ; that where-ever they go, they may be known what name they belong to ; with particular marks of their pofts and dignities ; as I fhall defcribe to your Reverences afterwards. The grand Pophar's colour, who was defcended from the eldeft fon of the ancient Pophar, was a flame colour, or approaching nigh the rays of the fun, becaufe he was chief prieft of the fun. Our new regent's colour was green, fpangled with funs of gold, as your Reverences faw in the picture ; the green reprefenting the fpring, which is the chief feafon with them. The third colour is a fiery red, for the

the fummer. The fourth is yellow, for
autumn; and the fifth purple, reprefenting the gloominefs of winter; for thefe
people, acknowledging the fun for the immediate governor of the univerfe, mimic
the nature of his influence as nigh as they
can. The women obferve the colours of
their refpective tribes, but have moons of
filver intermixed with the funs, to fhew
that they are influenced in a great meafure
by that variable planet. The young vir-
gins have the new moon; in the ftrength
of their age the full moon; as they grow
old, the moon is in the decreafe proportionably. The widows have the moon expreffed juft as it is in the change; the defcendents of the daughters of the firft Pophar were incorporated with the reft.
Thofe of the eldeft daughter took the eldeft fon's colour, with a mark of diftinction,
to fhew they were never to fucceed to the
popharfhip, or regency, till there fhould be
no male iffue of the others at age to govern.
This right of elderfhip, as thefe people underftand it, is a little intricate; but I fhall
explain it to your Reverences more at
large, when I come to fpeak more particularly of their government. When they
are fent out into foreign countries, they
take what habit or colour they pleafe, and
generally go all alike, to be known to each
other; but they muft not appear in their
own

own country but in their proper colours, it being criminal to do otherwife. They carry marks alfo of their families, that in cafe any mifdemeanor fhould be committed, they may know where to trace it out; for which reafon, now they drew near their own country, they were to appear in the colours of their refpective nomes; all but myfelf, who had the fame garment I wore at Grand Cairo, to fhew I was a ftranger, though I wore the Pophar's colour afterwards, as being his relation, and incorporated in his family. When they were all arrayed in their filken colours, fpangled with funs of gold, with white fillets round their temples, ftudded with precious ftones, they made a very delightful fhew, being the handfomeft race of people this day in the univerfe, and all refembling each other, as having no mixture of other nations in their blood.

The fun had now broke through the clouds, and difcovered to us the profpect of the country, but fuch a one as I am not able to defcribe; it looked rather like an immenfe garden than a country : at that diftance I could fee nothing but trees and groves; whether I looked towards the hills or vales, all feemed to be one continued wood, though with fome feemingly regular intervals of fquares and plains, with the glittering of golden globes or
                                                                            funs

funs through the tops of the trees, that it
looked like a green mantle fpangled with
gold. I afked the Pophar, if they lived
all in woods, or whether the country was
only one continued immenfe foreft. He
fmiled and faid, when we come thither,
you fhall fee fomething elfe befides woods ;
and then bid me look back, and compare
the dreary-fands we had lately paffed with
that glorious profpect we faw before us :
I did fo, and found the difmal barrennefs
of the one enhanced the beautiful delight
of the other. The reafon, fays he, why
it looks like a wood, is, that, befides innumerable kinds of fruits, all our towns,
fquares, and ftreets, as well as fields and
gardens, are planted with trees, both for
delight and conveniency, though you will
find fpare ground enough for the produce
of all things fufficient to make the life of
man eafy and happy. The glittering of
gold through the tops of the trees, are golden funs on the tops of the temples and
buildings : we build our houfes flat and
low on account of hurricanes, with gardens of perfumed ever-greens on the top of
them ; which is the reafon you fee nothing
but groves.

We defcended gradually from off the deferts through the fcattered fhrubs, and
were faluted every now and then with a
gale of perfumes quite different from what

are brought to the Europeans from foreign parts. The fresh air of the morning, together with their being exaled from the living flocks, gave them such a fragrancy as cannot be expressed. At length we came to a spacious plain a little shelving, and covered with a greenish coat, between mofs and grass, which was the utmost border of the defert; and beyond it a small river, collected from the hills, as it were weeping out of the sands in different places; which river was the boundary of the kingdom that way. Halting here, we discovered a small company of ten persons, the same number, excluding me, with ours, advancing gravely towards us : they were in the proper colours of the Nomes, with spangled suns of gold, as my companions wore, only the tops of their heads were sprinkled with dust, in token of mourning. As soon as they came at a due distance, they fell flat on their faces before the Pophar, without saying a word, and received the golden urns with the earth which we bro't along with us. Then they turned, and marched directly before us, holding the urns in their hands as high as they could, but all in a deep and mournful silence. These were deputies of the five Nomes sent to meet the urns. We advanced in this silent manner without saying one word, till we came to the river, over which was a

stately

stately bridge with a triumphal arch on the top of it, beautified with funs of gold, moft magnificent to behold. Beyond the bridge, we immediately paffed through a kind of circular grove, which led us into a moft delightful plain, like an amphitheatre, our filence was broke with fhouts of joy that rended the very fkies; then the whole multitude falling flat on their faces, adoring the urns, and thrice repeating their fhouts and adorations, there advanced ten triumphant chariots, according to the colours of the Nomes with funs as before; nine of the chariots were drawn with fix horfes each, and the tenth with eight for the Pophar regent. The five deputies, who were the chief of each Nome, with the urns and companions, mounted five of the chariots, the other five were for us, two in a chariot; only being a fupernumerary, I was placed backwards in the Pophars chariot, which he told me was the only mark of humiliation and inequality I would receive. We were conducted with five fquadrons of horfe, of fifty men each, in their proper colours, with ftreamers of the fame, having the fun in the centre, though the oppofite avenue, till we came into another amphitheatre of a vaft extent, where we faw an infinite number of tents of filk of the colour of the Nomes, all of them fpangled with golden funs:
here

here we were to rest and refresh ourselves. The Pophar's tent was in the centre of his own colour, which was green, the second Nome in dignity, in whose dominions and government we now were.

I have been longer in this description, because it was more a religious ceremony than any thing else, these people being extremely mysterious in all they do*. I shall explain the meaning to your Reverences as briefly as I can. The stopping before we came to the bridge on the borders of those inhospitable deserts, and walking in that mournful silent manner, not only expressed their mourning for their deceased ancestors, but also signified the various calamities and labours incident to man in this life, where he is not only looked upon to be, but really is, in a state of banishment and mourning; wandering in sun-burnt deserts, and tossed with storms of innumerable lawless desires, still sighing after a better country. The passage over the

---

* The ancient Egyptians were so mysterious, particularly in their religious ceremonies, and arcana of government, that, in all probability, the ancient fables, which very few yet understand rightly, had their rise from them; though the learned Bochart, in his Phaleg, derives them chiefly from the Canaanites, who dispersing themselves all over the world, when they fled from Joshua, imposed upon the credulous Greeks by the different significations of the same words in their language. It is observable by the by, that the most ancient languages, as the Hebrew, with its different dialects, of which the Canaanean or Phœnician language was one, the Chinese language, &c. had a great many significations for the same word, either from the plain simplicity or poverty of the ancient languages, or more probably from an affected mysteriousness in all they did.

bridge,

bridge, they would have to betoken man's
entrance into rest by death. Their shouts
of joy, when the sacred urns arrived in
that glorious country, not only signified
the happiness of the next life, (for these
people universally believe the immortality
of the soul, and think none but brutes can
be ignorant of it), but also that their ancestors, whose burial-dust they brought
along with them, were now in a place of
everlasting rest.

[*Inquisitor.* I hope you don't believe so
of Heathens, let them be ever so moral men, since we have no assurance
of happiness in the next life mentioned
in the Holy Scripture, without faith
in Christ.

Gaudentio. No, Reverend Fathers, I
only mention the sense in which these
men understand the mysteries of their
religion. As I believe in Christ, I
know there is no other name under
heaven by which men can be saved.

Inquisitor. Go on.]

Every ceremony of these people has some
mystery or other included in it; but there
appeared no harm in any of them; except
their falling prostrate before the dust,
which looked like rank idolatry: but they
said still, they meant no more than what

was merely civil, to fignify their refpect for their deceafed parents*.

I fhall not as yet detain your Reverences with the defcription of the beauties of the country through which we paffed, having fo much to fay of the more fubftantial part; that is, of their form of government, laws, and cuftoms, both religious and civil; nor defcribe their prodigious magnificence, though joined with a great deal of natural fimplicity, in their towns, temples, fchools, colleges, &c. Becaufe, being built moftly alike, except for particular ufes, manufactures, and the like; I fhall defcribe them all in one, when I come to the great city of Phor, otherwife called, in their facred language, No-om†: for if I fhould ftay to defcribe the immenfe riches, fertility, and beauties of the country, this relation, which is defigned as a real account of a place wherein I lived fo many years, would rather look like a romance than a true relation. I fhall only tell your Reverences at prefent, that after having taken a moft magnificent repaft,

* See the remarks before on that head, and the accounts of the worfhip of the Chinefe, who were originally Egyptians, in the difputes between the Dominicans and Jefuits, where the latter maintained the idolatrous ceremonies and offerings made to their deceafed anceftors, to imply nothing but a natural and civil refpect. The Dominicans, on the contrary, very juftly held them to be idolatry, as they were judged to be, and condemned as fuch by Clement XI.

† Jofephus againft Appion diftinguifhes two languages of the ancient Egyptians, the one facred, the other common. Their facred language was full of myfteries, perhaps like the Cabala of the Jews.

consifting

confifting of all the heart of man can conceive delicious, both of fruits and wines,
while we ftaid in thofe refrefhing tabernacles,
we paffed on by an eafy evening's journey
to one of their towns, always conducted
and lodged in the fame triumphant manner, till we came to the head of that Nome,
which I told your Reverences was the
green Nome, belonging to the Pophar
regent, fecond in dignity of the whole empire. Here the urn of duft belonging to
that Nome was repofited in a kind of gold-
en tabernacle, fet with precious ftones of
immenfe value, in the centre of a fpacious
temple, which I fhall defcribe afterwards.
After a week's feafting and rejoicing, both
for the reception of the duft, and the fafe-
return of the Pophar and his companions,
together with his exaltation to the regency,
we fet out in the fame manner for the
other Nomes, to repofit all the urns in
their refpective temples. Thefe are five,
as I informed your Reverences before.
The country is fomething mountainous,
particularly under the line, and not very
uniform, though every thing elfe is; con-
taining valleys, or rather whole regions
running out between the deferts; befides
vaft ridges of mountains in the heart of
the country, which inclofe immenfe riches
in their bowels. The chief town is fituated
as nigh as poffible in the middle of the
Nomes,

Nomes, and about the centre of the country, bating those irregularities I mentioned. The four inferior Nomes were like the four corners, with the flame-coloured Nome, where the grand Pophar, or regent *pro tempore* resided, in the centre of the square. Their method was to go to the four inferior Nomes first, and reposit the urns, and then to complete all at the chief town of the first Nome. These Nomes were each about eight days very easy journey over. Thus we went the round of all, which I think, as I then remarked, was a kind of political visitation at the same time. At length we came to the great city of Phor, or No-om, there to reposit the last urn, and for all the people to pay their respects to the grand Pophar, if in being, or else to the regent. By that time, what with those who accompanied the procession of the urns, and the inhabitants of that immense town, more people were gathered together, than one would have almost thought had been in the whole world; but in such order and decency, distinguished in their ranks, tribes, and colours, as is not easy to be comprehended. The glittering tents spread themselves over the face of the earth. .

I shall here give your Reverences a description of the town, because all other great towns or heads of the Nomes are
built

built after that model, as indeed the lesser towns come as nigh it as they can, except, as I said, places for arts or trades, which are generally built on rivers or brooks, for conveniency; such is the nature of the people, that they affect an exact uniformity and equality in all they do, as being brothers of the same stock.

The town of Phor, that is, the Glory or No-om, which signifies the house of the sun, is built circular, in imitation of the sun and its rays, It is situated in the largest plain of all the kingdom, and upon the largest river, which is about as big as our Po, rising from a ridge of mountains under the line, and running towards the north, where it forms a great lake, almost like a sea, whose waters are exhaled by the heat of the sun, having no outlet, or sink under ground in the sands of the vast deserts encompassing it. This river is cut into a most magnificent canal, running directly through the middle of the town. Before it enters the town, to prevent inundations, and for other conveniencies, there are prodigious basons, and locks, and sluices, with collateral canals, to divert and let out the water, if need be. The middle stream forms the grand canal, which runs through the town, till it comes to the grand place; then there is another lock and sluice which dividing it into two semicircles or wings, and

and carrying it round the grand place, forms an island with the temple of the sun in the centre, and meeting again oppofite to where it divided, fo goes on in a canal again. There are twelve bridges with one great arch over each, ten over the circular canals, and two where they divide and meet again. There are alfo bridges over the ftrait canals, at proper diftances. Before the river enters the town, it is divided by the firft great lock into two prodigious femicircles encompaffing the whole town. All the canals are planted with double rows of cedars, and walks the moft delightful that can be imagined. The grand place is in the centre of the town, a prodigious round, or immenfe theatre, encompaffed with the branches of the canal, and, in the centre of that, the temple of the fun. This temple confifts of three hundred and fixty-five double marble pillars, according to the number of the days of the year*, repeated with the ftories one above another, and on the top a cupola open to the fky for the fun to be feen through. The pillars are all of the Corinthian order†, of a marble as white as fnow;

                                    and

* Our author feems to be a little out in this place; for it is certain the ancient Egyptians did not make their year to confift of fo many days, unlefs you will fay, that thefe people, being very great aftronomers, were more exact in their obfervations.

† It is generally uppofed, that the different orders of pillars, as the Doric, the Ionic, Corinthian, &c. came firft from the Greeks, as their appellations

and fluted. The edges of the flutes, with
the capitals burnished, are all gilt. The
inner roofs or the vast galleries on these
pillars, are rained with the sun, moon,
and stars, expressing their different motions; with hieroglyphics known only to
some few of the chief elders or rulers. The
outsides of all are doubly gilt, as is the
dome or grand concave on the top, open
in the middle to the sky. In the middle of
this concave is a golden sun, hanging in the
void, and supported by golden lines or
rods from the edges of the dome. The
artificial sun looks down, as if it were shi-
ning on a globe of earth, erected on a pe-
destal altar-wise, opposite to the sun, according to the situation of their climate to
that glorious planet; in which globe or
earth are inclosed the urns of their deceased
ancestors. On the inside of the pillars, are
the seats of the grandees or elders, to hold
their councils, which are all public. Opposite to the twelve great streets, are so
many entrances into the temple, with as
many magnificent stair-cases between the

appellations, being Greek, would make us believe; but the famous and
ancient palace of Persepolis, notwithstanding its Greek name, where
there were hieroglyphics and inscriptions in characters none could understand, besides other reasons, shew that the invention came from
Egypt or from the ancient Chaldeans, or rather from Seth, Noah, and
the ancient Hebrews. It is likewise very observable, that the invention
of arts and sciences came from the east, and can be traced no higher
than Noah's flood; unless you will allow the fables of Seth, alledged by
the learned Josephus in his antiquities, quoted above. All which is a
very natural confirmation of the account given by Moses, against our
modern sceptics.

entrances,

entrances, to go into the galleries or places
where they keep the regifters of their laws,
&c. with gilt baluftrades looking down into the temple. On the pedeftals of all the
pillars were ingraven hieroglyphics and
characters known to none but the five
chief Pophars, and communicated under
the greateft fecrecy to the fucceffor of any
one of them, in cafe of death, lofs of fen-
fes, and the like. I prefume, the grand
fecrets, and *arcana* of 'ftate, and, it may
be, of their religion, arts, and fciences, are
contained therein. The moft improper de-
corations of the temple, in my opinion,
are the flutings of the pillars, which rather look too finical for the auguft and
majeftic fimplicity affected by thefe people
in other refpects.

The fronts of the houfes round the grand
place are all concave, or fegments of circles, except where the great ftreets meet,
which are twelve in number, according to
the twelve figns of the zodiac, pointing to
the temple in ftrait lines like rays to the
centre, This vaft round is fe' with double rows and circles of ftately cedars before
the houfes, at an exact diftance; as are all
the ftreets on each fide, like fo many
beautiful avenues, which produce a moft
delightful effect to the eye, as well as conveniency of fhade. The crofs ftreets are
fo many parallel circles round the grand
place

place and temple, as the centre, making greater circles as the town enlarges itself. They build always circular-wise till the circle is complete; then another, and so on. All the streets, as I said, both straight and circular, are planted with double rows of cedars. The middle of the areas between the cuttings of the streets are left for gardens and other conveniences, enlarging themselves as they proceed from the centre or grand place. At every cutting of the streets, is a lesser circular space set round with trees, adorned with fountains, or statues of famous men; that, in effect, the whole town is like a prodigious garden, diftinguished with temples, pavilions, avenues, and circles of greens; so that it is difficult to give your Reverences a just idea of the beauty of it. I forgot to tell your Reverences, that the twelve great streets open themselves as they lengthen, like the *radii* of a wheel, so that at the first coming into the town, you have the prospect of the temple and grand place directly before you; and from the temple a direct view of one of the finest avenues and countries in the world. Their principal towns are built after this form. After they have taken a plan of the place, they first build a temple; then leave the great area, or circular market-place, round which they build a circle of

P

houses,

houfes, and add others as. they increafe,
according to the foregoing defcription;
ridiculing and contemning other countries,
whofe towns are generally built in a con-
fufed number of houfes and ftreets, without any regular figure. In all the fpaces
or cuttings of the ftreets, there are either
public fountains brought by pipes from a
mountain at a confiderable diftance from
the town ; or, as I faid before, ftatues of
great men holding fomething in their hands
to declare their merit ; which, having no
wars, is taken, either from the invention
of arts and fciences, or fome memorable
action done by them for the improvement
and good of their country. Thefe they
look upon as more laudable motives, and
greater fpurs to glory, than all the trophies
erected by other nations, to the deftroyers
of their own fpecies. Their houfes are
built all alike, and low, as I obferved before, on account of ftorms and hurricanes,
to which the country is fubject; they are
all exactly of a height, flat-roofed, with
artificial gardens on the top of each*, full
of flowers and aromatic fhrubs ; fo that
when you look from any eminence down
into the ftreets, you fee all the circles and

* The ancient Babylonians had artificial gardens, or hort penfiles,
on the tops of their houfes, as early as the great Semiramis; though
Herodotus derives their invention from a later Babylonian queen, who
being a Mede by nation, and loving woods, and not being permitted to
go out of the palace, had thofe artificial gardens made to divert her.

avenues

avenues like another world under you; and if on the level, along the tops of the houfes, you are charmed with the profpect of ten thoufand different gardens meeting your fight where-ever you turn; infomuch, that I believe the whole world befides cannot afford fuch a profpect. There are a great many other beauties and conveniences according to the genius of the people; which, were I to mention, would make up a whole volume. I only fay, that the riches of the country are immenfe, which in fome meafure are all in common, as I fhall fhew when I come to the nature of their government; the people are the moft ingenious and induftrious in the world; the governors aiming at nothing but the grandeur and good of the public, having all the affluence the heart of man can defire, in a place where there has been no war for near three thoufand years; there being indeed no enemies but the inhofpitable fands around them, and they all confider themfeives as brothers of the fame ftock, living under one common father; fo that it is not fo much to be wondered at, if they are arrived to fuch grandeur and magnificence, as perfons in our world can fcarce believe or conceive.

When the ceremonies for the reception of the urns were over, religious ceremonies with thefe people always taking place

of

of the civil,*, they proceeded to the inauguration of the Pophar regent; which was performed with no other ceremony, for reason, I shall tell your Reverences afterwards, but placing him in a chair of state with his face towards the east, on the top of the highest hill in the Nome, to shew that he was to inspect, or overlook all, looking towards the temple of the sun, which stood directly eastward of him, to put him in mind that he was to take care of the religion of his ancestors in the first place. When he was thus placed, three hundred sixty-five of the chief of the Nome, as representatives of all the rest, came up to him, and making a respectful bow, said, *Eli Pophar*, which is as much as to say, *Hail father* of our nation; and he embracing them as a father does his children, answered them with *Cali Benim*, that is, *My dear children*. As many of the women did the same. This was all the homage they paid him, which was esteemed so sacred as never to be violated. All the distinction of his habit was one great sun

* The most polite nations of antiquity, even among the Heathens, gave the preference to religion, before all other considerations. As for the Christian religion, though of late persons of some wit, little judgment, and no morals, call it in question, it is well known, men become more men as they become Christians. The light of faith brought in learning, politeness, humanity, justice, and equity, instead of that ignorance, and a brutal barbarity, that overspread the face of the earth; and the want of it will lead us in time into the same enormities which religion has taught us to forsake; on which account it is the part of all wise governments to countenance, and preserve religion.

OB.

on his breaft, much bigger than that of any of the reft. The precious ftones alfo, which were fet in the white fillet binding his forehead, were larger than ordinary, as were thofe of the crofs circles over his head, terminated on the fummit with a large tuft of gold, and a thin plate of gold in the fhape of the fun, faftened to the top of it horizontally; all of them, both men and women, wore thofe fillet-crowns with a tuft of gold, but no fun on the top, except the Pophar.

As foon as the ceremonies and rejoicings were over, which were performed in tents at the public expenfe, he was conducted, with the cheerful acclamations of the peo-ple, and the found of mufical inftruments, to a magnificent tent in the front of the whole camp, facing the eaft, which is look-ed upon as the moft honourable, as firft feeing the rifing fun; and fo on, by eafy journeys, till he came to the chief town of that Nome. The reafon why thefe cere-monies were performed in the different Nomes, was to fhew that they all depended on him, and becaufe the empire was fo very populous, it was impoffible they could meet at one place. I cannot exprefs the careffes I received from them, efpecially when they found I was defcended from the fame race by the mother's fide, and fo nearly related to the Pophar. When I

P 2   came

came firſt into their company, they all
embraced me, men and women, with the
moſt endearing tenderneſs; the young
beautiful women did the fame, calling me
brother, and catching me in their arms
with ſuch an innocent aſſurance, as if I
had been their real brother loſt and found
again. I cannot ſay but fome of them expreſſed a fondneſs for me that feemed to be
of another fort, and which afterwards gave
me a great deal of trouble; but I imputed
it to the nature of the fex who are unac-
countably more fond of ſtrangers, whom
they know nothing of, than of perfons of
much greater merit, who converfe with
them every day. Whether it proceeds
from the want of a fufficient folidity in
their judgment, or from a levity and fickle-
neſs in their nature, or from the ſpirit of
contradiction, which makes them fond of
what they moſtly ſhould avoid; or thinking that ſtrangers are not acquainted with
their defects, or, in fine, are more likely to
keep their counfel; be that as it will, their
mutual jealoufies gave me much uneafinefs
afterwards. But to ſay a word or two
more of the nature of the people, before I
proceed in my relation: as I told your
Reverences, they are the handſomeſt race
of people I believe nature ever produced,
with this only difference, which fome may
think a defect, that they all are too much
like:

like one another : but if it be a defect, it
proceeds from a very laudable caufe ; that
is, from their fpringing from one family,
without any mixture of different nations
in their blood* ; they have neither wars,
nor traffic with other people, to adulterate
their race, for which reafon they know
nothing of the vices fuch a commerce
often brings along with it. Their eyes are
fomething too fmall, but not fo little as
thofe of the Chinefe ; their hair is generally
black, and inclined to be a little cropped
or frizzled †, and their complexion brown,
but their features are the moft exact and
regular imaginable ; and in the mountainous parts towards the line, where the air
is cooler, they are rather fairer than our
Italians ‡ ; the men are univerfally well
fhaped, tall and flender, except through
fome accidental deformity, which is very

* Tacitus fays much the fame of the Germans, Ipfe eorum opinioni-
bus accedo, qui Germaniæ populos nullis aliarum nationum connubiis
infectos, propriam et finceram et tanquam fui fimilem gentem exflitiffe
arbitrantur *. I agree, fays he, with their opinion, who think the people of Germany fo peculiarly like one another, becaufe they have not
been corrupted by marriages with other nations. They were noted in
Auguftus's time to have blue eyes as moft of the native Germans have
to this day. I remember I faw a review of a German regiment in the
city of Milan, where almoft every one of the common foldiers had blue
eyes. No wonder therefore, if thefe Africans, our author fpeaks of,
fhould be fo like one another.

† The ancient Egyptians, according to Herodotus and Bochart were
fo.

‡ Though our Italians are fomething more fwarthy than the northern
Tramontani ; yet our ladies keeping much in the houfe from their child-
hood, have very fine fkins. and excel all others for delicacy of features †.

* Tacitus de moribus Germanorum.
† I fancy Signior Rhedi never faw our American beauties.

rare ;

rare; but the women, who keep themfelves much within doors, are the moft
beautiful creatures, and the fineft fhaped
in the world, except, as I faid, being too
much alike. There is fuch an innocent
fweetnefs in their beauty, and fuch a native modefty in their countenance, as cannot be defcribed. A bold forwardnefs in
a woman is what they diflike; and to give
them their due, even the women are the
moft chafte I ever knew, which is partly
owing to the early and provident care of
their governors. But as I defign to make
a feparate article of the education of their
young people, I fhall fay no more at prefent on that head.

The vifitations which we made to carry
the urns, gave me an opportunity of feeing
the greateft part of their country as foon as
I came there; though the Pophar, with a
lefs retinue, and with whom I always was,
vifited them more particularly afterwards.
The country is generally more hilly than
plain, and in fome parts even mountainou;
there are, as I faid, vaft ridges of mountains, which run feveral hundred miles,
either under, or parallel to the equator.
Thefe are very cold, and contribute very
much to render the climate more tempe-
rate than might otherwife be expected,
both by refrigerating the air with cooling
breezes, which are wafted from thence
OVER

over the reft of the country, and by supp-
plying the plains with innumerable rivers
running both north and fouth, but chiefly
towards the north*. Thefe hills, and the
great woods they are generally covered
with, are the occafion of the country's
being fubject to rains†; there are vaft
forefts and places, which they cut down
and deftroy as they want room, leaving lefs
groves for beauty and variety, as well as
ufe and conveniency. The ruins and hilli-
nefs of the country make travelling a little
incommodious, but then they afford numberlefs fprings and rivulets, with fuch delicious vales, that, adding this to the ho-
nefty and innocence of the inhabitants, one
would think it a perpetual paradife. The
foil is fo prodigious fertile, not only in
different forts of grain and rice, with a fort
of wheat much larger and richer in flower
than any Indian wheat I ever faw; but
particularly in an inexauftible variety of
fruits, legumes, and eatable herbs of fuch
nourifhing juice, and delicious tafte, that
to provide fruit for fuch numbers of people

---

* It is remarkable that moft 'prings rife from the north fide of the
hills, and more rivers run northward than fouthward, at leaft on this
fide of the line, though the obfervation does not always hold; the reafon may be, for that there are more mifts and dews hanging on the north
fide, becaufe the fun dries up the moifture on the fouth fide of the mountains, more than on the north; though perhaps all fprings don't rife from,
rain and mifts, &c. yet moft do.
† It is well known to the naturalifts, that great woods and hills collect
clouds and vapours, and confequently caufe it to rain more there than in
other places.

is.

is the least of their care.   One would think
the curse of Adam had scarce reached that
part of the world ; or that Providence had
proportioned the fertility of the country to
the innocence of the inhabitants ; not but
the industry and ingenuity of the people,
joined with their perpetual peace and rest
from external and almost internal broils,
contribute very much to their riches and
fertility.   Their villages being most of
them built on the rivulets for manufactures
and trades, are not to be numbered.   Their
hills are full of metallic mines of all sorts,
with materials sufficient to work them ; filver is the scarcest, and none more plentiful than gold ; it comes out oftentimes in
great lumps from the mineral rocks, as if
it wept out from between the joints, and
was thrown off by the natural heat of the
earth, or other unknown causes : this gold
is more ductile, easier to work, and better
for all uses, than that which is drawn from
the ore.   Their inventions not only for
common conveniences, but even the magnificence of life, are astonishing.   When I
spoke of their fruits, I should have mentioned a small sort of grape that grows
there naturally, of which they make a
wine, sharp at first, but which will keep
a great many years, mellowing and im-
proving as it is kept ; but the choicest
grapes, which are chiefly for drying, are
cultivated

cultivated among them, and a very little pains does it. Their wines are more cordial than inebriating ; but a smaller sort, diluted with water, makes their constant drink. I don't remember I ever saw any horned beasts in the country, except goats of a very large size, which serve them for milk, though it is rather too rich : deer there are innumerable, of more different kinds than are in Europe. There is a little beast seemingly of a species between a roe and a sheep, whose flesh is the most nourishing and delicious that can be tasted ; these make a dish in all their feasts, and are chiefly reserved for that end. Their fowl, wild and tame, make the greatest part of their food, as to flesh-meat, of which they don't eat much, it being, as they think, too gross a food. The rivers and lakes are stored with vast quantities of most exquisite fish, particularly a golden trout, whose belly is of a bright scarlet colour, as delectable to the palate as to the eye. They suppose fish to be more nourishing and easier of digestion than flesh, for which reason they eat much more of it ; but having no rivers that run into the sea, they want all of that kind.

Their horses, as I observed before, are but small, but full of mettle and life, and extremely swift ; they have a wild ass longer than the horse, of all the colours of the

raint irks most

rainbow, very ftrong and profitable for
burden and drudgery; but their great
carriages are drawn by elks; the dromedaries are for travelling over the fands.
The rivers, at leaft in the plain and low
countries, are cut into canals, by which
they carry moft of their provifion and effects all over the country. This is only a
fmall fketch of the nature of the country,
becaufe I know thefe matters don't fall under the cognifance of your Reverences, fo
much as the account of their religion, morals, cuftoms, laws, and government. Yet
I muft fay that for riches, plenty of all
delicacies of life, manufactories, inventions
of arts, and every thing that conduces to
make this mortal ftate as happy as is poffible, no country in the known world can
parallel it; though there are fome inconveniences, as your Reverences will obferve
as I go on with my relation.

Before I come to the remaining occurrences of my own life, in which nothing
very extraordinary happened till I came
away, unlefs I reckon the extraordinary
happinefs I was placed in, as to all things
of this life, in one of the moft delicious
regions of the univerfe, married to the regent's daughter, whofe picture is there
before you, and the deplorable lofs of her
with my only remain'ig fon. [Here he
could not refrain from weeping for fome
time.]

time], as well as the prefent ftate to which I am reduced ;' though I muft own I have received more favourable treatment than could well be expected : I fhall give your Reverences a fuccinct account of their religion, laws, and cuftoms, which are almoft as far out of the common way of thinking of the reft of the world, as their country.

Of their Religion.

The religion of thefe people is really idolatry in the main ; though as fimple and natural as poffible for Heathens. They indeed will not acknowledge themfelves to be Heathens, in the fenfe we take the word ; that is, worfhippers of falfe gods*, for they have an abhorrence of idolatry in words as well as the Chinefe, but are idolaters in effect, worfhipping the material fun, and paying thofe fuperftitious rites to their deceafed anceftors ; of which part of their religion your Reverences have had a full account already. Thefe people however acknowledge one fupreme God, maker of all things, whom they call El†, or the

* This opinion was very ancient, and came originally from Egypt, where Pythagoras learned it: though perhaps not liking this way of employing it, he altered it quite from what thefe men held, which is the lefs irrational of the two. Though, with Signor Gaudentio's leave, I can never believe, thefe wife men really held that opinion, but only underftood it allegorically: I muft own, at the fame time, one of the ancients did hold the other metempfychofis.

† The old Arabians by Al, or perhaps El, mean fomething very grand or high, as Al-Cair, for Grand Cair, Alchymy for the higheft chymiftry, &c. I wonder Signor Redi took no notice of this in his remarks.

moft high of all. This they fay natural
reafon teaches them from an argument,
though good in itfelf, yet formed after a
different way of arguing from other people:
they fay all their own wifdom, or that of
all the wifeft men in the world put together, could never form this glorious world
in all its caufes and effects, fo juftly adapted
to its refpective ends, as it is with refpect
to every individual fpecies. Therefore the
author of it muft be a being infinitely
wifer than all intellectual beings. As for
the notion of any thing producing itfelf
without a prior caufe, they laugh at it,
and afk why we don't fee fuch effects produced without a caufe? hence they hold
one only independent caufe, and that there
muft be one, or nothing could ever be produced. Though they make a god of the
fun, they don't fay he is independent as
to his own being : but that he received it
from this El. Some of the wifer fort,
when I argued with them, feemed to acknowledge the fun to be a material being
created by God ; but others think him to
be a fort of wicegerent, by whom the El
performs every thing, as the chief inftrumental caufe of all productions. This is
the reafon ha they addrefs all their prayers to the fun, though they allow all power
is to be referred originally to the El. The
men look upon the moon to be a material
being,

being, dependent on the fun; but the women feem to make a goddefs of her, by reafon of the influence fhe has over that fex; and foolifhly think fhe brings forth every month when fhe is at the full, and that the ftars are hers and the fun's children. They all of them; both men and women, reft fatisfied in their belief, without any difputes or ftudied notions about a being fo infinitely above them, thinking it much better to adore him in the infcrutability of his effence, in-an humble filence, than to be difputing about what they cannot comprehend; all their fearch is employed in fecond caufes, and the knowledge of nature as far as it may be ufeful to men.

> [*Inquifitor.* I hope you don't deny but that fome men may have wrong notions of the Deity, in which they ought to be fet right by wifer and more learned men than themfelves; by confequence all fearches and difputes about the being and nature of God are not to be condemned.

> *Gaudentio.* No, may it pleafe your Reverences, for I prefume you only underftand me now as reprefenting other people's opinions, not my own, which is entirely conformable to what the Catholic church teaches. I often told the Pophar, to whom I could fpeak
my

my mind with all the freedom in the
world, that as no mortal man could
pretend to tell what belonged to the
incomprehenſibility of God's eſſence,
yet our reaſon obliging us to believe
his being; it was neceſſary, by the
ſame reaſon, that we ſhould be inſtructed by himſelf, or ſome lawgiver
immediately commiſſioned by him;
leſt we ſhould err in ſo material a
point. This lawgiver we Chriſtians
believe he did ſend, by giving us his
only Son, who was capable of inſtruct-
ing us in what belonged to the eternal Godhead : that he did not only
give us the juſteſt notions we could
poſſibly have, but confirmed the truth
of what he ſaid, by ſuch ſigns and
wonders as none but one ſent from
God could perform.

Inquiſiter. Go on:]

When I ſaid, they addreſs all their prayers, and moſt of the external actions of
their worſhip to the ſun, it is on account
of their believing him to be the phyſical
cauſe of the production of all things by his
natural influence; which, though the wiſer
ſort of them, when you came to reaſon
more cloſely, will grant to be derived from
the Fl, and ſome of them will own him to
be a mere material being, moved by a
prior cauſe, yet the generality of them
                                          don't

don't reflect on this; but are really guilty
of idolatry in worfhipping a mere creature.
Neverthelefs, as to the moral effects of
the univerfe, or the free actions of men
with refpect to equity, juftice, goodnefs,
uprightnefs, and the like, which they allow
to be properly the duty of rational creatures; and of much greater confequence
than the phyfical part of the world: this,
I fay, they all refer to the fupreme being,
whofe will it is they fhould be merciful,
good, juft, and equitable to all, agreeable
to the juft notions of the all-wife author
of their exiftence, whofe fupreme reafon
being incapable of any irregular bias, ought
to be the rule of his creatures that depend
on him, and are in fome meafure partakers
of his perfections. They confirm this notion by a very proper comparifon; as for
example, to act contrary to the laws of
nature in phyfical productions, i. to produce monftrous births, &c. fo to act contrary to the ideas of the fupreme reafon in
moral cafes, muft be a great deformity in
his fight.

I own I was charmed with this natural
way of reafoning, and afked them further,
whether they believed the fupreme being
troubled himfelf about the moral part of
the world; or the free actions of men?
They feemed furprifed at the queftion, and
afked me, whether I thought it was poffible

Q 2

he should leave the noblest part out of his
care, when he took the pains (that was
their expreffion) to create the leaft infect
according to the moft exact rules of art
and knowledge, beyond all that the art of
man can come up to? I afked them again,
what were the rules, which it was his will
that free agents, fuch as man for inftance,
fhould follow in the direction of their
lives? They told me, reafon, juftice, and
equity, in imitation of the fupreme reafon
in him; for, faid they, can you think the
fupreme being can approve of the enormous actions committed by men; or that
any vile practices can be according to the
juft ideas of his reafon; if not, they muft
be contrary to the beft light of reafon, not
only in God, but man, and therefore
liable to be punifhed by the juft governor
of all.

I fubmit thefe notions to your Reverences better judgment, but I thought them
very extraordinary for perfons who had
nothing but the light of nature to direct
them; it is pity but they had been as
right in their more remote inferences as
they were in thefe principles. The fum
therefore of the theoretical part of their
religion, is

Firft, that is the fupreme intellectual, rational moft noble of all beings;
that it is the duty of all intellectual beings
to

to imitate the juft laws of reafon in him,
otherwife they depart from the fupreme
rule of all their actions, fince what is contrary to the moft perfect reafon in God,
muft be contrary to our own, and by confequence of a deformity highly blameable
in his fight ; all their prayers, and whatever they afk of this fupreme being, is, that
they may be juft and good as he is.   •

Secondly, that the fun is the chief, at
leaft inftrumental caufe of their bodies, and
all other phyfical effects. Your Reverences
know better than I can inform you, that
this is wrong: to him they addrefs their
prayers for the prefervation of their lives,
the fruits of the earth, &c.

Thirdly, that their parents are the more
immediate inftrumental caufe of their natural being, which they derive partly from
the El, and partly from the fun, and they
reverence them the more on this account,
as being the vicegerents of both, and believe them to be immortal, as to the fpiri-
tual or intellectual part, and confequently
able and ready to affift them according to
the refpect they fhew them by reverencing
their tombs and honouring their memories.
Though, upon a nicer examination, I found
that the fuperftitious worfhip they pay to
their deceafed anceftors, was as much a
politic as a religious inftitution, becaufe
their government being patriarchal, this
                                    inviolable

inviolable ▮▮▮ect they shew t
re▮▮s ▮▮ ▮▮ obey their el
vernors, ▮▮ ▮ly with the m
observance, but even with a fil
alacrity.

There are some other points
sequence, and reducible to t
heads, which your Reverences ▮
in the course of my relation.
immortality of the soul, rewar
▮nishments in another life, they b
though they have an odd way
ing them. They ▮▮ppose, wi
hesitation, that t▮ ▮oul is a ▮
pendent of matter, ▮▮o its effer
faculties of thinking, willing, a▮
which mere matter, let it be
▮o fine, and actuated by the q▮
the most subtile motion, ca▮▮v
ble of; but their notion ▮▮▮ei
ence with the El, before they
into bodies, is very confused. T
and punishments in the next li
lieve will chiefly consist in thi
proportion as their actions have
formable to the just ideas of tl
being in this life, partaking stil
more of his infinite wisdom, so
will approa▮ ▮▮ ▮arer to th
intelligence ▮▮ ▮▮ divine m▮
next. But if their actions in tl
been inconsistent with the supr▮

in God, they fhall be permitted to go on
for ever in that inconfiftency and difagree-
ment, till they become fo mónftroufly
wicked and enormous, as to become abominable even to themfelves..

*Of their opinion concerning the tranfmigration
of fouls, and the fcience of phyfiognomy.*

I found the wifeft of them held the metempfychofis, or the tranfmigration of
fouls *, not as a punifhment in the next
life, as fome of the ancient Heathen philofophers did, but as a punifhment in this;
the chief punifhment in the next was explained above. This tranfmigration of
fouls is quite different from the received
notion of the word. Inftead of believing,
as the ancients did, that the fouls of wicked and voluptuous, men, after their deaths,
tranfmigrated into beafts according to the
fimilitude of their vitious inclinations, till,
paffing through one animal into another,
they were permitted to commence men
again; I fay, thefe people, inftead of believing this, hold a metempfychofis of
quite a different nature; not that the fouls
of men enter into brutes, but that the fouls

---

* This notion of the tranfmigration of the fouls of brutes into men
and women in this life, particularly into the latter, was not unknown
to the ancients, though explained fomething after a different way: witnefs a remaining fragment of Simonides, a very ancient Greek poet, to
that effect.

of brutes enter into the bodies of men, even in this life.. They say, for example, that the bodies of men and women are such delicate habitations, that the souls of brutes are perpetually envying them, and contriving to get into them; that, unless the divine light of reason be perpetually attended to, these brutal souls steal in upon them, and chain up the rational soul, so that it shall not be able to govern the body, unless it be to carry on the designs of the brutal soul, or- at best only make some faint efforts to get out of its slavery. I took it at first, that this system was merely allegorical, to shew the similitude between the passions of men when not directed by reason, and those of brutes. But, upon examination, I found it was their opinion, that this transmigration did really happen; insomuch that in my last journey with the Pophar into Egypt, when he saw the Turks, or other strange nations, nay several Armenian and European Christians, he would say to me in his own language, there goes a hog, there goes a lion, a wolf, a fox, a dog, and the like; that is, they believe the body of a voluptuous man is possessed by the soul of a hog, of a lustful man by that of a goat, a treacherous man by that of a fox, a tyrannical man by that of a wolf, and so of the rest: This belief is instilled into them so early, and

with

with fo much care, that it is of very great
benefit to keep them within the bounds of
reafon. If a ycung man finds himfelf inclined to any of thefe paffions, he addreffes
himfelf immediately to fome perfon whom
he thinks of fuperior wifdom, who affures
him that the foul of fome certain brute is
endeavouring to furprife and captivate his
rational foul, and take poffeffion of its
place. This makes them always watchful,
and upon their guard againft their own
paffions, not to be furprifed by fuch a
mercilefs enemy. Their immediate reme-
dy is, to look ftedfaftly at the divine light
that fhines within them, and compare it
with its original, till by the force of its rays
they drive away thofe brutal fouls, which,
as foon as fully difcovered in their treacherous attacks, (for they come on, fay they,
by ftealth, not daring to attack that divine
light directly), are eafily repulfed, before
they have obtained poffeffion, though it
cofts a great deal of pains to diflodge them,
when once they are got in. The fear of
being abandoned to the flavery of thefe
brutal fouls is fo deeply imprinted in them
from their infancy, that they look upon the
temperance and regularity of their lives to
be in a great meafure owing to this doctrine. The fame notions hold with their
women; into whom their mothers and
governeffes inftil them, as the wife men
do

do to the men; only they believe the brutal
fouls that enter into women, are of a different fpecies from thofe that enter into men.
They fay, for inftance, that of a cameleon
makes them falfe and inconftant; that of
a peacock, coquettifh and vain; that of a
tygrefs, cruel and ill-natured; and fo of
the reft. They add another difference between men and women, that when thefe
brutal fouls are entered into them, they are
much harder to be driven out from them,
than from the men; befides that thefe
brutal fouls will lurk undifcovered in women a great while, and are often fcarce
difcernible, till the age of five and twenty
or thirty; whereas in moft men they difcover themfelves prefently after their entrance.

It was on account of this doctrine, as I
found by repeated obfervations, that they
were fo addicted to the ftudy of phyfiognomy, laying down rules to know by the
countenance, the lines of the face, and un-
guarded looks of men, whether the brutal
foul has got poffeffion or not, in order to
apply proper remedies. This fcience, however uncertain and doubtful among Chriftians, (who have greater affiftance of grace
and virtue to refift their paffions, thofe
treacherous invaders), is brought to greater perfection and certitude than one would
imagine, among fuch of thefe people, who,
having

having no fuch affiftance, take little care to cultivate and moderate their vitious inclinations, unlefs they are apprifed and forewarned of the danger. Therefore their wife men, whenever they come in company of the younger fort, confider attentively with themfelves all the lineaments of the countenance, complexions, motions, habit of body, conftitution, tone of the voice, make and turn of the face, nofe, ears, &c. but particularly they obferve the ftructure and glances of the eye, with innumerable figns proceeding from it, by which they pretend to difcover thofe paffions. I fay, they pretend to know by thefe what brutal foul lays fiege to the rational foul, or whether it has already taken poffeffion of its poft. If they are ftrangers, they prudently take care to avoid their company, or at leaft are on their guard not to have any dealings with them in matters obnoxious to the brutal foul they think them poffeffed by. But if the perfon attacked by thefe brutal fouls be of their own nation, they immediately forewarn fuch to be on his guard, by which, and the dread they have entertained from their youth of thefe brutal enemies, they are kept in fuch order, that, as I faid, I never faw fuch moral people in my life. The worft is, they are extremely inclined to be proud, and have too great a value for

R   themfelves,

themselves, despising in their hearts all other nations as if they were nothing but brutes in human shape*. However, their wife men take as much care as possible to correct this fault, as far as the ignorance of the law of grace will allow; by putting them often in mind of the miseries and infirmities of human life, which being real evils, must be in punishment of some fault; that the most perfect are liable to death, which makes no distinction between them and the rest of the world. Besides, humility, and a commiseration for the defects of others, is one of the rays of the divine light that is to guide them. From such documents and instructions of the wiser sort, though they do not care to have any correspondence with other people, seeing them so possessed with those brutal souls, yet they are a most courteous and compassionate people in all their behaviour.

Of their laws and customs.

Over and above what has been said already of the nature and customs of these people, I shall here observe that their laws are very few in number; but then they are

---

* The Chinese, whom I have proved to be descended from the first Egyptians, are subject to the like pride and contempt of other people; saying that all other nations have but one eye, whereas nature has given them two: signifying thereby, how much wiser they think themselves than other men.

prodigious

prodigious exact in the observance of them.
I have often heard the Pophar, contrary to
his custom, make very severe reflections
on the lawyers of other countries, who
make laws upon laws, and add precepts
upon precepts, till the endless number of
them makes the fundamental part to be
forgotten; leaving nothing but a confused
heap of explanations; which may cause ignorant people to doubt, whether there is
really any thing meant by the laws, or not.
If I forbid my son, says he, to do any
wrong to any one, what need is there of
reckoning up all the particulars by which
a person may be wronged? Shew but the
fact on both sides, any man of sense and
equity can tell, if there be any wrong done.
For if you multiply an infinity of circum-
stances, it will be much more difficult to
decide what is right, or what is wrong,
than if you precisely and absolutely forbid
all injury whatsoever. It is almost incredible, with what nicety and equity, and
how soon, their judges determine the few
disputes they have among them. To
weigh the merits of the cause by the weight
of the purse, would be counted by them
one of the greatest enormities. There are
no courts for disputes of this nature; all
is done by laying the case before their public assemblies, or before any one or two
prudent and just men; and the affair is
finally

finally decided at once. All the law for *meum* and *tuum* among them is, *Thou shalt do no wrong to any one*, without entering into any further niceties. Such explanatory suppositions, say they, oftener shew people how they may ingeniously contrive to do an injury, than how to avoid it.

Their laws therefore are nothing but the first principles of natural justice, explained and applied by the elders, in the public hearing of all who have a mind to come in when the facts are brought into dispute.

The worship of the Deity, and that excessive and even superstitious reverence they pay to their parents, both alive and dead, is so carefully inculcated to them from their infancy, that there is no need of any written law to inforce it. They look on a man to be possessed with some brutal soul, who should pretend to call in question or neglect this duty.

There is a positive law among them, not to shed human blood voluntarily*. They

* The people defending from Mizraim, who might know the patriarch Noah, and might have learned by tradition the punishment of Cain for the murder of his brother Abel, carried that opinion to an excess. Be there people who they will, or not be at all, I cannot but observe, how inexcusable the wickedness of men was from the beginning, without blaming God, as some libertines do, for leaving them in ignorance.

The wicked Ham, or Cham, was in the ark with Noah, and lived many years before the deluge, (the truth of which is attested by ancient history as well as by sacred scripture,) and saw the dreadful punishment inflicted on the world for sin; could not he have learned godliness, and the reward for it, of his father Noah? Could not Ham have taught his own children, they theirs; and so on? But they corrupted their own ways, and thereby shewed the necessity of a revelation.

carry

carry this fundamental law of nature to
such a height, that they never put any one
to death, even for murder, which very
rarely happens; that is, once in several
ages. If it appears that a person has really
murdered another, a thing they think almost impossible, the person convicted is
shut up from all commerce of men, with
provisions to keep him alive as long as nature allows. After his death the fact is
proclaimed, as it was when they shut him
up, over all the Nomes. His name is
blotted out of their genealogies; then
his dead body is mangled just in the same
manner as he killed the innocent, and afterwards burnt to ashes, which are carried
up to the highest part of the deserts, and
then tossed up into the air, to be carried
away by the winds blowing from their own
country: nor is he ever more to be reckoned as one of their race, and there is a general mourning observed throughout the
kingdom for nine days.

There is also an express law against adultery and whoredom, which are likewise
punished after death. If persons are caught
in adultery, they are shut up apart till
death; then they are exposed naked as
they were surprised, and the body of the
women treated after the most ignominious
manner for three days. After which,
they are burnt, and their ashes dispersed

as before *.　Whoredom is only punifhed, in the man, by chaining him to a he-goat, and the women to a falt bitch, and leading thus round the Nome.　All in the refpective Nome, men and women, are to be prefent at the more fignal punifhments ; and parents are obliged to explain to their children the wickednefs and horror of the crime, for a warning for the future.　I forgot to tell your Reverences, that if the woman brings forth by adultery, the child is preferved, till able to be carried with them when they go into Egypt, and there given to fome ftranger, with ample provifion for its maintenance, but never to be heard of more†.

There is alfo one particular I fhould have mentioned, relating to injuftice.　If, for example, the elders find there has been any confiderable injuftice done, the criminal is obliged to reftore nine times the value.　If any one be convicted to have impofed upon the judges, he is to be fent out to the fkirts of the country, to live by himfelf for a time proportionable to his guilt, with a mark on his forehead, for all

* See the learned Bifhop of Meaux's univerfal hiftory, concerning the Egyptians, par. 3. and of their punifhments after death.

† With our author's leave, this is not fuch a foft and compaffionate part, to turn innocent children out among people whofe cuftoms they had fuch a horror of, only for their parents faults. For though the maxim be good, Beware a breed, yet the care they took of their youth, and the moral inftruction they gave them, might make them abhor the crimes of their parents.

perfons

perfons to avoid him, left he fhould inftil
his principles into others. All other matters
are regulated rather by cuftom, than by
laws, which will be feen, when I come to
the form of their government, and other
particular inftitutions.

Of their form of Government.

Their form of government, as I had the
honour to acquaint your Reverences before,
is patriarchal, which they preferve inviola-
bly, being the moft tenacious people in the
world of their primitive inftitutions.   But
the order of the fucceffion is extremely particular, in order to keep up the equality of
brotherhood and dignity as exact as they
can. Your Reverences, I prefume, remember that they all fprung from one family
(and lived as fuch when they were driven
out of Egypt), the head of which was
prieft of the fun.   This government they
had obferved ever fince mifraim took poffeffion of that land for his habitation. But
when they were fecured from all the world
in the firft vale, as was mentioned before,
they eftablifhed that form of government
after a particular manner. The firft Pophar
fettling in that vale with his five fons, and
as many daughters with their hufbands, governed them during life, as father or patriarch of them all.   Their prodigious veneration

ration for their parents, and feparation from all other people, render this form infinitely more practicable than can well be imagined. As they were children of one man, the intereft of the whole was the intereft of every particular. All the nation of the firft tranfmigration were children, grandchildren, or great-grandchildren of the good old man who conducted them thither. Having no wars, or voyages at fea, nor commerce with the diftempers as well as vices of other nations, who generally differ in their way of living as well as their climate; having nothing of this, I fay, to deftroy their people, they not only increafed prodigioufly, without plurality of wives, but by that and their almoft primitive way of living, they preferved their lives to great old age, moft of them living above hundred and fifty years. The firft Pophar (fay their memoirs) lived till an hundred and fifty-five, and his eldeft fon his fucceffor, more robuft ftill, to a hundred and fixty. Prefently after his eftablifhment in the firft vale, he divided his fmall dominions into five Nomes, or governments, under his five fons, as was obferved before. All were to be fubordinate to the eldeft; but it was only a patriarchal fubordination, relating to the whole. The other governors, and indeed all fathers of families, were entire minifters of the laws in their refpective

families;

families ; but thefe laft were liable to the
infpection of the more immediate fuperiors,
and all to that of the Grand Pophar, affifted with fuch a number of counfellors as
were eftablifhed afterwards. To give your
Reverences a more diftinct idea of this wonderful government, it will come much to
the fame, whether we defcend from the
chief Pophar to every refpective family, or
from thefe upwards. The particularities
of the fucceffion I fhall confider afterwards.
However, it will be eafier feen if we take
them when their numbers were not fo great,
at the firft beginning of their eftablifhment.

The Pophar, then, having diftinguifhed
the bounds of every Nome, I mean in their
firft tranfmigration, each fon took poffeffion of it for himfelf and pofterity. While
each fon's children were unmarried, they
continued under the government of their
father, who made ufe of as much land as
was fufficient for the conveniencies and
pleafures, as well as the neceffaries of life.
But as foon as any fon was married, or at
leaft when he could be called a father of a
family, the father, with confent of the Pophar, alloted him likewife a fufficient quantity for the fame end : fo they fpread and
enlarged themfelves as it were from the centre to a father extent, much in the fame
manner as they build their towns, till they
had

had occupied the whole Nome. Here you will say, thefe people muft in procefs of time increafe *ad infinitum*, without lands fufficient to maintain them. This was really the cafe in the firft plantation, which was fo entirely occupied by them, that if the famous Pophar. who brought them into the vaft continent they now enjoy, had not made that glorious difcovery with the danger of his life, they muft have returned into Egypt, or ate up one another ; but where they are at prefent, they have room enough, notwithftanding their numbers, for feveral ages. However, I often reprefented to the Pophar, that it muft come to that at laft : the thought made him uneafy at firft, and at length put him on a further difcovery, as your Reverences will fee in the fequel. But fuch vaft numbers of them betaking themfelves to arts and manufactures, and the country being fo prodigioufly fertile, there does not appear any great difficulty in that refpect. Of all arts they look upon agriculture as the firft in dignity next to the liberal fciences, fince that nourifhes all the reft ; but it comes fo eafily, and the fruits and legumes are fo rich and delicious, that they have little more trouble than to gather them : befides, having two fummers, and two fprings, each different feafon produces its peculiar fruits. But to return to the idea of their government,

government, each father of a family go-
verns all his defcendents, married or unmarried, as long as he lives. If his fons
are fathers, they have a fubordinate power under him ; if he dies before he comes
to fuch an age, the eldeft fon, or the eldeft
uncle, takes care of them, till they are fufficient to fet up a family of themfelves.
The father, on extraordinary occafions, is
liable to be infpected by five of the moft
prudent heads of that diftrict ; thefe by
five of the five adjacent diftricts chofen by
common confent ; thefe laft, by the heads
of the five Nomes, and all the Nomes by
the Grand Pophar, affifted with three hundred fixty-five elders, or fenators, chofen
out of every Nome. What is moft particular in this government is, that they are
all abfolute in fome manner, and independent, as looking on themfelves as, all equal
in birth ; yet in an entire dependency of
natural fubordination or elderfhip, which
runs through the whole œconomy, as your
Reverences will fee when I come to the
fucceffion. They are in the fame manner
lords and proprietors of their own poffeffions, yet the Pophar and governors can
allot and difpofe of all for the public emo-
lument, becaufe they look on him to be as
much the father of all, as the immediate
natural father is of his proper children,
and even in fome fenfe their natural father

by

by right of elderſhip, becauſe they ſprung originally from õne man, whom the Grand Pophar repreſents. To this, that natural, õr politic, or even ſuperſtitious reſpect they ſhew to their parents, contributes ſo much; that they never diſpute, but, on the contrary, revere, the regulations made by their ſuperiors ; being ſatisfied that they are not only juſt and good, but that it is their own act, ſince it is done by virtue of a ſubordination to which they all belong.

The ſucceſſion of elderſhip has ſomething very particular, and even intricate in it. To expreſs at the ſame time the ſuperiority of the elder ſon and the equality of independence, I ſhall endeavour to explain to your Reverences, as well as I can, the right thereof. The eldeſt ſon of the firſt Pophar is always Grand Pophar, when he is of age to govern, which, as I ſaid, is at fifty at ſooneſt ; but if the direct line fails, not the uncle's ſon, nor any one in that Nome, but the right heir of the next Nome; and ſo of all the five Nomes. If they ſhould fail in all the Nomes, the right heir of the ſecond ſon of the firſt Nome, and ſo of all the reſt. This, they ſay, has happened ſeveral times ſince their firſt eſtabliſhment, which is not much to be wondered at, if they are ſo ancient as they pretend. Thus, though the grand popharſhip be confined to the eldeſt in ſome ſenſe, in effect it belongs to them all; but if the next heir be a minor, as he is a'ways judged to be till he is fifty years of age, the eldeft of that age of the fecond fon of the next Nome, is regent till the heir be out of his minority, and fo on : infomuch that, in order to divide the fuperiority among them as equally as poffible, he who has the next rignt to be Grand Pophar, is never to be regent. All other public officers, teachers of arts and fciences, overfeers of all the public employments, &c. are conftituted by the Grand Pophar, and fanhedrim, with affociates of every Nome.

More particulars of their public œconomy.

Though, as I faid, the Pophar is in fome fenfe the proprietor of the whole country, as head of the government and chief patriarch; yet the paradox of this government confiits in this, that they are joint lords, acknowledging no inequality, but merely elderfhip, and the refpect due to dignitaries, which they efteem as their own, or redounding to themfelves, becaufe they all give their confent to their election for the public good. In a word, the whole country is only one great family governed by the laws of nature, with proper officers, conftituted by the whole, for order and common prefervation. Every individual looks on himfelf as a part of that great family. The Grand Pophar is the common father, efteeming all the reft as children and brothers, calling them univerfally by that name, as they all call one another brothers, bartering and exchanging their commodities as one brother would do with another ; and not only fo, but they all join in building their towns, public places, fchools, &c. laying up all the ftores and provifions, over and above the prefent confumption, in public places, for the ufe of the whole, with overfeers and infpectors, conftituted by the common confent, who are to take care chiefly, that no diforder be committed. Thus every one contributes to all public expenfes, feafts, and the like, which on fome occafions are extremely magnificent ; affecting external grandeur in all refpects. Thus alfo every man, where-ever he goes, enters into what houfe he pleafes, as if it were his own home ; this they are doing perpetually throughout the whole country, rather vifiting than merchandifing : exchanging the rarities of each refpective place with thofe of other parts, juft like friends making prefents to one another ; fo that all the roads are like ftreets of great towns, with people going backward and forward perpetually. They do this the more frequently to keep up a correfpondence between the Nomes, left

diſtance of place ſhould cauſe any forget-
fulneſs of their being of one family. The
plenty of the country affords them every
thing that nature can call delightful, and
that with fuch eaſe, that infinite numbers
are employed in trades and arts, according
to their genius, or inciinations; which, by
their continual peace and plenty, their
long eſtabliſhment in one country, and
under one form of government, the natural ingenuity of the people, the early
knowledge of arts, which they brought
with them out of Egypt; by the improve-
ments their wife men make in them from
time to time; and from what they learn
when they pay their viſits to their deceaſed
anceſtors, they have brought to prodigious
perfection. One may ſay of them, that
they are all maſters, and all ſervants; every
one has his employment; generally ſpeaking, the younger ſort wait on the elders,
changing their offices as is thought proper
by their ſuperiors, as in a well-regulated
community. All their children univerſally
are taught at the public expenſe, as children of the government, without any diftinction but that of perſonal merit. As
the perſons deputed for that end, judge
of their genius, or any particular inclination, they are difpoſed afterwards to thoſe
arts and callings for which they ſeem moſt
proper; the moſt ſublime ſciences are the

                                        moſt

moft in refpect with them, and are chiefly
the employment of their great men and
governors, contrary to the cuftom of other
countries ; the reafon of which is, becaufe
thefe being never chofen till they are fifty
years of age, they have had more time to
improve themfelves, and generally are
perfons of more extenfive capacities. They
rightly fuppofe, that perfons who excel
others in the moft rational fciences, are
not only fitteft to govern a rational people,
but alfo moft capable of making themfelves mafters of what they undertake ; not
but fuch men, knowing the governors are
chofen out of that rank, have an eye in
their ftudies to the rules and arts of governing, which are communicated at a
diftance by them, according to the talents
they remark in the fubjects. They do not
do this out of any fpirit of ambition, employments being rather an honorary trouble than an advantage, but for the real
good of the whole. Agriculture, as I faid,
has the next place in honour after the liberal arts ; and next to that, thofe arts are
moft efteemed which are moft neceffary ;
the laft of all are thofe which are of leaft
ufe, though perhaps the moft delightful.

Since every one is employed for the
common good more than for themfelves,
perhaps perfons may apprehend that this
gives a check to induftry, not having that
fpur

fpur of private intereft, hoarding up riches, or aggrandizing their families, as is to be found in other nations. I was apprehen- five of this myfelf, when I came to under- ftand their government; but fo far from it, that poffibly there is not fuch an induf- trious race of people in the univerfe. They place their great ambition in the grandeur of the country, looking on thofe as narrow and mercenary fpirits, who can prefer a part to the whole: they pride themfelves over other nations on that account ; each man having a proportionable fhare in the public grandeur, the love of glory and praife feems to be their greateft paffion. Befides, their wife governors have fuch ways of ftirring up their emulation by pub- lic honours, harangues, and panegyrics in their affemblies, with a thoufand other ways of fhew and peagantry, and this for the moft minute arts, that were it not for that fraternal love ingrafted in them from their infancy, they would be in danger of raifing their emulation to too great a height. Thofe who give indications of greater wifdom and prudence in their con- duct than others, are marked out for go- vernors, and gradually raifed according to their merit. Whoever invents a new art has a ftatue erected according to the ufe- fulnefs of it, with his name and family inferted in public records. Whoever dif-

tinguiſhes himſelf by any particular excel-
lency, has ſuitable marks of diſtinction
paid him on public occaſions, as garlands,
crowns, acclamations, ſongs, or hymns in
his praiſe, &c. It is incredible how ſuch
rewards as theſe encourage induſtry and
arts in minds ſo affected with glory as theſe
people are: on the other hand, their greateſt puniſhments, except for capital crimes,
which are puniſhed as above, are by public diſgraces.

But now I am ſpeaking of their youth;
as they look upon them as ſeeds of the
commonwealth, which if corrupted in the
bud will never bring forth fruit, ſo their
particular care is laid out in their education, in which I believe they excel all nations.
One cannot ſay there is one in the whole
nation who may be called an idle perſon,
though they indulge their youth very
much in proper recreations, endeavouring
to keep them as gay as they can, becauſe
they are naturally inclined to gravity. Beſides daily recreations, they have ſet times
and ſeaſons for public exerciſes, as riding,
vaulting, running, but particularly hunting wild beaſts, and fiſhing for crocodiles
and alligators, in their great lakes, which I
ſhall deſcribe to your Reverences on another occaſion; yet they are never ſuffered
to go alone, that is, a company of young
men together without grave men and perſons

fons in authority along with them, who are a guard to them in all their actions.: nay, they are never suffered to fleep together, each lying in a fingle bed, though in a public room, with fome grave perfon in the fame room with them. Their women are kept much in the fame manner, to prevent inconveniences which I fhall touch upon when I come to the education of their women : and this fo univerfally,.that as there are no idle companions to lead them into extravagancies, fo there are no idle and loofe women to be found to corrupt their minds. Their whole time, both for men and women, is taken up in employments, or public recreations, which, with the early care to inftruct them in the fundamental principles of the morality of the country, prevents all thofe diforders of youth we fee elfewhere. Hence too comes" that ftrength of body and mind in their men, and modeft blooming beauty in their women ; fo that among this people nature feems to have kept up to its primitive and original perfection. Befides, that univerfal likenefs in them, proceeding from their conjugal fidelity and exclufion of all foreign mixture in their breed, (where all the lineaments of their anceftors, direct and collateral, meet at laft in their offspring), gives the parents the comfort of feeing their own bloom and youth renewed in

their

their children ; though in my opinion this universal likenefs is rather a defect ; not but the treasures of nature are fo inexhauftible, that there are fome diftinguifhing beauties in every face.   Their young men and women meet frequently, but then it is in their public affemblies, with grave people mixed along with them.   At all public exercifes the women are placed in view to fee and be feen, in order to infpire the young men with emulation in their performances.   They are permitted to be decently familier on thofe public occafions, and can chufe their lovers refpectively, according to their liking, there being no fuch thing as doweries, or intereft, but mere perfonal merit in the cafe ; but more of this afterwards when I fhall fpeak more particularly of the education of their women and marriages.   This is a fhort fketch of the government and œconomy of a people, who are as much diftinguifhed from the cuftoms of others, as they are feparated by their habitation and country.

Inquifitor. You feem, Sir, to have a very high idea of this patriarchal government, and look upon it according to the law of nature ; I hope you don't deny but perfons may be obliged by the law of nature to obey their forms of government, as well as a patriarchal one ?

Gaudentio.

Gaudentio. No, Reverend Fathers, by no means, I don't enter into comparisons, but relate matter of fact. It is not to be doubted, but different forms of government may be proper for different nations; and where once a form of government is lawfully established, persons are obliged to obey, to avoid anarchy and confusion; as for example, whoever should endeavour to subvert a monarchical government once lawfully established, must break in upon the laws of right and justice, which are obligations of the law of nature.

Inquisitor. Read on.

Second *Inquisitor.* Under favour, I must ask him a question or two first. I think Signor Gaudentio, you make the Grand Pophar to be both prince and priest; that is, to be vested both with temporal and spiritual power. Is it your opinion that the spiritual power is subject to the temporal?

Gaudentio. I speak of Heathens, Reverend Fathers, and a Heathenish worship, where the Grand Pophar was both prince of the people, and chief priest of the sun by his place. I acknowledge no head of the church but his Holiness, as most agreeable to the primitive institution of our religion.

Here

Here he went on in his exalted notions of the sovereign Pontiff, partly being a Roman Catholic, but chiefly, in all appearance, because he was before the Inquisition; for which reason the publisher thought fit to leave it out.

Gaudentio. Is it your Reverences pleasure that I go on with my history?

Inquisitor. Ay, ay, read on.]

The education of their women, and marriages.

As for their women, the Pophar told me it was what gave them the most trouble of any thing in their whole government; that by their records their anceftors had held frequent confultations after what manner they were to be managed, there being great difficulties to be feared either from allowing them liberty, or keeping them under reftraint. If you allow them liberty, you muft depend on their honour, or rather caprice, for your own; if you keep them under confinement, they will be fure to revenge themfelves the firft opportunity; which they will find in fpite of all you can do. The rules, faid he, by which men are governed, will not hold with women; folid reafon, if you can make them fenfible of it, will fome time or other have an influence on moft men; whereas humour is what predominates in women.

women. Hit that, you have them ; mifs
it, you do nothing : and yet they are fo far
from being an indifferent thing in the
commonwealth, that much more depends
on the right management of them than
people imagine. Licentioufnefs of youth
draws innumerable misfoutunes on any
government, and what greater incentives
for licentioufnefs than lewd women, whether common proftitutes, wanton ladies, or
adultereffes? For all loofe women belong
to one of thefe claffes. Our women, continued he, are extremely beautiful, as you
fee, our men ftrong and vigorous ; conjugal fidelity therefore and chaftity muft
be the ftrongeft bonds to keep them in
their duty. As for our young men, we
fteep them in perpetual employment, and
animate them to glory by every thing that
can move generous minds ; with our women, we endeavour the fame by ways
adapted to their genius. But our greateft
care of all is, to make marriage efteemed
by both parties the happieft ftate that can
be wifhed for in this life. This we believe
to depend on making the woman, rather
than the man, happy and fixed in her
choice ; becaufe, if the perfon be impofed
upon her, contrary to her own inward inclination, diflike, or revenge, or perhaps
a more fhameful paffion, will make her
feek for relief elfewhere ; and where women

m\:n are not virtuous, men will be lewd.
We therefore permit the woman to chufe
entirely for herself, and the men to make
their addreffes where they pleafe : but the
woman is to diftinguifh her choice by fome
fignal occafion or other, and that too not
without great difficulties cn both fides,
which being furmounted, they efteem
themfelves arrived at the happy part of all
their wifhes. The moft ardent and tried
love determines the choice : this endears
the man to her on the one hand, and the
difficulty of finding any woman who has
not the fame inducements to love her hufband, leaves him no encouragement for his
lawlefs defires among married women ; and
the fingle women are either fo early engaged with their lovers, or fo poffeffed
with the uotion that a married man cannot
belong to her, that his fuit would be entirely vain. In a word, we do not allow
the leaft temporal intereft to interfere in
the choice, but rather wifh our young people fhould be mutually attracted by efteem
and affection. The whole bufinefs of
courtfhip is to prove their conftancy, and
to make them fo : when we are well affured of this, all obftacles are removed. We
found this method to have the leaft inconveniencies of any, and the beft means to
preferve conjugal fidelity, on which the
good of families fo much depends.

When

When our nation, continued he, began to grow very populous, and the country full of riches and plenty ; the promiscuous conversation of our young men and wo-men, with some neglect on the part of the governors, was the occasion that the bounds of our innocent anceftors were not suffici-ent to keep them in their duty ; ftrange diforders were crept in among our youth of both fexes ; our men grew enervated and effeminate, our women wanton and inflamed ; unnatural abufes wafted their conftitution ; fo that we loft thoufands of our young men and women, without knowing what was the caufe ; even in the married ftate, the women began not to be contented with one man : on which ac-count our anceftors had almoft refolved to keep all our women from the fight of men till they were married, and then to deliver them up to their hufbands, who fhould have a defpotic right over them, as I am informed they have in other nations. They imagined this to be a certain means to afcertain the legitimacy of their child en, and to prevent jealoufy, the firft caufe, however diffembled, of the man's diflike to his wi e.   Others objected againft this fevere difciple, and faid it was making the moft beautiful part of the creation mere flaves, or at leaft mere properties ; that it was to give a fatal check to the glory of a

T   free

free people, to deprive the hufband of the
voluntary love of his moiety, and take a-
way the moft endearing part of conjugal
happinefs.   To this the feverer fide anfwered, that their abufes of liberty fhewed
they were fcarce capable of making a proper
ufe of it.   However a medium betwixt
both carried it for that time.   The injuries
of the married ftate, and the corruption of
youth, which was the occafion of it, were
judged to be of fuch confequence to the
commonwealth, that, refolved to put a
ftop to it at any rate, all the wife men and
governors confulted together, and refolved
unanimoufly to put the laws I mentioned
againft adultery and whoredom in execution, caufing proclamations to be made for
that intent throughout the whole empire.
All corruptors of youth of both fexes were
fhut up immediately, with the regulations
I related above, of having grave perfons
always in the company of young people,
whether men or women.   They married
off all that were of age for it, as faft as
they could ; but quickly found the number of inhabitants did not increafe as
ufual, their native vigour being exhaufted
or debelitated by their unnatural abufes.
. . . .
[*Some paragraphs feem wanting in this part
of Gaudentio's narrative which doubtlefs
were very curious.*]   There

There is one peculiar method allowed by them, in which they differ from all other nations; for whereas this last endeavor to preserve their young people from love, left they should throw themselves away, or make disadvantageous matches; the former, having no interested views in that respect, encourage a generous and honourable love, and make it their care to fix them in the strictest bonds they can, as soon as they judge, by their age and constitution, of their inclinations: this they do sometimes by applauding their choice, but mostly by raising vast difficulties, contrived on purpose, both to try and inhance their constancy. They have histories and stories of heroic examples of fidelity and constancy in both sexes; but particularly for the young women, by which they are taught rather to suffer ten thousand deaths, than violate their plighted faith. One may say they are a nation of faithful lovers; the longer they live together, the more their friendship increases, and infidelity in either sex is looked upon as a capital crime. Add to this, that being all of the same rank and quality, except the regard paid to eldership, and public employments; nothing but personal merit, and a liking of each other, determines the choice; there must be signal proofs produced, that the woman prefers the man before all others,

as

as the fervice muft be diftinguifhed in the fame manner. Where this is, approved of by the governors or elders, if the woman infifts on her demands, it is an inviolable law that that man muft be her hufband. Their hands are firft joined together in public, then they clafpe each other in the clofeft embrace, in which pofture the elder of the place, to fhew that this union is never to be diffolved, takes a circle of the fineft tempered fteel, woven with flowers, and firft lays it over their necks, as they are thus clafping each other, then round their breafts, or hearts, to fignify that the ardency of their love muft terminate in an indiffoluble friendfhip ; which is followed by infinite acclamations and congratulations of the whole affembly. I believe the world cannot furnifh fuch examples of conjugal chaftity as are preferved between them by thefe means. Widowers and widows never marry fingle perfons, and but rarely at all, except left young ; when they are to gain each other as before. By fuch prudent precautions infinite diforders and misfortunes to the commonwealth are prevented, proceeding not only from difproportionate and forced marriages, but from the licentioufnefs of idle perfons, who either marry for money, or live on the fpoil of other people, till they can get an advantageous match. This is a fhort fketch of

their

their government and cuſtoms, which I thought would not be unacceptable to your Reverences, though a great many other cuſtoms of leſs moment will occur in the ſequel of my life, to which I now return.

The Pophar regent made choice of me for one of his attending companions, with the other young men who came home with us; he had a great many other attendants and officers, deputed by common conſent to wait his orders as regent; theſe were changed every five years, as were thoſe attending the governors of the other Nomes, on account of improvement; for, being all of equal quality, they endeavour to give them as equal an education as is poſſible, changing their employments, and waiting on one another in their turns, by the appointment of their reſpective governors, except thoſe whoſe genius or choice determines them to arts and ſciences, according to their œconomy deſcribed before. I muſt only add, that having ſuch a high value for their race, no one thinks it a diſgrace to perform the meaneſt offices, being all to be attended in like manner themſelves when it comes to their turns, each looking on the honours done to every branch of their government, as their own. Hence all their public ranks and ceremonies are the moſt magnificent that can be imagined;

T 2   there

there is fcarce any thing done even in en-
tertainments between the private tribes,
but there are proper officers deputed for it,
and all expenfes paid out of the common
ftock, with deputies and overfeers for every thing.   Their houfes are all open to one
another with a long gallery, which runs
from the end of one range of building to
the other.   The women's apartments join
together ; with the men of each family
joining to their own women, that is, their
wives, fifters, and dau hters.   The women
have their fubaltern officers like the men.
The firft apartment of every break of a
ftreet belongs to the men, then the wo-
mens belonging to them, then the women
of the next family joining to them, and
their men beyond them, and fo on, with
large public halls at proper diftances for
public affemblies ; fo that every thing they
do is a fort of paradox to us, for they are
the freeft and yet ftricteft people in the
world ; the whole nation, as I obferved
before being more like one univerfal regular college, or community, than any thing
elfe.   The women are perpetually employed as well as the men ; it is their bufinefs
to work all the fine garments for themfelves and the men, which being much the
fame except devices and flowers for their
friends and lovers, are made with lefs
difficulty ; the chief difference is in the
wearing

wearing them. But the chief diftinction of fexes is in the ornaments of their necks, and hair. Crowns and fillets are worn by all, juft after the model of the little picture your Reverences faw in the cabinet; all their tapeftry, embroidery, and the like, with infinite other curiofities, are the works of their women, fo that the chief qualification of their women or ladies, for they are all fuch, is to excel at the loom, needle, or diftaff. Since I came there, by the Pophar's defire, they have added that of painting, in which I believe, the vivacity of their genius will make them excel all the reft of the world. Not teaching for hire, I thought it no difgrace in me to inftruct fuch amiable fcholars in an art no man ought to be afhamed of. It is a thing unknown with thefe people for young ladies of any degree, or even young men, to have nothing elfe to mind or think of but vifits and drefs. When I gave them an account of the lives of our quality and gentry, they cried out, What barbarians! Can any thing become beauty more than knowledge and ingenuity? They feemed to have fuch a contempt, and even a horror for a life of that nature, that the young ladies afked me with great concern, if our ladies had any lovers? as if it were impoffible to love a woman who had nothing to recommend her, but what nature gave her. In fine, by

by the defcription I gave of the idle life of
our ladies, they judged them to be no
more than beautiful brutes. They afked
me alfo, if I did not think myfelf fortunate
by my captivity, where I met with ladies,
who thought the ornaments of the mind
more defirable than thofe of the body, and
told me they imputed what they faw in
me, to my good fortune of being borne of
their race by the mother's fide ; nay, could
fcarce believe but my father had a mixture
of their blood fome way or other. I affured them, I efteemed myfelf very happy to
be in the midft of fo many charms of body
and mind ; and added, that though they
had the ineftimable happinefs of being born
all of one race, without any mixture of
foreign vices, yet, in effect, all the world
were originally brothers and fifters, as
fpringing from one pair, fince men and
women did not rife out of the ground like
mufhrooms. This I faid, to give them a
little hint of natural and revealed religion,
which are infeparably linked together. But
to return to myfelf : The Pophar being my
neareft relation, took me into his own fa-
family, as his conftant companion and attendant, when he was not on the public
concerns : where I likewife accompanied
fometimes, and received moft diftinguifhing marks of his favour. He would often
confer with me, and inftruct me in their
ways

ways and cuftoms, and the polity of their
government, inquiring frequently into the
particularities of our governments, both
civil and religious. He never endeavoured
to perfuade me to conform to their religious ceremonies, and my own good fenfe
told me it was prudence not to meddle
with them. I rather thought he feemed
inclined to have more favourable fentiments
of our religion, as fuch, than his own,
though he was prodigioufly bigotted to
their civil cuftoms; faying, it was impoffible ever to preferve a commonwealth,
when they did not live up to their laws;
which would be as few, and as fimple as
poffible. For when once people come to
break in upon fundamentals, all fubfequent
laws would not have half the ftrength as
primary ones. To thefe he added many
other reflections, that fhewed him a man
of confummate wifdom, and worthy the
high poft he bore. He had had two fons,
both dead, and two daughters living; the
one was about ten years old, when I arrived there, (it is we your Reverences faw
in that picture), the other born the year
before the Pophar fet out for Grand Cairo.
His lady, much younger than himfelf,
fhewed fuch frefh remains of beauty, as
demonftrated that nothing but what fprung
from herfelf, could equal her; both the
Pophar and his confort looked on me as
their

their own fon, nor could I expect greater
favour had I really been fo. I took all the
care imaginable not to render myfelf unworthy of it, and both revered and loved
them beyond what I am able to exprefs ;
though indeed, as I obferved, the whole
race of them was nothing but a kingdom
of brothers and friends ; no man having
the leaft fufpicion or fear of one another.
They were fo habituated to the obfervance
of their laws, by their natural difpofitions
and the never-ceafing vigilancy of their governors, that they feemed to have a greater horror for the breach of their laws, than
the punifhments attending it ? faying, that
infinite diforders might be committed by
the malicious inventions of men, if there
was nothing but fear to keep them in their
duty. Such force has education and the
light of nature rightly cultivated ; for myfelf I was left to follow what liberal employment I had a mind to. Philofophy, mufic, and painting had been the chief part
of my ftudy and diverfion, till my unhappy captivity and the lofs of my bro her ;
but as I was fallen among a nation of philofophers, that noble fcience, the miftrefs
of all others, made up the more ferious
part of my employment ; though at fometimes, by the Pophar regent's earneft defire, I applied myfelf to the other two, particularly painting. They had a great many
old-

old.fashioned musical instruments, and an infinite number of performers in their way, who attended their feasts and public rejoicings; but their music, both vocal and instrumental, was not near so perfect as one might have expected of so polite a people, and did not come up to the elevated genius of our Italians. Their philosophy chiefly turned on the more useful part of it, that is, the mathematics and direction of nature: in the moral part of it they have a system, or rather notion, of which I forgot to acqaint your Reverences before; it is a too high and exalted notion of providence, if that expression may be allowed, by which they imagine all things to be so governed in this world, that whatever injury a man does to another, it will be returned upon him or his posterity, even in this world, in the same manner, or even in a greater degree, than what he did to others.

[*Iquifitor.* You will be pleased to explain your own sentiments in this particular, since we hope yon don't deny that fundamental law of nature and religion, *viz.* That the divine providence presides over all things; and as for sublunary things, we presume you believe that providence does not only shew itself in the wonderful production and harmony conspicuous in all natural causes and effects, beyond all the

the wit. and art of men ; but alfo o-
ver the moral part, that is, the free
actions of men, by fuitable rewards
and punifhments in this world or the
next, to make an equal and juft com-
penfation for all the good and evil of
this life, as God is the juft and equal
father of all. So pray explain yourfelf, that we may know your real fentiments on that head.

Gaudentio. I hope, Reverend Fathers, I
fhall convince you, my fentiments are
really orthodox in this point ; no man
has more reafon to magnify Providence than myfelf; but Heathenifh
people may carry a juft belief to fuperftition. That there is a providence
over the phyfical part of the world,
no man who has any juft knowledge
in nature can be ignorant, fince he
may be convinced by the leaft infect,
every thing being adapted to its peculiar ends, with fuch art and knowledge in the author of it, that all
art and knowledge of men cannot
do the like; and by confequence
not being able to make itfelf, it muft
be produced by a caufe infinitely
knowing and forefeeing. Then,
as to the moral part of the world, the
fame reafon fhews, that fince the great
creator defcends fo low as to take care

of

of the leaft infect, it is incredible to
think that the nobleft part of the
world, that is, the free actions of men
fhould be without his care. But as
he has given them the glorious endow-
ments of free will, the fame providence knows how to adapt the direction of them by ways and means fuitable to their beings; that is, by let-
ing them know his will, and propof-
ing fuitable rewards and punifhments
for their good and bad actions; which
rewards and punifhments, it is evident, are not always feen in this life,
fince the wicked often profper, and
the good fuffer, but by confequence
muft be referved for another ftate.

But thefe people not having a juft notion
of the next life, though they believe
a future ftate, carry matters fo far,
that they think every injury done to
another, will be fome way or other
retaliated upon the aggreffor, or his
pofterity, in this life; only they fay,
the punifhment always falls the heavi-
er the longer it is deferred. In this
manner do they account for all the
revolutions of the earth, that one
wicked action is punifhed by another;
that the defcendents of the greateft
monarchs have been loft in beggary
U   for

for almoft endlefs generations, and the
perfons that difpoffeffed them treated
after the fame manner by fome of the
defcendents of the former; and fo on:
which notion, in my opinion, is not
juft, fince a fincere repentance may
wipe off the moft grievous offences.
But as perfons, generally fpeaking,
are more fenfibly touched with the
punifhments of this life, it is not to
be doubted but there are often moft
fignal marks of avenging providence
in this life, in order to deter the
wicked.

Inquifitor. Go on.]
Finding the Pophar had a prodigious
fancy for painting, by fome indifferent
pieces he had picked up, I applied myfelf,
with extraordinary diligence, to that art,
particularly fince he would have me teach
his daughter, whofe unparalleled charms,
though but in the bud, made me infenfible
to all others. By frequent drawing, I not
only pleafed him and others, but almoft
myfelf; every one there men and women,
were to follow fome art or fcience; the
Pophar defired me to impart my art to
fome of the young people of both fexes,
faying there were very great encourage-
ments for the inventors of any new arts,
which I might juftly claim a title to. I did
fo, and before I left the place, I had the
                                    pleafure

pleasure to see some of them equal, or even excelling their master.

These were the chief employments of me leisure-hours; though I was forced to leavy them for considerable intervals, to attend the Regent in the private visitations of his charge, which he did frequently from time to time, sometimes to one Nome, sometimes to another, having an eye over all, both officers and people. These visitations were rather preservatives against, than remedies for, any disorders., He used to say, that the commonwealth was like a great machine with different movements, which if frequently visited by the artist, the least flaw being taken notice of in time, was not only soon remedied, but was a means of preserving all the rest in a constant and regular motion; but if neglected, would soon disorder the motions of the other parts, and either cost a great deal to repair or bring the whole machine to destruction. Unless on public solemnities, which were always very magnificent, the Pophar (not to burden his people) went about without any great train, accompanied by only an assisting elder or two, the young Pophar, and myself. He had frequent conversations with the subalterns, and even with the meanest artisans, calling them his children; and they having recourse to him as their common father. For the first five years of
his

his regency, the only difficulty we had of any moment to determine was an affair of the moft delicate nature I ever heard; though it does not concern myfelf, I fhall relate it to your Reverences for the peculiar circumftances of it, being a cafe entirely new, as well as unprovided for by the laws of their conftitution.

The cafe was this: Two twin-brothers had fallen in love with the fame woman, and fhe with them. The men and the woman lived in different parts of the fame Nome, and met accidentally at one of their great folemnities; it was at the feaft of the fun, which is kept twice a year, becaufe, as I informed your Reverences, their kingdom lies betwean the tropics, but more on this fide the line than the other. This fituation is the occafion that they have two fprings and two fummers. At the beginning of each fpring there are great feafts in every Nome, in honour of the fun; they are held iu the open fields, in teftimony of his being the immediate caufe (in their opinion) of the production of all things. All the facrifice they offer to him are five little pyramids of incenfe, according to the number of their Nomes, placed on the altar in plates of gold till they take fire of themfelves. Five young men and as many women are deputed by the governors to perform the office of placing the pyramids

of

of incenfe on the altar: they are clad in
their fpangled robes of the colour of the
Nome, with crowns on their heads, marching up two by two, a man and a woman,
between two rows of young-men and women, placed theatre-wife one above another; and make the moft beautiful fhow
that eyes can behold. It happened that
one of the twin.brothers was deputed, with
the young lady I am fpeaking of, to make
the firft couple for the placing the incenfe
on the altar. They marched up on different fides till they came to the altar: when
they have placed the incenfe, they falute
each other, and crofs down, the men by
the ranks of the women, and the women
by the men, which they do with a wonderful grace becoming fuch an auguft affembly.
The defign of this is to encourage a deco-
rum in the carriage of the young people,
and to give them a fight of each other in
their greateft luftre. When the five couple
have performed their ceremony, the other
ranks come two by two to the altar, falut-
ing each other, and croffing as before: by
which means the young people have an
opportunity of feeing every man and woman of the whole company, though the
placing of them is done by lot. If they
have not any engagement before, they generally take the firft liking to one another
at fuch interviews, and the woman's love

and choice being what determines the marriage, without any view of intereft, being,
as I faid, all equal in quality, the young
gallants make it their bufinefs to gain the
affection of the perfon they like by their
future fervices.. To prevent inconveniencies of rivalfhip at the beginning, if the
man be the perfon the woman likes, he
prefents her with a flower juft in the bud,
which fhe takes and puts in her breaft. If
fhe is engaged before, fhe fhews him one,
to fignify her engagement; which if in the
bud only, fhews the courtfhip is gone no
further than the firft propofal and liking ;
if half blown, or the like, it is an emblem
of further progrefs; if full blown, it fignifies that her choice is determined, from
whence they can never recede ; that is, fhe
can change the man that prefents it, but he
cannot challenge her till fhe has worn it
publicly. If any diflike fhould happen after that, they are to be fhut up, never to
have any hufband. If fhe has no engagement, but does not approve of the perfon,
fhe makes him a low courtefy, with her
eyes fhut till he is gone away. The women, it is true, for all this, have fome
little coquetifh arts, diffembling their affections now and then, but not often. If
the man be engaged, he wears fome favour
or other to fhew it ; if he likes not the woman, he prefents her with nothing ; if the
                                          woman

woman fhould make fome extraordinary advances, without any of his fide, fl:e has liberty to live a maid, or to be difpofed of among the widows, being looked upon as fuch, who, by the by, marry none but widowers. But to return to the twins. It happened that the brother who went with the lady to the altar, feeing fhe had no bud upon her breaft, fell in love with her, and fne with him ; the awe of the ceremony hindered them from taking any further notice of one another at that time. As fhe went down the ranks, the other brother faw her, and fell in love with her likewife, and contrives to meet her with a' bud in his hand, juft as the ceremony ended; which fhe accepts of taking him to be the perfon who had marched up with her to the altar ; but being obliged to go off with the other young ladies, whether the concern fhe had been in, in performing the ceremony before fuch an illuftrious affembly, or the heat of the weather, or the joy fhe conceived in finding her affection reciprocal, or all together, had fuch an effect, that fhe fell into a fainting-fit among her companions ; who opening her bofom in hafte, not minding the flower, it fell down, and was trod under foot. Juft as fhe was recovered, the brother who performed the ceremony, came up and prefented his bud; fhe thinking it had been

that

that she had loft, received it with a look that shewed he had made a greater progrefs in her affections than what that flower exprefied. The laws not permitting any further converfation at the juncture, they retired to their refpective habitations. Some time after, the brother who had the luck to prefent the firft flower, whom for diftinction I fhall call the younger brother, as he really was, found a way to make her a vifit by ftealth, at a grated window which, as I obferved, was publicly prohibited by the wife governors, but privately connived at to enhance their love. He came to her, and, after fome amorous converfation, makes bold to prefent her the more advanced mark of his affection ; which fhe accepted of, and gave him in return a fcarf worked with hearts feparated by little brambles, to fhew there were fome difficulties for him to overcome yet : however, they gave one another mutual affurances of love, and he was permitted to profefs himfelf her lover, without declaring her name, for fome private reafons fhe had. Not long after, the elder brother came, and procured an opportunity of meeting her at the fame window. The night was very dark, fo that he could not fee the fecond flower which fhe had in her bofome : only fhe received him with greater figns of joy and freedom than he expected ; but reflecting on the

figns

figns he had remarked in her countenance, and after her illnefs by a fort of natural vanity for his own merits, flattered himfelf that her paffion was rather greater than his, excufed himfelf for being fo long without feeing her, and added, that if he were to be guided by the height of his flame, he would fee her every night. She reflecting how lately fhe had feen him, thought his diligence was very extraordinary, but imputed it to the ardour of his paffion; in fine, fhe gave him fuch affured figns of love, that he thought in himfelf he might pafs the middle ceremony, and prefent her with the full-blown flower, to make fure of her. She took it; but told him fhe would not wear it for fome time, till fhe had paffed fome forms, and had further proof of his conftancy; but, for his confirmation of her affection, fhe put out her hand as far as the grate would permit, which he kiffed with all the ardour of an inflamed lover, giving her a thoufand affurances of his fidelity, and fhe in return gave him a riband with two hearts interwoven with her own hair, feparated only with a little hedge of pomegranates almoft ripe, to fhew that the time of gathering the fruit was nigh at hand. Thus were the three lovers in the greateft degree of happinefs imaginable; the brothers wore her favours on all public occafions, congra-

t ulating

tulating each other for the fuccefs in their amours; but, as lovers affect a fecrecy in all they do, never telling one another who were the objects of their affection. The next great feaft drew on, when the younger brother thought it was time to prefent the laft mark of his affection in order to demand her in marriage, which was ufually performed in thofe public folemnities. He told her he hoped it was now time to reward his flame, by wearing the open flower, as a full fign of her confent, and gave her a full-blown artificial carnation, with gold flames and little hearts on the leaves, interwoven with wonderful art and ingenuity. She thinking it had been a repitition of the ardour of his affection, took it, and put it in her bofom with all the marks of tendernefs, by which the fair fex in all countries know how to reward all the pains of their lovers in a moment. Upon this he refolved to afk her of her parents; which was the only thing neceffary on his fide, the woman having right to demand any man's fon in the kingdom, if he had but prefented her with the laft mark of his affection. The elder brother having given in his fome time before, thought the parents approbation was the only thing wanting on his fide, and refolves the fame day on the fame thing. They were ftrangely furprifed to meet one another;

ther; but feeing the different favours, they did not know what to make of it. When the father came, they declared the caufe of their coming, in terms which fully expreff- ed the agony of their minds: the father was in as great concern as they were, affur- ing them he had but one daughter, who, he was confident, would never give fuch encouragement to two lovers at the fame time, contrary to their laws; but feeing their extreme likenefs, he gueffed there muft be fome miftake. Upon this the daughter was fent for; who, being inform- ed it was to declare her confent in the choice of her lover, came down with four flowers in her bofom, not thinking but the two full blown had belonged to the fame perfon, fince fhe had received two before fhe had worn the firft. The defcription the poets give of the goddefs Venus rifing out of the fea, could not be more beautiful than the bloom that appeared in her cheeks when fhe came into the room. I happen- ed to be there prefent, being fent before by the Pophar, to let the father know of the regent's intended vifit; that being a confiderable officer, he might order his concerns accordingly. As foon as the young lady heard the caufe of their com- ing, and faw them indiftinguifhably like each other, with the public figns of her favours wrought with her own hand,
which

which they brought along with them, she creamed out, "I am betrayed!" and immediately fell in a swoon, flat on the floor, almost between her two lovers. The father, in a condition very little better, fell down by his daughter, and bathing her with his tears, called to her to open her eyes, or he must die along with her. The young men stood like statues, with rage and despair in their looks at the same time. I being the only indifferent person in the room, though extremely surprised at the event, called her mother and women to come to her assistance; who carried her into another room, undressed her, and, by proper remedies, brought her at last to herself. The first word she said was, " Oh! Berilla, what have you done? All the rest was nothiing but sobs and sighs, enough to melt the hardest heart. When she was in a condition to explain herself, she declared, she liked the person of the man who went up with her to the altar; that some time after the same person, as she thought, had presented her with the first marks of his affection, which she accepted of, and in fine had given her consent by wearing the full-blown flower; but which of the two brothers it belonged to, she could not tell; adding, that she was willing to submit to the decision of the elders, or

to

to undergo what punifhment they thought
fit for her heedlefs indifcretion; but pro-
tefted, that fhe never defigned to entertain two perfons at the fame time, but
took them to be the fame perfon. The
care of their marriages being one of the
fundamentals of their government, and
there being no provifion in the law for
this extraordinary cafe, the matter was
referred to the Pophar regent, who was
to be there in a few days; guards in the
mean time were fet over the brothers,
for fear of mifchief, till a full hearing.
The affair was difcuffed before the Pophar
regent, and the reft of the elders of the
place. The three lovers appeared before
them, each in fuch agony as cannot be
expreffed. The brothers were fo alike,
it was hard to diftinguifh one from the
other. The regent afked them, which of
the two went up to the altar with the
young lady; the elder faid it was he;
which the younger did not deny. The
lady being interrogated, owned fhe defigned to entertain the perfon that went up
with her to the altar, but went no further than the firft liking. Then they afked which of the two brothers gave the
firft flower; the younger faid, he prefumed he did, fince he fell in love with her
as fhe went down the ranks, and contrived to give her the flower as foon as

V   the

the ceremony was over, not knowing of his brother's affection, neither did she bear any mark of engagement, but accepted of his service; the lady 'likewise owning the receipt of such flower, but that she lost it, fainting away in the croud; but when, as she thought, he restored it to her, she did not like him quite so well, as when she received it the first time, supposing them to be the same person. Being asked who gave her the second, third, and last mark of engagement, it appeared to be the younger brother, whose flower she wore publicly in her bosom; but then she received the full-blown flower from the elder brother also. The judges looked at one another for some time, not knowing well what to say to the matter. Then the regent asked her, when she gave her consent, if she did not understand the person to be him that went up with her to the altar? She owned she did; which was the elder: but in fact had placed her affections on the person who gave her the first flower, which was the younger. Then the two brothers were placed before her, and she was asked, that, supposing she were now at liberty, without any engagement, which of the two brothers she would chuse for her husband? she stopped, and blushed at the question, but at length said, the younger had been more assiduous in his court-
ship;

fhip ; and with that burft into tears, caft-
ing a look at the younger brother, which
eafily fhewed the fentiments of her heart.
Every one was in the laft fufpenfe how the
regent would determine the cafe ; and the
young men expreffed fuch a concern in
their looks, as if the final fentence of life
and death, happinefs or mifery, was to be
pronounced to them.   When the regent,
with a countenance partly fev.ere as well as
grave, turning towards the young lady,
Daughter, faid he, your ill fortune, or indifcretion, has deprived you from having
either of them : both you cannot have,
and you have given both an equal right ;
if either of them will give up their right,
you may marry the other, not elfe.   What
do you fay, fons ? fays he, will you contribute to make one of you happy ? They
both perfifted they would not give up their
right till the laft gafp.   Then, fays the regent, turning to the lady, who was almoft
dead with fear and confufion, fince neither
of them will give up their right, I pronounce fentence on you to be fhut up from
the commerce of men, till the death of one
of your lovers ; then it fhall be left to your
choice to marry the furvivor.   So giving
orders to have her taken away, the court
was going to break up, when the younger
brother falling on his knees, cries out, I
yield my right, rather than the adorable

Berilla

Berilla fhould be miferable on my account ;
let me be fhut up from the commerce of
men, for being the occafion of fo divine a
creature's misfortune.   Brother, take her
and be happy; and you divine Berilla,
only pardon the confufion my innocent
love has brought upon you ; and then I
fhall leave the world in peace.   Here the
whole court rofe up, and the young man
was going out, when the regent ftopped
him ; Hold, fon, fays he, there is a greater happinefs preparing for you than you
expect; Berilla is yours, you alone deferve
her, you prefer her good to your own ;
and as I find her real love is for you, here
join your hands, as I find your hearts are
already.   They were married immediately;
the regent leaving behind him a vaft idea,
not only of his juftice, but wifdom, in fo
intricate a cafe.   I drew an hiftorical piece
of painting of this remarkable trial, expreffing as nigh as I could the poftures and
agonies of the three lovers, and prefented
it to the divine Ifyphena, the regent's
daughter, telling her, that if fhe were to
accept of flowers, as that young lady did,
fhe would ruin all the youths of Mezorania.
She received it blufhing, and faid fhe
fhould never receive any but from one
hand, nor even that, if fhe thought fhe
fhould do him any harm; adding, that
fhe thought her father had given a juft
                              judgement

judgement; then waved the difcourfe with fuch innocence, yet knowledge of what fhe faid, that I was furprifed to the laft degree ; not being able to guefs whether I had offended her or not.

Thefe vifitations in the company of the Pophar, gave me an opportunity of feeing all the different parts and chief curiofities of the whole empire. Their great towns, efpecially the heads of every Nome, were built, as I faid, much after the fame form, differing chiefly in the fituation, and are principally defigned for the winter-refi-dence, for their courts and colleges, but particularly for inftructing and polifhing their youth of both fexes; and fuch admi-rable care and œconomy, to avoid all diffo-lutenefs and idlenefs, that, as I obferved before, there is no fuch thing known, as for perfons to have no other bufinefs on their hands but vifits and drefs ; efteeming thofe no better than brutes and barbarians, who are not conftantly employed in im-proving their natural talents in fome art or fcience. Their villas, or places of pleafure, are fcattered all over the country, with moft beautiful variety : the villages and towns built for manufactures, trades, con-veniency, of agriculture, &c. are innume-rable; their canals, and great lakes, fome of them like little feas, are very frequent, according as the nature of the country will

allow ; with pleafure-houfes and pavilions,
built at due diftances round the borders,
interfperfed with iflands and groves, fome
natural, fome artificial, where at proper
feafons you might fee thoufands of boats
fkimming backwards and forwards, both
for pleafure and the profit of catching fifh,
of which there is an inexhauftible ſtore.
There are alfo vaft forefts of infinite variety
and delight, diftinguifhed here and there
with theatrical fpaces or lawns, either natural, or cut out by art, for the conveniency of pitching their tents in the hot feafons,
with fuch romantic ſcenes of deep vales,
hanging woods, and precipices, natural
falls, and cafcades, or rather cataracts of
water over the rocks, that all the decora-
tions of art are nothing but foils and fhadows to thofe majeſtic beauties of nature ;
befides glorious profpects of different kinds
over the edges of the mountains where we
paffed in our vifitations, fometimes pre-
fenting us with a boundlefs view over the
moft delicious plains in the world ; in other
places, having our view terminated with
other winding hills, exhaling their reviving perfumes from innumerable fpecies of
natural fruits and odoriferous fhrubs.—
Travelling thus by eafiy journeys, ftaying
or advancing in our progrefs as we thought
fit, I had an opportunity of admiring with
infinite delight the effects of induftry and
liberty,

liberty, in a country where nature and art feemed to vie with each other in their different productions. There was another extraordinary fatisfaction I received in thefe vifitations, which was the opportunity of feeing, and partaking of their grand matches, or rather companies, if I may ufe the expreffion, of hunting and fifhing. All the young people with their governors, or all who are able or willing to go, at particular feafons difperfe themfelves for thefe hunts all over the kingdom : the country being fo prodigious fertile, that it furnifhes them, almoft fpontaneoufly, with whatever is neceffary, or even delectable for life, the people living in fome meafure in common, and having no other intereft but that of a well-regulated cummunity. They leave the towns at certain feafons, and go and live in tents for the conveniency of hunting and fifhing, according as the country and feafons are proper for each recreation ; the flat part of the country (though it is generally more hilly than champaign) is flocked with prodigious quantities of fowl and game, as pheafants, partridges of different kinds, much larger than our wild hens; turkeys, and peacocks, with other fpecies of game, which we have not in Italy; hares almoft innumerable, but no coneys that ever I faw ; unlefs we call coneys a leffer fort of hare, which feed and run a-
long

long the cliffs and rocks, but don't burrow
as ours do. There is alfo a fmall fort of
wild goat, much lefs than ours, not very
fleet, of a very high tafte, and prodigious
fat. They take vaft quantities of all forts
but ftill leave fufficient ftock to fupply next
feafon, except hurtful beafts, which they
kill whenever they can. But their great
hunts are in the mountains and woodland
parts of the country, where the forefts are
full of infinite quantities of maft and fruits,
and other food for wild beafts of all kinds;
but particularly ftags of four or five different fpecies; fome of which, almoft as big
as a horfe, keep in the wildeft parts, whofe
flefh when dry and feafoned with fpices,
is the richeft food I ever tafted. Their
wild fwine a e of two kinds, fome vaftly
large, others very little, not much bigger
than a lamb, but prodigious fierce. This
laft is moft delicate meat, feeding on the
mafts and wild fruits in the thickeft part
of the groves; and multiplying exceedingly, where they are not difturbed, one
fow bringing fixteen or eighteen pigs; fo
that I have feen thoufands of them caught
at one hunting match, and fent in prefents
to the other parts of the kingdom. where
they have none; which is their way in all
their recreations, having perfons appointed
to carry the rarities of the country to one
another, and to the governors, parents,
and

and friends left behind. When they go out to their grand hunt, they chuse some open vale, or vast lawn, as far in the wild forests as they can ; where they pitch their tents, and make their rendezvous : then they send out their most courageous young men, in small bodies, of ten in a company, well-armed, each with his spear and his fusil hung on his back, which last of late years they find more serviceable against the wild beasts than spears, having got samples of them from Persia. These go quietly through the wildest parts of the forest at proper distances, so as to meet at such place, which is to view the ground, and find a place proper to make their stand, and pitch their toils. They are often several days out about this ; but are to make no noise, nor kill any wild beast, unless attcacked, or they come upon him in his couch, at unawares, that they may not disturb the rest. When they have made their report, several thousands of them surround a considerable part of the forest, standing close together for their mutual assistance, making as great a noise as they can, with dogs, drums, and rattles, and other noisy instruments, to frighten the game towards the centre, that none may escape the circle. When this is done, all advance in a breast, encourage their dogs, sounding their horns, beating their drums

and

and rattles, that the moſt courageous beaſts are all rouſed, and run before them towards the centre, till by this means they have driven together ſeveral hundreds of wild beaſts, lions, tygers, elks, wild boars, ſtags, foxes, hares, and in fine all ſorts of beaſts that were within that circle. It is moſt terrible to ſee ſuch a heap of cruel beaſts gathered together, grinning and roaring at one another, in a moſt frightful manner : but the wild boar is the maſter of all. Whoever comes neareſt him in that rage, even the largeſt lion, he ſtrikes at him with his tuſks, and makes him keep his diſtance. When they are brought within a proper compaſs, they pitch their toils round them, and incloſe them in, every man joining cloſe to his neighbour, holding out their ſpears to keep them off. If any beaſt ſhould endeavour to make his eſcape, which ſome will do now and then (particularly the wild boars), they run againſt the points of the ſpears, and make very martial ſport. I was told, that a prodigious wild ſow once broke through three files of ſpears, overturned the men, and made a gap, that ſet all the reſt a running almoſt in a body that way, ſo that the people were forced to let them take their career, and loſt all their labour. But now they have men ready with their fuſils to drop any beaſt that ſhould offer to turn ahead.

When

When they are inclofed, there is moft terrible work, the greateft beafts fighting and goring one another, for rage and fpite, and the more fearful running into the toils for fhelter. Then our men with their fufils, drop the largeft as faft as they can. When they intend to fhoot the wild boars, three or four aim at him at a time, to be fure to drop him or difable him, otherwife he runs full at the laft that wounded him, with fuch fury, that fometimes he will break through the ftrongeft toils; but his companions all join their fpears to keep him off. When they have dropped all that are dangerous, and as many as they have a mind, they open their toils, and difpatch all that are gafping. I have known above five hundred head of beafts of all forts killed in one day. When all is over, they carry off their fpoil to the rendezvous, feafting and rejoicing, and fending prefents as before.

There is oftentimes very great danger, when they go through the woods to make difcovery of their hunts; becaufe, if, in fmall companies, fome ftubborn beaft or other will attack them directly; every man, therefore, as I faid, has a fufil flung at his back, and his fpear in his hand for his defence. Being once in one of their parties, we came upon a prodigious wild boar, as he was lying in his haunt; fome

of

of us were for paffing by him, but I thought
fuch a noble prey was not to be let go ; fo
we furrounded him, and drew up to him,
with more courage and curiofity, than prudence ; one of my companions, who was
my intimate friend, being one of thofe who
conducted me over the deferts, went up
nigher to him than the reft, with his fpear
in his hands, ftretched out ready to receive
him, in cafe he fhould come at him ; at
which the beaft ftarted up of a fudden, with
a noife that would have terrified tht ftout-
eft hero, and made at him with fuch fury,
that we gave him for loft. He ftood his
ground with fo much courage, and held
his fpear fo firm and exact, that he run it
exactly up the mouth of the beaft, quite
into the inner part of his throat ; the boar
roared, and fhook his head in a terrible
manner, endeavouring to get the fpear out,
which if he had done, all the world could
not have faved the young man. I, feeing
the danger, ran in with the fame preeipi-
tancy, and clapping the muzzle of my gun
almoft clofe to his fide, a little behind his
fore-fhoulder, fhot him quite through the
body ; fo he dropped down dead before us.
Juft as we thought the danger was over,
the fow, hearing his cry, came rufhing on
us, and that fo fuddenly, that before I
could turn myfelf with my fpear, fhe ftruck
at me behind with her fnout, and pufhing
on,

on, knocked me down with her impetuo-
sity; and the place being a little shelving,
she came quite tumbling over me, which
was the occasion of saving my life. Asham-
ed of the foil, but being well apprifed of
the danger, I was fcarce got up on my feet
and on my guard, when, making at me
alone, though my companions came in to
my affiftance, she pushed at me a fecond
time with equal fury. I held my fpear
with all my might, thinking to take her
in the mouth; but miffing my aim, I took
her juft in the throat, where the head and
neck join, and thruft my fpear with fuch
force, her own career meeting me, that I
ftruck quite through her windpipe, the
fpear fticking fo faft in her neck-bone, that
when she dropt, we could fcarce get it out
again. She toffed and reeled her head a
good while before she fell; but her windpipe being cut, and bleeding inwardly, she
was choaked. My companions had hit her
with their fpears on the fide and back; but
her hide and briftles were fo thick and
hard, they did her very little damage.—
They all applauded my courage and victory, as if I had killed both the fwine. But
I, as juftice required, gave the greateft
part of the glory, for the death of the
boar, to the courageous dexterity of the
young man, who had expofed himfelf fo
generoufly, and hit him fo exact in the

W   throat.

throat. We left the carcafes there, not being able to take them with us; but marking the place, we came afterwards with fome others to carry them off. I had the honour to carry the boar's head on the point of my fpear; which I would have given to the young man, but he re-fufed it, faying, that I had not only kill-ed it, but faved his life into the bargain. The honour being judged to be me by eve-ry one, I fent it as a prefent to the di-vine Ifyphena; a thing allowed by their cuftoms, though as yet I never durft make any declarations of love: fhe accepted of it, but added, fhe hoped I would make no more fuch prefents; and explained herfelf no further.

Thefe people having no wars, nor fin-gle combats with one another, which laft are not allowed for fear of deftroying their own fpecies, have no other way of fhew-ing their courage, but againft wild beafts; where, without waiting for any exprefs or-der of their fuperiors, they will expofe themfelves to a great degree, and fome-times perform exploits worthy the greateft heroes.

Their fifhing is of two kinds; one for recreation and profit; the other to deftroy the crocodiles and allagators, which are on-ly found in the great lakes, and the rivers that run into them, and that in the hotter

and

and champaign parts of the country. In
some of the lakes, even the largest, they
cannot live: in others they breed prodi-
giously.   As they fish for them only to
destroy them, they chuse the properest
time for that purpose, that is, when the
eggs are hatching; which is done in the
hot sands, by the sides of the rivers and
lakes. The old ones are not only very ravenous at that time, but lie lurking in the
water near their eggs, and are so prodigious fierce, that there is no taking their
eggs, unless you first contrive to kill the
old ones. Their way to fish for them is
this : They beat at a distance, by the sides
of the rivers and lakes, where they breed,
which makes the old ones hide themselves
in the water. Then twenty or thirty of
the young men row quietly backward and
forward on the water where they suppose
the creatures are ; having a great many
strong lines with hooks, made after the
manner of fish-hooks, well armed as far
as the throat of the animal reaches. These
hooks they fasten under the wings of ducks
and water-fowls, kept for the purpose,
which they let drop out of the boat, and
swim about the lake. Whenever the ducks
come over the places where the creatures
are, these last strike at them, and swallow
the poor ducks immediately, and so hook
themselves, with the violence and check of
the

the boat. As foon as one is hooked, they
tow him, floundering and beating the water, at a ftrange rate, till they have him
into the middle of the water at a diftance
from the reft of his companions, who all
lie nigh the banks ; then the other boats
furround him, aud dart their harping-
fpears at him, till they hill him. Thefe
harping-fpears are pointed with the fineft
tempered fteel, extremely fharp, with
beards to hinder them from coming out of
his body ; there is a line faftened to the
fpear, to draw it back, and the creature a-
long with it; as alfo to hinder the fpear
from flying too far, if they mifs their aim.
Some of them are prodigious dexterous at
this ; but there is no piercing the creature
but in his belly, which they muft hit as he
flounces and rolls himfelf in the water. If
a fpear hits the fcales of his back, it will
fly off as from a rock, not without fome
danger to thofe who are very nigh, tho'
· they generally know the length of the
firing. I was really apprehenfive of thofe
ftrange fierce creatures at firft, and it was
a confiderable time before I could dart with
any dexterity ; but the defire of glory, and
the applaufes given to thofe that excel, who
have the fkins carried like trophies before
their miftreffes, thefe, and the charms of
the regent's daughter, fo infpired me, that
I frequently carried the prize.

It

It is one of the fineft recreations in the
world ; you might fee feveral hundred
boats at a time, either employed, or as
fpectators, with fhouts and cries, when the
creature is hit in the right place, that make
the very banks tremble.   When they have
killed all the old ones, they fend their people on the fhore, to rake for the eggs, which
they burn and deftroy on the fpot; not
but fome *will be hatched before the reft,
and creep into the water, to ferve for fport
the next year. They deftroy thefe animals,
not only for their own fecurity in the ufe
of the lakes, but alfo to preferve the wild
fowl and fifh, which are devoured and deftroyed by the crocodiles.

But the fifhing on the great lake Gilgol,
or lake of lakes, is without any danger ;
there being no allagators in that water ;
and is only for recreation, and the profit of
the fifh.   The lake is above a hundred Italian miles in circumference.   At proper
feafons, the whole lake is covered with
boats ; great numbers of them full of ladies
to fee the fport, befide what are on the
iflands and fhores, with trumpets, haut-
boys, and other mufical inftruments, play-
ing all the while.   It is impoffible to defcribe the different kinds of fifh the lake
abounds with ; many of them we know
nothing of in Europe ; though they have
fome like ours, but much larger, as pikes,

or a fish like a pike, two or three yards long : a fish like a bream, a yard and a half over ; carps forty or fifty pound weight ; they catch incredible numbers of them : fome kinds in one part of the lake, fome in another. They fish in this manner, and afterwards feaft on what they catch, for a fortnight or three weeks, if the feafon proves kind, retiring at night to their tents, either on the iflands or fhore, where there are perfons employed in drying and curing what are proper for ufe ; fending prefents of them into other parts of the country, in exchange for venifon, fowl, and the like. Though there are noble lakes and ponds, even in the forefts, made by the inclofures of the hills and woods, that are ftored with excellent fish ; yet they are entirely deftitute of the beft fort ; that is, fea fish, which we have in fuch quantities in Europe. When this fishing is over, they retire to the towns, becaufe of the rainy feafons, which begin prefently after.

I am now going to enter on a part of my life, which I am in fome doubt, whether it is proper to lay before your Reverences, or not : I mean the hopes and fears, the joys and anxieties of a young man in love ; but in an honorable way, with no lefs a perfon than the daughter of the regent of this vaft empire. I fhall not however, enter into
the

the detail of the many various circumftances attending fuch a paffion ; but fhall juft
tuch on fome particular paffages, which
were very extraordinary, even in a paffion
which generally of itfelf runsinto extremes.
Your Reverences will remember, that
there is no real diftinction of quality in
thefe people, nor any regard either to intereft or dignity, but merely to perfonal
merit ; their chief view being to render
that ftate happy which makes up the better
part of human life. I had nothing therefore to do in this affair, but to fix my
choice, and endeavour to pleafe and be
pleafed. My choice was foon determined ;
the firft time I faw the incomparable Ifyphena, the regent's daughter, though fhe was
then but ten years old, ten thoufand bud-
ding beauties appeared in her, with fuch
unutterable charms, that though I as good
as defpaired of arriving at my wifhed for
happinefs, I was refolved to fix there, or
no where.

I obferved when I was firft introduced
into her company by the regent her father,
that fhe had her eye fixed on me, as a ftranger, as I fuppofed, but yet with more than
a girlifh curiofity. I was informed afterwards, that fhe told her playfellows, that
that ftranger fhould be her hufband, or no
one. The wife Pophar her father had obferved it, and whether it was from his
                                    knowledge

knowledge of the fex, and their unaccountable fondnefs for ftrangers, or whether he
difapproved of the thought, I cannot tell,
but he was refolved to try both our con-
ftances to the utmoft. I was obliged by the
Pophar to teach her and fome other young
ladies, as well as fome young men, to paint;
but it was always in the father or mother's
company. Not to detain your reverences
with matters quite foreign to, and perhaps
unworthy your cognifance, it was five
years before I durft let her fee the leaft
glimmering of my affection. She was now
fifteen, which was the height of her bloom.
Her father feeing fhe carried no mark of
any engagement, afked her in a familiar
way, if her eyes had made no conquefts;
fhe bluihed, and faid, fhe hoped not. He
told me alfo as a friend, that I was older
than their cuftoms cared to allow young
men to live fingle; and with a fmile afked
me, if the charms of the Baffa's daughter
of Grand Cairo had extinguifhed in me all
thoughts of love. I told him there were
objects enough in Mezorania, to make one
forget any thing one had feen before, but
that being a ftranger I was willing to be
thoroughly acquainted with the genius of
the people, left I fhould make any one unhappy. I was juft come back from one of
our vifitations, when I was ftruck with
the moft lively fenfe of grief I ever felt in
my

my life. I had always obferved before, that
Hyphena never wore any fign of engagement, but then I found fhe carried a bud
in her bofom. I. fell immediately upon
it; which fhe perceiving, came to fee me
without any bud, as fhe ufed to go before,
keeping her eyes upon me to fee what effect
it would have. Seeing her continue without any marks of engagement, I recovered, and made bold to tell her one day, that
I could not but pity the miferable perfon,
whoever he was, who had loft the place in
her bofom he had before; fhe faid uncon-
cernedly, that both the wearing and taking
away the flower from her bofom, was done
out of kindnefs to the perfon. I was then
fo taken up with contrary thoughts, that I
did not perceive fhe meant to try whether
fhe was the object of my thoughts or not.
However, finding fhe carried no more
marks of engagement, I was refolved to
try my fortune for life or death; when an
opportunity offered beyond my wifh. Her
mother brought her to perfect a piece of
painting fhe was drawing: I obferved a
melancholy and trouble in her countenance
I had never feen before; that moment the
mother was fent for to the regent, and I
made ufe of it to afk her, what it was that
affected her in fo fenfible a manner? I pronounced thefe words with fuch emotion
and concern on my own part, that fhe

might

might eafily fee I was in fome very great
agony.   She expreffed a great deal of confufion at the queftion, infomuch, that
without anfwering a word, fhe got up, and
went out of the room, leaving me leaning
againft the wall almoft without life or motion.   Other company coming, I was rouf-
ed out of my lethargy, and flunk away to
my own apartment, but agitated with fuch
numberlefs fears, as left me almoft deftitute of reafon.   However, I was refolved
to make a moft juft difcovery, and to be
fully determined in my happinefs or mifery.   There was a greated window on the
back fide of the palace, where I had feen
Ifyphena walk fometimes, but never dared
to approach ; I went thither in the evening,
and feeing her by herfelf, I ventured to it,
and falling on my knees, afked her for heaven's fake what was the matter, or if I had
offended her ? She immediately burft into
tears, and juft faid, " Afk no more," and
withdrew ; though I cannot fay with any
figns of indignation.   Some time after, I
was fent for to inftruct her in the finifhing
of her piece.   I muft tell your Reverences,
that I had privately drawn that picture of
her which you faw, and put the little boy
in afterwards.   In a hurry I had left it behind me in my clofet, and the Pophar finding it by accident, had taken it away without my knowledge : and fhewn it to the
mother ;

mother; and making as if he did not
mind Ifyphena, who ftood by, and faw it
(as fhe thought, undifcerned), feemed to
talk in a threatening tone to the mother
about it. When I came in, I had juft courage enough to caft one glance at Ifyphena,
when, methought, I faw her eyes meet
mine, and fhew a mixture of comfort and
trouble at the fame time. As this fubject
cannot be very proper for your Reverences
ears, I fhall comprife in half an hour
what coft me whole years of fighs and folicitude, though happily crowned at laft with
unfpeakable joys. This trouble in Ifyphena was, that having made herfelf miftrefs
of the pencil, fhe had privately drawn my
picture in miniature, which fhe kept fecret-
ly in her bofom, and it having been difcovered by the mother, as that which I had
drawn was by the father, to try her conftancy he had expreffed the utmoft indignation at it : but Ifyphena's greateft trouble was, left I fhould know and take it for
a difcovery of her love, before I had made
any overtures of mine. In progrefs of
time we came to an eclairciffement : fhe
received my two firft flowers : but becaufe
I was half a ftranger to their race, we were
to give fome more fignal proof of our love
and conftancy than ordinary ; we had frequently common occafions offered us, fuch
as might be looked upon as the greateft
trials.

trials. She was the paragon not only of the kingdom, but poffibly of the univerfe, for all perfection, that could be found in the fex. He ftature was about the middle fize, the juft proportion of her fhape made her really taller than fhe feemed to be; her hair was black* indeed, but of a much finer glofs than the reft of the fex, nor quite fo much curled, hanging down in eafiy treffes over her fhoulders, and fhading fome part of her beautiful cheeks. Her eyes, though not fo large as our Europeans, darted fuch luftre, with a mixture of fweetnefs and vivacity, that it was impoffible not to be charmed with their rays: her features were not only the moft exact, but inimitable and peculiar to herfelf. In fine, her nofe, mouth, teeth, turn of the face, all concurring together to form the moft exquifite fymmetry and adorned with a bloom beyond all the blufhes of the new-born aurora, rendered her the moft charming, and the moft dangerous object in nature. The nobleft and gaeft youths of all the land, paid their homages to her adorable perfections, but all in vain: fhe avoided doing hurt where fhe could do no good; fhe did not fo much fcorn, as fhut her eyes to all her offers, though fuch a treafure gave me ten thoufand anxieties before I knew what fhare I had in it: but when once fhe received my

* The author being an Italian, did not think black hair fo beautifal.

addreſſes, the ſecurity her conſtant virtue
gave me was proportionable to the im-
menſe value of her perſon. For my part,
I had ſome trials on my ſide. I was ſur-
rounded with beauties, who found a great
many ways to ſhew me they had no diſlike
to me. Whether being a ſtranger, of different features and make from their youth,
gave them a more pleaſing curioſity, or the
tallneſs of my ſtature, ſomething exceeding any of theirs, or the gaiety of my
temper, which gave me a freer air than is
uſual with them, being, as I obſerved, naturally too grave, (be that as it will), Iſyphena's bright ſenſe eaſily ſaw I made ſome
ſacrifices to her. But we had greater trials
than theſe to undergo, which I ſhall briefly relate to your Reverences, for the par-
ticularity of them. When I thought I
was almoſt arrived at the height of my
happineſs, being aſſured of the heart of
the divine Iſyphena, the Pophar came to
me one day with the moſt ſeeming concern in his countenance I ever marked in
him, even beyond that of the affair with
the great Baſſa's daughter: after a little
pauſe, he told me, he had obſerved the
love between his daughter and myſelf;
that, out of kindneſs to my perſon, he had
conſulted their wiſe men about it, who all
concluded; that, on account of my being
a ſtranger, and not of their race by the

X　father's

father's fide, I could never marry his
daughter; fo that I muft either folemnly
renounce all pretenfions to her; or be fhut
up for ever without any commerce with
his people, till death. But, fays he, to
fhew that we do juftice to your merit, you
are to have a public ftatue erected in your
honour, becaufe you have taught us the
art of painting; which is to be crowned
with a garland of flowers by the moft
beautiful young woman in the kingdom;
thus you will live to glory, though you
are dead to the world. But if you will renounce all pretenfions to my daughter, we
will furnifh you with riches, fufficient,
with the handfomenefs of your perfon, to
gain the greateft princefs in the world,
provided you will give a folemn oath never
to difcover the way to this place. I fell
down on my knees before him, and cried
out, " Here take me, fhut me up, kill me,
" cut me in a thoufand pieces, I will never
" renounce Hyphena."—He faid no more,
but that their laws muft be obeyed. I obferved tears in his eyes, as he went out,
which made me fee he was in earneft. I
had fcarce time to reflect on my miferable
ftate, or rather was incapable of any reflection at all, when four perfons came in
with a difmal heavinefs in their looks, and
bade me come along with them; they
were to conduct me to the place of my
confinement.

confinement. In the mean time, the Pophar goes to his daughter, and tells her
the same thing; only adding that I was
to be sent back to my own country, loaded
with such immense riches as might procure me the love of any woman in the
world: for, says he, those barbarians
(meaning the Europeans) will m rry their
daughters to any one who has but riches
enough to buy them; the men will do the
same with respect to the women; let the
woman be whose daughter she will, if she
had but money enough to purchase a kingdom, a king would marry her. Before he
had pronounced all this, Isyphena had not
strength to hear it out, but fell down in a
swoon at his feet: when she was come to
herself, he endeavoured to comfort her,
and added, that she was to have the young
Pophar's son, a youth about her age; for
though he was not old enough to govern
he was old enough to get children. He
went on and told her, I was to have a statue erected in honour of me, to be crowned by the fairest woman in all Mezorania,
which, says he, is judged to be yourself,
and, if you refuse it, Amnophilla is to be
the person. This was the most beautiful
woman next Isyphena, and by some thought
equal to her, whose sighs of approbation
and liking to my person I had taken no notice of, for the sake of Isyphena. She answered

fwered with a refolution that was furprifing, even to her father, That fhe would,
die before fhe would be wanting to her
duty, but that their laws allowed her to
chufe whom fhe pleafed for her hufband,
without being undutiful; that as to the
crowning of the ftatue, fhe accepted of it,
not for the reafon he gave, but to pay her
laft refpects to my memory, who, fhe was
fure, would never marry one elfe. As for
the young Pophar, fhe would give her anfwer when this ceremony was over. When
all things were ready for it, there was public proclamation made in all parts of the
Nome, that whereas I had brought into the
kingdom, and freely communicated to
them the noble art of painting, to have a
public ftatue erected in my honour, to be
crowned with a crown of flowers by the
faireft woman in all Mezorania. Accordingly, a ftatue of full proportion, of the
fineft polifhed marble, was erected in one
of their fpacious fquares with my name ingraven on the pedeftal in gold characters,
fetting forth the fervice I had done to the
commonwealth, &c. The ftatue had the
picture of Ifyphena in one hand, and the
emblems of the art in the other. The laft
kindnefs I was to receive, was to be permitted to fee the ceremony with a per-
fpective glafs, from the top of a high tower
belonging to the place of my confinement,
                                        from

from whence I could difcern every minute
circumftance that paffed. Immediately the
croud opened ta make way for Ifyphena,
who came in the regent's triumphant chariot, drawn by eight white horfes, all ca-
parifoned with gold and precious ftones,
herfelf more refplendent than the fun they
adorned. There was a fcaffold with a
throne upon it juft clofe to the ftatue, with
gilt fteps for her to go up to put the crown
on the head of it. As foon as fhe appeared,
a fhout of joy ran through the whole croud,
applauding the choice of her beauty,
and the work fhe was going to perform ;
then proclamation was made again for the
fame intent, fetting forth the reafons of
the ceremony. When all was filent, fhe
fteps from the throne by degrees with
the crown in her hand, holding it up to
be feen by all, fupported by Amnophilla
and Menifa, two of the moft beautiful vir-
gins after herfelf. There appeared a ferenity in the looks of Ifyphena beyond what
could be expected, exprefling a fixed refo-
folution at the fame time. As foon as fhe
had put the crown on the head of the
ftatue, which was applauded with repeated fhouts and acclamations, she ftood fill
for fome time, with an air that fhewed fhe
was determined for fome great action ;
then turning to the officers, ordered them
to make proclamation, that every one

shou'd

should remark what she was going to do. A profound filence enfuing through the whole affembly, she went up the fteps again, and taking out the moft confpicuous flower in the whole crown, firft put it in the right hand of the ftatue, and then clapped it into her bofom, with the other two she had received from me before, as a fign of her confent for marriage, which could not be violated.   This accafioned a shout ten times louder than any before, applauding fuch an heroic act of conftancy, as had never been feen in Mezorania. The regent ran up to her, and embracing her with tears of joy trickling down his cheeks, faid, she should have her choice, fince she had fulfilled the law, and fupplied all defects by that extraordinary act of fidelity: and immediately gave orders to have that heroic action regiftered in the public records, for an example and encouragement of conftancy to pofterity.   But the people cried out, Where is the man! where is the man! let their conftancy be rewarded immediately. . .

Here the reader, as well as the publifher, will lament the irreparable lofs of the fheets, which were miflaid at his coming over.   He does not pretend to charge his memory with what they contained ; juft having time to run them over in the Italian, when Signor Rhedi got them copied
                                                out

out for him. As far as the publisher re-
members, the lost sheets contained several
discourses between the Pophar and Gau-
dentio, concerning religion, philosophy, po-
litics, and the like; with the account of
the loss of his wife and children, and
some other accidents that befel him during
his stay in the country, which, as we shall
see, induced him to leave the place, with
several curious remarks of Signor Rhedi;
all which would doubtless have given a
great deal of satisfaction to the reader.
But no one can be so much concerned for
the loss as the publisher, since they cannot
now be repaired, by reason of the death of
the same Signor Rhedi, never to be suffici-
ently regreted by the learned world.]

Thefe difcourfes* made very great im-
preffions on the mind of a perfon of fo
much penetration as the regent was, infomuch that he feemed refolved, when his
regency was out, which wanted now but
a year, to go along with me into Europe,
during the ſtay he was to make at Grand
Cairo, that he might have an opportunity of examining matters at the fountainhead; wifely judging a confideration of
fuch confequence, as that of religion, to be
no indifferent thing. For my own part, notwithftanding the beauty and riches of the
country, I could find no fatisfaction in a

* Probably about the Chriſtian religion.

place

place where I had loft all that was dear to
me, though I had the comfort to have my
deat Ifyphena, and her three children, all
baptized by my own hand before they died :
neither could length of time allay my grief;
but, on the contrary, every thing I faw revived the memory of my irreparable lofs.
I confidered the inftability of the fleeting
joys of this world, where I thought I had
built my happinefs, for a man of fortune, on the moft folid foundation. But
alas ! all was gone as if it had been but a
dream, and the adorable Ifyphena was ro
more. The good old Pophar was in a very
little better condition, having loft his deareft
daughter, and his little grandchildren, particularly the eldeft boy, who is that picture
with his mother. This reflection on the
vanity of human felicity, made him more
difpofed to hear the truths of our divine
religion, fo that he was refolved to go
and fearch further into the reafons for
it.   There was another yet more forcible
reafon induced me to folicit the Pophar for
my return to my native country, which
was the care of my future ftate. I had
lived fo many years without the exercife
of thofe duties our church obliges us to
perform, and, though I had not been
guilty of any great crimes, I was not willing to die out of her bofom : however,
to do all the good I could to a country
where

where I had once enjoyed fo'much happinefs, this being the laft year we were to
ftay, I at length perfuaded the regent, that
there might be fome danger of an invafion
of his country, from the appofite fide towards the fouthern tropics; at leaft, I did
not know, but there might be fome habitable climate not fo far over the fands,
as towards Libya and Egypt. I had often fignified my thoughts to him in that
refpect. I told him, that though his kingdom was fafe, and inacceffible to all but
ourfelves on that fide, it was impoffible,
it might be nigher 'the great ocean on
the oppofite one, or that the fands might
not be of fuch extent; or, in fine, there
might be ridges of mountains, and from
them rivers running into the ocean, by
which, in procefs of time, fome barbarous
people might afcend, and difturb their long
uninterrupted reft, without any fence to
guard againft fuch an emergency. This
laft thought alarmed him; fo we were refolved to make a new trial, without com-
municating the defign to any but the chief
council of five, where we were fure of inviolable fecrecy. What confirmed me in
my notion was, that, when we were on the
utmoft point of our mountains fouthward, looking over the deferts, I could
perceive fomething like clouds, or fogs,
hanging always towards one part. I im-
                                    agined

agined them to be fogs covering the tops
of some great mountains, which must
be habitable vales.   Being refolved to
make a trial, we provided all things accordingly, and fet out from   the furtheft
part of the kingdom fouthwards, taking
only five perfons in our company, fteering
our courfe directly towards that point of
the horizon, where I obferved the thick
air always hanging towards one place. We
took provifions and water but for ten
days, leaving word that they fhould not
trouble themfelves about us, unlefs we
made a confiderable ftay, becaufe in cafe
we found mountains, we fhould always
find fprings and fruits to fubfift on, by
making a further fearch into the country :
otherwife, if we faw no hopes at the five
days end, we would return the other five,
and take frefh meafures.   The third day
of our voyage, we found the deferts not
fo barren as we expected, the ground
grew pretty hard ;   and the fourth
day we difcovered fome tufts of mofs and
fhrubs, by which we conjectured we fhould
foon come to firm land ; the evening of
that day we difcovered the tops of hills,
but further off than we thought ; fo that
though we travelled at a great rate all that
night and moft of the next day, we could
only arrive at the foot of them the fifth
day at night.   After fome little fearch we

* came

came to a fine fpring, and, to our comfort, no figns of inhabitants ; if there' had, we fhould have returned immediately to take further advice. The next morning we got up to the top of the higheft hill to difcover the country ; but found it to be only the point of a vaft mountainous country, like the worft part of our Alps, though there were fome fertile vales and woods, but no footfteps of its ever having beeninhabit-ed, as we believed, fince the creation. Find-ing we could make good provifion for our return, we were in no great pain about time ; but wandering from place to place, viewing and obferving every way. After proceeding along thofe craggy hills and pre-. cipices in this manner for five days, they began to leffen towards our right, but feemed rather to increafe the other way : at length, in the moft difmal and horrid part of the hill-brow, one of our young men thought he fpied fomething like the . figure of a man, fitting by a little fpring under a craggy rock juft below us ; we fent three of our people round another way to keep him from running into the wood, while the Pophar and myfelf ftole quietly over the rock where he was. As foon as he faw us, he whips up a broaken chink in the rock, and difappeared immie-diately : we were fure he could not get from us ; fo we clofed and fearched, till

we

we found a little cave in the windings of, the rock, where was his retiring place. His bed was made of mofs and leaves, with little heaps of dried fruits, of different forts, for his fuftenance. When he faw us, he was furprifed, and rufhed at us like a lion, thinking to make his way through us, but being all five at the mouth of the cave, he ftood ready to defend himfelf a-gainft our attempts. Viewing him a little nigher, we faw he had fome remains of an old tattered coat, and part of a pair of breeches, with a ragged fafh, or girdle, round his waift, by which, to our great furprife, we found he was an European. The Pophar fpoke to him in Lingua Fran-ca, and afked him who, or what he was; he fhook his head as if he did not under-ftand us. I fpoke to him in French, Italian, and Latin, but he was a ftranger to thofe languages; at length he cried out *Inglis, Inglis.* I had learned fomething of that lan-guage, when I was ftudent at Paris: for knowing my father had a mind I fhould learn as many languages as I could, I had made an acquaintance with feveral Englifh and Scotch ftudents in that univerfity, par-ticularly with one F. Johnfon, an English Benedictine; and could fpeak it pretty well for a foreigner, but had almoft forgot it for want of ufe. I bid him take cou-rage, and fear nothing, for we would do
him

him no harm.   As foon as ever he heard
me fpeak Englifh, he fell down on his
knees, and begged us to take pitty on him,.
and carry him to fome habitable country,
where he might poffibly get an opportunity of returning home again, or at
leaft, of living like a human creature.   Upon this he came out to us, but looked more
like a wild beaft, than a man; his hair,
beard, and nails were grown to a great
length, and his mien was as haggard, as if
he had been a great while in that wild
place ; though he was a ftout well-built
man, and fhewed fomething above the
common rank.   We went down to the
fountain together, where he made me to
underftand, that his father was an Eaft-
India merchant, and his mother a Duch
woman of Batavia ; that he had great part
of his education in London ; but being
very extravigant, his father, whofe natural fon he was, had turned him off, and
fent him to Batavia, to his mother's friends;
that, by his courage and induftry, he was
in a fair way of making his fortune, being
advanced to a lieutenant in the Dutch
guards at Batavia ; but was unhappily caft
away on the coaft of Africa, where they
had been on a particular adventure : That
he and his companions, four in number,
wardering up in the country to feek provifions, were taken by fome ftrange bar-

barians, who carried them a vast unknown
way into the continent, designing to eat
them, or sacrifice them to their inhuman
gods, as they had done his companions.
But being hale and fat at the time of his
taking, they reserved him for some particular feast : That, as they were carrying
him through the woods, another party of
barbarians, enemies to the former, met
them, and fell a fighting for their booty :
which he perceiving, knowing he was to
be eaten if he staid, slunk away in the scuf-
fle into the thickest woods, hiding himself
by day, and marching all night he did not
know where, but, as he conjectured, still
higher in the country. Thus he wandered
from hill to hill, and wood to wood, till
he came to a desert of sands, which he was
resolved to try to pass over, not daring to
return back, for fear of falling into the
hands of those merciless devourers. He
passed two days and two nights without
water, living on the fruits he carried with
him, as many as he could, till he came to
this mountanious part of the country,
which he found uninhabited ; taking up
his abode in that rock, where he never had
any hopes of seeing a human creature again :
neither did he know himself where he was,
or which way to go back. In fine, he told
us he had lived in that miserable place, now
upwards of five years. After we had comforted

forted him, as well as we could, I afked
him, which way the main fea lay, as near
as he could guefs, and how far he thought
it was to it? He pointed with his hand towards the fouth, a little turning towards
the eaft, and faid, he believed it might be
thirty or forty days journey; but advifed
us never to go that way, for we fhould certainly be devoured by the barbarians.   I
afked him whether the country was habitable from that place down to the fea; he
told me yes, except that defert he had paffed; but whether it was broader in other
places, he could not tell.

All the time he was fpeaking, the Pophar
eyed him from top to toe; and calling me
afide, What monfter, fays he, have we got
here? There is a whole legion of wild
beafts in that man. I fee the lion, the goat,
the wolf, and the fox, in that one perfon.
I could not forbear fmiling at the Pophar's
fkill in phyfiognomy, and told him we
fhould take care he fhould do no harm.
Then I turned to the man, and afked him,
whether he would conform himfelf to the
laws and rites of the country, if we carried him among men again, where he fhould
want for nothing. He embraced my knees,
and faid, he would conform to any laws
or any religion, if I would but let him
fee a habitable country again.   I ftarted at
the man, and began to think there was
                                    fome

fome truth in the Pophar's fcience. However, I told him, if he would but behave like a rational creature, he fhould go along with us: but he muft fuffer himfelf to be blindfolded, till he came to the place. He ftartled a little, and feemed to be prodigious fufpicious, left we fhould deceive him. But on my affuring him on the faith of a man, that he fhould come to no harm; he confented.

After we had refrefhed ourfelves, being both glad and concerned for the informaiion we had received of the nature of the country, which was the intent of our journey, in order to guard againft all inconveniencies, we covered his eyes very clofe, and carried him back with us, fometimes on foot, fometimes on one of the fpare dromedaries, till we arrived fafe from where we fet out. Then we let him fee where he was, and what a glorious country he was come into. We cloathed him like ourfelves, that is, in our travelling-drefs, to fhew he was not an entire ftranger to our race. He feemed loft in admiration of what he faw, and embraced me with all the figns of gratitude imaginable. He readily conformed to all our cuftoms, and made no fcruple of affifting at all their idolatrous ceremonies, as if he had been as good a Heathen as the beft of them. Which I feeing without declaring myfelf to be a Chriftian, told

told him I had been informed, the people
of the country where he was educated,
were Chriſtians ; and wondered to ſee him
join in adoring the ſun.   Pugh ! ſays he,
ſome bigotted people make a ſcruple, but
moſt of our men of ſenſe think one religion
is as good as another.   By this I perceived
our ſavage was of a new ſet of people,
which I had heard of before I left Italy,
called *Politici**, who are a ſort of Atheiſts
in maſquerade.   The Pophar, out of his
great ſkill in phyſiognomy, would have
no converſation with him, and commanded me to have a ſtrict eye over him.   However, the information he had given us of
the poſſibility of invading the kingdom
the way he came, anſwered the intent of
our voyage, and my former conjectures ;
about which there was a grand council
held, and orders given to ſecure the foot
of our outermoſt mountain ſouthwards,
which ran a great way into the deſert ; ſo
that it was ſufficient to guard againſt any
of thoſe barbarous invaders of the continent.   But to return to our European ſavage ; for he may be juſtly called ſo, being
more dangerous in a commonwealth, than
the very Hickſoes themſelves ; though he
was a perſon who had a tolerably civi-

---

* Theſe Politici were forerunners of modern free-thinkers, whoſe
principles tend to the deſtruction of all human ſociety, as our author
ſhews incomparably well by and by.

lized education, bating the want of all fenfe of religion, which was owing to his perpetual converfation with libertines : He had a fmattering of moft kinds of polite learning, but without a bottom in any refpect. After he had been with us fome time, his principles began to fhew themfelves in his practice. Firft, he began to be rude with our women ; married or fingle, it was all alike to him ; and, by an unaccountable fpirit of novelty or contradiction, our women feemed to be inclined to be very fond of him ; fo that we were at our wits ends about him. Then he began to find fault with our government, defpifing and condemning all our ceremonies and regulations: but his great aim was, to pervert our youth, enticing them into all manner of liberties, and endeavouring to make them believe, that there was no fuch thing as moral evil in nature ; that there was no harm in the greateft crimes, if they could but evade the laws and punifhments attending them. As I had endeavoured to create a confidence in him, he came to me one day, and faid, that, fince I was an European as well as himfelf, we might make ourfelves men for ever, if I would join with him : You fee, fays he, thefe men cannot fight ; nay, will rathe, be killed themfelves, than kill any one elfe : can't you fhew me the way out of this country,

country, where we will get a troop of ftout fellows well armed, and come and plunder all the country? we fhall get immenfe riches, and make ourfelves lords and mafters of all. I heard him with a great deal of attention, and anfwered him, that I˜ thought the project might eafily take, only for the horrid wickednefs of the fact; efpecially for us two, who had received fuch favours from the Pophar and his people; he, in his being delivered from the greateft mifery; and myfelf, in having been freed from flavery, and made one of the chief men of the kingdom: that the action would deferve to be branded with eternal infamy, and the blackeft ingratitude: befide the infinite villanies, injuftices, crimes, and deaths of innocent perfons, who muft perifh in the attempt; which would always ftare us in the face, and torment us with never-ceafing ftings of confcience till our death. Confcience! fays he, that is a jeft; a mere engine of prieft-craft: all right is founded in power: let us once get that, and who will difpute our right? As for the injuftice of it, that is a mere notion; diftinction of crimes, mere bigotry, and the effect of education, ufhered in under the cloak of religion. Let us be but fuccefsful, and I will anfwer for all your fcruples. I told him, it was a matter not to be refolved on fuddenly;

and

and that 1 would confider on it. But I bid him be fure to keep his matters to himfelf. I went immediately to the Pophar, and gave an account of what had paffed. He was ftruck with horror at the recital ; not fo much for the confequences, as that human nature could be brought to fuch a morfftrous deformity. If, fays he, your Europeans are men of fuch principles, who would not fly to the furtheft corner of the earth, to avoid their fociety ? Or rather, who can be fure of his life among fuch people ? Whoever thinks it no greater crime in itfelf, to kill me, than to kill a fly, will certainly do it, if I ftand in his way. If it were lawful, continued he, by our conftitutions to kill this man, he deferves a thoufand deaths, who makes it lawful to deftroy all the world befides. I anfwered, that all the Europeans were not men of his principles, nor even thofe of his nation, who were generally the moft compaffionate and beft natured men in the world. But that he was of a new fet of wretched people, who called themfelves *Deifts*, and interorly laughed at all religion and morality, looking upon them as mere engines of policy and prieft-craft. Interiorly ! fays he ; yes, and would cut any man's throat ex eriorly and actually, if it were not for fear of the gallows. Shut him up, cried he, from all commerce of

men,

men, left his breath should infect the whole world; or rather, let us send him back to his cave, to live like a wild beast; where if he is devoured by the favages, they do him no injury, on his own principles. I reprefented to him, that we were juft on our journey back to Grand Cairo, where we might carry him blindfold, that he fhould not know our way over the fands, and there give him his liberty; but that we would fhut him up till then. This being agreed on, I took a fufficent number of men, to feize him; and to do it without any mifchief, for he was as ftout as a lion, we contrived to come upon him in his bed, where we caught him with one of our young women. Three of our men fell upon him at once, and kept him down, while the reft tied his hands and legs, and carried him into a ftrong-hold, whence it was impoffible for him to efcape. The woman was fhut up apart, according to our laws. When he found himfelf taken, he called me by the moft cruel names he could think on, as the moft wicked and treacherous villain that ever was, thus to betray him, and the truft he had put in me. Yes, fays I, it is a crime to difcover your fecrets, and no crime in you to fubvert the government, and fet all mankind a-cutting one another's throats, by your monftrous principles: fo I left him for the present.

prefent. Some time after, I went to him, and told him, our council had decreed he fhould be carried back from whence he came, and be delivered over to the favages, either to be devoured by them, or to de-fend himfelf by his principles, as well as he could. He cried out, Sure we would not be guilty of fuch horrid barbarity ! Bar-brrity ! faid I; that is a mere jeft : they will do you no injury ; if your flefh is a ra-rity to them, when they have you in their power, they have full right to make ufe of it. He begged by all that was dear, we would not fend him to the favages ; but rather kill him on the fpot. Why, fays I, you are worfe than the greateft canibals ; becaufe they fpare their friends, and only eat their enemies ; whereas your princi-ples fpare no body, and acknowledge no tye in nature. At length he owned him-felf in a miftake, and feemed to renounce his errors ; when I told him, if he would engage his moft folemn promife, to fuffer himfelf to be blindfolded, and behave peaceably, we would carry him to a place where he might find an opportunity to re-turn to his own country. But, fays I, what fignify promifes and engagements in a man who laughs at all obligations, and thinks it as juft and lawful to break them, as to make them ? No, he curfed himfelf with the moft dreadful imprecations, if he

were

were not tractable in all things we fhould command him. But, fays he again, won't you deliver me back to the favages? I anfwered in the fame tone, fhould we do you any wrong, if we did? At length, to appeafe him, I promifed him faithfully we would put him in a way to return into his own country: but bid him confider, if there were no fuch thing as right and wrong, what would, or what fecurity could there be in human life?

In a few weeks, the time drew on for our great journey to Grand Cairo, where I was in hopes of feeing my native country once more. All things were now as good as ready; the Pophar and myfelf had other defigns than ufual, and were in fome pain to think of leaving that once fo happy country. Though, as I faid, all things that could make me happy, were buried with my dear Ifyphena. The Pophar had fome ferious thoughts of turning Chriftian; the evidences of our religion were foon perceived by a perfon of his deep penetration; though perfons of little learning, and great vices pretend they don't fee them. But, like a wife man, he was refolved to examine into it, in the places where it was exercifed in the greateft fplendour. We provided a good quantity of jewels, and as much gold as we could well carry, for our prefent expenfes at

Grand

Grand Cairo, and elsewhere, in future ex-
igencies. I went to my Deist in his grot-
to, and threw him in as much gold and
jewels as were sufficient to glut his avarice,
and make him happy in his brutal way of
thinking. But I would not truft myfelf
with him alone, for all his promifes, as
he, on his fide, expreffed ftill a diffidence
of trufting any body; I fuppofe from the
confcioufnefs of his own vile principles.
Then I threw him a blinding-cap, which
we had made for him, that he fhould not
fee our way over the deferts. This cap
was made like a head-piece, with breath-
ing places for his mouth and nofe, as well
as to take in nourifhment, opening at the
back part, and clafping with a fpring behind, that being once locked, he could not
open it himfelf. He put it on his head
two or three times, before he durft venture
to clofe it. At laft he clofed it, and he
was as blind as a beetle. We went to him
and tied his hands, which he let us do quietly enough; but ftill begged us that we
would not betray him to the favages. I
bid him think once more, that now his
own interior fence told him, that to betary
him would be a crime; by confequence
there was fuch a thing as evil.

All things being in readinefs, we mounted our dromedaries. The Pophar and all
the reft kiffed the ground as ufual; I did
the

the fame, out of refpect to the place which
contained the remains of my never too
much lamented Ifyphena, the afhes of whofe
heart are in the hollow of the ftone, whereon is her picture. Not to mention the ceremonies of our taking leave, we were
conducted in a mournful manner over the
bridge, and lanched once more into the
ocean of fands and deferts, which were
before us. Our favage was on a dromedary which followed the reft, but led by a
cord faftened to one of them, for fecurity.
It ftumbled with him twice or thrice, and
threw him off once, but without any great
hurt. But the fear of breaking his neck
put him into a great agony; and though
he was as bold as a lion on other occafions,
he was prodigioufly ftartled at the thoughts
of death. We arrived at Grand Cairo
at the ufual period of time, without
any particular difafter. As foon as we
were fettled, the Pophar ordered me to
fend the Deift packing as foon as we could.
This brutal race, fays he, next the cannibals, are fitteft company for him. I un-
locked the blinding-helmet, and told him,
we had now fulfilled our promife; that he
was at Gaand Cairo, where he might find
fome way or other to return into Europe;
and, to convince him, carried him to fome
European merchants who affured him of
the fame. Delivering to him his gold and

Z   jeweis,

jewels, I begged him to reflect on his obligations to us, and the greatful acknowledgments due to our memory on that account: we had taken him from a miserable solitude, where he lived more like a wild beaft than a man; and where he was in danger of being found and devoured by the cannibals: we had brought him into one of the happieft countries in the world, if he would but have conformed to its laws; and now had given him his liberty to go where he pleafed, with riches fufficient to make him eafy, and benefits to make him grateful all his life. I then took my leave of him. But to our forrow we had not done with him yet. As foon as the Pophar and the reft had performed the ceremony of vifiting the tombs of their anceftors, or rather the places where the tombs had been, the good old man and myfelf began to think of meafurs for our journey into Italy. He ordered his people to ftay at Grand Cairo till the next annual caravan; and in cafe he did not return by that time, they were to go home, and he would take the opportunity of the next following caravan, becaufe he was upon bufinefs that nearly concerned him. We had agreed with a mafter of a fhip to carry us to Venice, which, as I had the honour to acquaint your Reverences before, was a French fhip, commanded by
                                        Monfieur

.Monfieur Godart. We had fixed the day to go aboard, when behold? our favage, at the head of a band of Turks, came and fiezed every one of us, in the name of the great Baffa. By great good fortune, while we ftaid at Grand Cairo, I had the grateful curiofity to inform myfelf what was become of the former Baffa's daughter, we left there five and twenty years ago. The people told me, the daughter was married to the Grand Sultan, and was now Sultanefs, mother to the prefent Sultan, and regent of the empire; adding that her brother was their prefent great Baffa. This lucky information faved all our lives and liberties. We were carried prifoners before the Great Baffa, the faithlefs favage accufing us of crimes againft the ftate; that we were immenfely rich, (a crime of itfelf fufficient to condemn us), and could make a difcovery of a country of vaft advantage to the Grand Signior. To be fhort, we had all been put to torture, had not I begged leave to fpeak a word or two in private to the Great Baffa. There I told him who I was; that I was the perfon who had faved his fifter's life, the now Emprefs; and, to convince him, told him all the circumftances except that of her love, though he had heard fomething of that too: I fhewed him the ring fhe had given me for a remembrance, (which he

alfo

alfo remembered), adding, that we were innocent men, who lived honeftly according to our own laws, coming there to traffic, like other merchants, and had been traduced by one of the greateft villains upon earth. In a word, this not only got us off, and produced us an ample paffport from the Grand Baffa for our further voyage ; but he alfo ordered the informing wretch to be feized, and fent to the galleys for life. He offered to turn turk if they would fpare him. But being apprifed of his principles, they faid he would be a dif. grace to their religion ; and ordered him away immediately. Upon which, feeing there was no mercy, being grown mad with rage and defpair, before they could feize his hands, he drew out a piftol, and fhot himfelf through the head ; not being able to find a worfe hand than his own. The Pophar, good man! bore thefe misfortunes with wonderful patience, though he affured me his greateft grief was to fee human nature fo far corrupted, as it was in that impious wretch, who could think the moft horrid crimes were not worth the notice of the fupreme governor of the univerfe. But fee, fays he, that providence can make the wicked themfelves the inftruments of its juft vengence: for can any thing be fo great a blot upon human nature as to be its own deftroyer, when the very brutes
will

will ftruggle for life till the laft gafp?
However, he was uneafy till he had left
that hateful place. Befides, there were
fome figns of the plague breaking out; fo
we went down to Alexandria as faft we
could. And to encourage Monfieur Godart, he made him a prefent beforehand of
a diamond of a conliderable value. We
fet fail for Candy, where Monfieur Godart was to touch, the 16th day of Auguft, *anno* 1712. But, alas! whether thefe
troubles, or not being ufed to the fea, or
fome infection of the plague he had caught
at Grand Cairo, or all together, is uncertain; but that great good man fell fo
dangeroufly ill, that we thought we fhould
fcarce get him to Candy. He affured me,
by the knowledge he had of himfelf and
nature, that his time was come. We put
in at the firft creek, where the land-air a
little refrefhed him; but it was a fallacious
crifis; for in a few days, all of us perceived his end drew near. Then he told me
he was refolved to be baptized, and die in
the Chriftian faith. I got him inftructed
by a Reverend prieft belonging to Monfieur Godart; his name was Monfieur Le
Grelle, whom I had formerly known when
he was a ftudent in the college for foreign
miffions; and, what was the only comfort
I had now left, I faw him baptized, and
yield up the ghoft with a courage becom-

ing the greateſt hero, and the beſt of men.
This was the greateſt affliction I ever had
in my whole life,' after the death of his
daughter. He left me all his effects, which
were ſufficient to make me happy in this
life, if riches could procure happineſs.

We had ſome days to ſtay, before Monſieur Godart could make an end of his bu-
ſineſs. I was walking in a melancholy po-
ſture along the ſea-ſhore, and reflecting on
the adventures of my paſt life, occaſioned
by thoſe very waters whereon I was looking, when I came, or rather my feet caried
me, to a hanging rock, on the ſide of the
iſland, juſt on the edge of the ſea, and where
there was ſcarce room enough for two or
three perſons to ſtand privately under covert,
very difficult to be diſcerned; where going
to ſit down, and indulge my melancholy
thoughts, I eſpied a Turk and two women,
as if concealed under the rock. My own
troubles not allowing me the curioſity to pry
into other people's concerns, made me turn
ſhort back again : but the elder of the two
women, who was miſtreſs of the other, ſee-
ing by my diſtreſs, that I was a ſtranger and
a Chriſtian, (being now in that habit), came
running to me, and falling on her knees,
laid hold of mine, and begged me to take
pitty on a diſtreſſed woman, who expect d
every moment to be butchered by one of the
moſt inhuman villains living, from whoſe
violence

violence they had fled and hid themſelves in
that place, in expectation of finding a boat
to convey him off.   I lifted her up, and
thought I ſaw ſomething in her face I ſeen
before, though much altered by years
and troubles.   She did the ſame by me,
and at length cried out, O heavens! it
cannot be the man I hope! I remembered
confuſedly ſomething of the voice, as well
as the face ; and, after a deal of aſtoniſh-
ment, found it was the Curdiſh lady, who
had ſaved my life from the pirate Hamet.
Oh! ſays ſhe, I have juſt time enough to
tell you, that we expected to be purſued by
that inhuman wretch, unleſs you can find
a boat to carry us off before he finds us,
otherwiſe we muſt fall a ſacrifice to his cruelty.   I never ſtaid to conſider conſequen-
ces, but anſwered precipitately, that I
would do my beſt ; ſo ran back to the ſhip
as faſt as I could, and with the help of the
firſt man brought the boat to the rock.   I
was juſt getting out to take hold of her
hand, when we heard ſome men coming
ruſhing in behind us, and one of them cried, Hold villain, that wicked woman ſhan't
eſcape ſo ; and fires a piſtol, which miſſing
the lady, ſhot the man attending her, into
the belly, ſo that he fell down preſently,
though not quite dead.   I had provided
myſelf with a Turkiſh ſcymitar, and a caſe
of piſtols, under my ſaſh, for my defence

on

on fhipboard ; I faw there was no time to
deliberate, fo I fired directly at them, for
there were three, and had the good luck to
drop one of them. But Hamet, as I found
afterwards, minding nothing but his revenge on the, woman, fired again, and
miffing the lady a fecond time, fhot her.
maid through the arm, and was drawing
his fcymitar to cleave her down, when I
ftept in before the lady ; but fhooting with
too much precipitancy, the bullets paffed
under his arm, and lodged in the body of
his fecond ; he ftarted back at the fire fo
near him, which gave me time to draw
my fcymitar. Being now upon equal
terms, he retired two or three paces, and
cried, Who art thou that ventureft thy
life fo boldly for this wicked woman ? I
knew his voice perfectly well, neither was
he fo much altered as the lady. I am the
man faid I, whofe life thou wouldft have
taken, but this lady faved it, whofe caufe
I fhall now revenge as well as my own, and
my dear brother's. We made no more
words, but fell to it with our fcymitars,
with all our might ; he was a brave ftout
man, and let me fee I fhould have work
enough to hew him down. After feveral
attacks, he gave me a confiderable wound
on my arm, and I cut him acrofs the cheek
a pretty large gafh, but not to endanger
his life ; at length the juftice of my caufe
                                     would

would have it, that ftriking of his turban
at one ftroke, and with another falling on
his bare head, I cut him quite into the
brains, that fome of them fpurted on my
fcymitar. He fell down, as I thought,
quite dead, but after fome time he gave a
groan, and muttered thefe words, Mahomet thou art juft, I killed this woman's
hufband, and fhe has been the occafion of
my death ; with thefe words he gave up
the ghoft. By this time the lady's attendant was dead ; fo I took the lady and her
woman without ftaying, for fear of further
difficulties, and putting them in the boat,
conducted them to the fhip. Monfieur
Godart was extremely troubled at the accident, faying we fhould have all the ifland
upon us, and made great difficulty to receive the lady ; but upon a juft reprefenta-
tion of the cafe, and an abundant recom-
penfe for his effects left behind, we got him
to take her in, and hoift fail for Venice as
faft as we could. The lady had now time
to thank me for her delivery, and I to con-
gratulate my happy fortune in being able
to make a return for her faving my life.
During our paffage, I begged her to give
us the hiftory of her fortunes fince I left
her, which I prognofticated then could not
be very happy, confidering the hands fhe
was fallen into. Says fhe, You remember
I made a promife to Hamet, that I would
marry

marry him on condition he would fave your life. Yes, Madam, faid I, and am ready to venture my own once more in return for fo great a benefit. You have done enough, fays fhe; and with that acquainted us, that when I was fold off to the ftrange merchants, Hamet carried her to Algiers, and claimed her promife. I was entirely ignorant, fays fhe, of his having a hand in the death of my dear lord; but, on the contrary, the villain had contrived his wickednefs fo cunningly, that I thought he had genceroufly ventured his own life to fave his, and being, as you know, a very handfome man, of no very inferior rank, and expreffing the moft ardent love for my perfon, and I having no hopes of returning into my own country, fulfilled my promife made on your account, and married him. We lived contentedly enough together for fome years, bating that we had no children, till his conftant companion, who was the man attending me at the rock, and was killed by that villain, fell out about a fair flave, which Omar, fo he was called, had bought, or taken prifoner in fome of their piracies. Hamet, as well as he, fell in love with her, and would have taken her for his concubine, but the other concealed her from him : they had like to have fought about it ; Hamet vowed revenge. The other, who was the honefter

man

man of the two, was advifed to be upon
his guard, and to deliver the woman to
him; which he never would confent to,
but was refolved to run all rifks, rather
than the young lady fhould fuffer any dif-
honor. In the mean time, her friends, who
were rich people of Circaffia, hearing
where fhe was, made intereft to have her
ranfomed, and taken from both of them,
by the authority of the Dey of Algiers,
who was otherwife no friend to Hamet.
This laft had been informed, that Omar,
becaufe he could not enjoy her himfelf,
contrived to have her ranfomed from his
rival, and I myfelf had a hand in the affair,
for which he threatened revenge on both of
us; and being alfo difgufted with the Dey,
he gave orders to have his fhips ready to
move, and follow his trade of piracy.
Then Omar informed me how Hamet had
murdered my firft hufband, by hiring the
Arabians to do it, while he pretended to
defend him to avoid my fufpicions, with
fuch circumftances of the fact, that I faw
the truth was too clear. The horror and
deteftation I was in, is not to be expreffed,
both againft myfelf, for marrying fuch a
monfter. Omar added, that he was certainly informed, that as foon as he had us
out at fea, he would make away with us
both; and told me, if I would truft myfelf with him, he would undertake to carry

me

me off in a boat, and conduct me into my own country. I was refolved to fly to the fartheft end of the earth to avoid his loathed fight ; fo refolved to pack up our moft precious things, and go along with him. He procured a boat to meet us, at a little creek of the ifland, by a perfon he thought he could confide in, but who betrayed the whole affair to Hamet. Of which alfo we had timely notice, and removing from the ftation where we expected the boat, and fled along the coaft as privately as we could, and hid ourfelves under the rock where you found us, expecting either to find fome favourable occafion to be carried off, or to die by the hand of Hamet, which we certainly had done, had not he met with his juft death by yours. The lady had fcarce given us this fhort account of her misfortunes, and we were not only congratulating her for her deliverance, but admiring the juftice of providence, which reached this villain, both to bring him to condign punifhment for the murder of the innocent Curd, and make him die by my hand, five and twenty years after he had robbed and killed my brother with all his crew, fold me for a flave, and attempted to kill me alfo, had not the ftrange lady faved my life : I fay, we were making fuch like reflections on this ftrange accident, when they told us from above, two veffels

feemed

feemed to come full fail upon us, as if they
were purfuing us with all their might. We
made all the fail we could, but our fhip
being pretty heavy loaded, we faw we muft
be overtaken. Some of us were refolved
to fight it out to the laft, in cafe they were
enemies. But Monfieur Godart would not
confent to it, faying the Baffa's paffport
would fecure us, or by yielding peaceably,
we might be ranfomed. They came up
to us in a fhort time, and faluted us with
a volley of fhot, to fhew what we were to
truft to. We ftruck our fails and let them
board us without any refiftance. Monfieur
Godart, with too mean a fpirit, as I thought,
told them with cap in hand, that he would
give them any fatisfaction, and affured them
he would not willingly fall out with the
fubjects of the Grand Signior. They feized every man of us, and fpying the lady
and me, There they are, faid they; the
adulterefs and her lover, with the fpoils of
her murdered hufband. Which words,
fhewing they were Turks in purfuit of us
from Candy, quite confounded Monfieur
Godart at once, and made me imagine, I
fhould have much ado to find any quarter.
They hauled us upon deck, making fhew
as if they were going to cut off my head.
I never thought myfelf fo nigh death before; but had the prefence of mind to
cry out in the hearing of the whole crew,

A a   that

that we were fervants of the Grand Sultanefs; and produced the paffport of the
Great Baffa her brother; charging them on
their peril not to touch us. This ftopt
their fury a little; fome cried out. Hold,
have a care what you do; others cried,
Kill them all for robbers and murderers,
the Sultanefs will never protect fuch villains as thefe. When the hurlyburly was
fomething appeafed, Monfieur Godart rea-
foned the cafe with them, and told them,
if they murdered us, they could uever
conceal it; fince all the crew of the three
fhips heard our appeal to the Sultanefs mother, the paffpoit fetting forth among
other things, that I had faved the life of
the Garnd Sultanefs. This brought them
to a demur. The chief of them began to
confult among themfelves what was beft to
be done. When I, begging leave to fpeak,
told them, if they would carry us to Conftantinople, we would willingly fubmit our
lives, and all that belonged to us, in cafe
the Sultanefs did not own the fact, and
take us into her protection : that, in cafe
they put us to death, fome one or other,
in fuch a number, would certainly inform
againft them, the confequences of which
they knew very well. I touched alfo but
tenderly on the death of Hamet, and our
innocence. The firft part of my fpeech
made them pafs over the other. They
demurred

demurred again, and at length refolved to carry us to Conftantinople, and proceed againft us by way of juftice, not doubting to make good prize of us, on account of our being Chriftians. Thus was our journey to Venice interrupted by this accident. When we came to the port, Monfieur Godart got leave to fend our cafe to Monfieur Savigni, the French refident; who found means to reprefent to the Sultanefs mother, that there was a ftranger in chains, who pretended to be the perfon who had faved her life, when fhe was at Grand Cairo, and would give her proofs of it, if he could be admitted to her Highnefs's prefence. I would not fend the ring fhe gave me, for fear of accidents. The Sultanefs gave orders immediately, I fhould be brought to her prefence; faying, fhe could eafily know the perfon, for all it was fo long before. I put on the fame kind of drefs I was in when fhe firft faw me, which, if your Reverences remember, was the travelling drefs of the Mezoranians. When I was brought into her prefence, I fcarce knew her, being advanced to a middle age, and in the attire of the Grand Sultanefs. She looked at me with a great deal of emotion, and bid me approach nigher. I immediately fell on my knees, and holding the ring in my hand which fhe gave me at parting, as if I were

making

making a present of it, Madam, said I, behold a flave, who had the honour to fave your Highnefs's life, and now begs his own, and that of his companions; and moft humbly requeft your Highnefs to accept of this jewel, as a token of our laft diftrefs. Inftead of anfwering me, which put me in great pain, as doubting whether I was right or not, fhe turned to her nigheft attendants, and faid in a pretty foft voice, It is he, I know him by his voice, as well as his drefs: and rifing off her feat, came and took the ring. Then looking attentively at it, Yes, Sir, faid fhe, I own the ring and bearer; and acknowledge you to be the one who faved my life. For which reafon, I give you yours, and all that belongs to you, forbidding all under pain of death, to give you the leaft trouble; and withal ordered a very rich Turkifh robe to be thrown over my fhoulders, as a fign of her favour. Immediate orders were fent to the port to fet Monfieur Godart and all his crew at liberty, and to feaft us as particular friends of the Grand Sultanefs. The company being difmiffed, fhe made a fign for me to ftay, having further bufinefs with me. When all were gone, but two of her chief favourite women, fhe came to me without any ceremony, and taking me in her arms, as if I had been her brother, embraced me with a

great

great deal of tendernefs; her joy to fee me,
making her lay afide her grandeur, and
yield to the tranfports of undifguifed nature.   She led me by the hand into a moft
magnificent apartment ; faying, Come, Signior Gaudentio, for fo I think you are called; after you have refrefhed yourfelf, you
fhall tell me your adventures.   She made
no fcruple to fit down with me, being now
not only miftrefs of herfelf, but of the
whole Ottoman empire, as well as fure of
her attendants.   We had a refrefhment of
all the rarities of the Eaft, with the richeft
wines for me, though fhe drank none herfelf: I long to hear your adventures, continued fhe, of fo many years abfence.   So
I told her in fhort, how I was carried by
that ftrange merchant into an unknown
country; without telling her the way we
went thither ; where I had married the regent's daughter.   She blufhed a little at
that part, and fhewed the remains of all
her former beauty.   But it put me in mind
of my own indifcretion, to touch on fuch
a nice point.   She paffed it off with a great
deal of goodnefs ; and, recovering myfelf,
I acquainted her of the reafons of my return, as well as how I was taken by Hamet
the firft time, which fhe had not, been acquainted with before; and laftly, how I
met with the fame Hamet again, killed him,
and by that means came into that misfor-

tune. I called it then a misfortune, faid I, but look upon it now to be one of my greateft happineffes ; fince, by that occafion, I have the honour of feeing your Highnefs in that dignity of which you are the moft worthy of any one in all the Ottoman empire. She feemed to be in admiration at the courfe of my life; and added, I think, Signor, you faid you were married; is your fpoufe dead? No, Madam, faid I: alas! fhe is dead, and all my children, and I am going to retire, and lead a private life in my native country. With thefe and other difcourfes we paffed the greateft part of the day, when fhe bid me go back to the fhip in public, attended with all the marks of her high favours ; but fhe faid fhe would fend for me privately in the evening ; for, added fhe, I have a thoufand other things to afk you. Accordingly I was introduced privately into the feraglio ; which fhe, being Sultanefs-regent, could eafily do. There fhe intirely laid afide her grandeur. We talked all former paffages cver again, with the freedom of friends and old acquaintances. In our converfation, I found fhe was a woman of prodigious depth of judgment, as indeed her wading through fo many difficulties, attending the inconftancy of the Ottoman court, particularly the regency, evidently fhewed. I made bold to afk her how fhe

arrived

arrived at that dignity, though she was the only person in the world that deserved it; and took the liberty to say in a familiar way, that I believed her Highness was now sensible of the service I did her, in refusing to comply with her former demands, since the fates had reserved her to be the greatest empress of the world, not the consort of a wandering slave. Had I not been entirely assured of her goodness, I should not have dared to have touched on that head. She blushed with a little confusion at first, but putting it off with a grave air, Grandeur, says she, does not always make people happy. Ten thousand cares attend a crown; but the indifference I have for all things, make mine sit easier than it might have done otherwise. It is true, continued she, that young people very seldom see their own good, and oftentimes run into such errors, by the violence of their passions, as not only to deprive them of greater blessings, but render their misfortunes irretrievable. Some time after you were gone, my father the Grand Bassa was accused by some underhand enemies, of mal-administration, a thing too frequent in our court, and privately condemned to be strangled. But having some trusty friends at the Porte, he had notice of it, before the orders came: he immediately departed from Grand Cairo, and took a

round.

round-about way towards Conftantinople, to prevent, as the way is, the execution of them. He fent me before to prepare matters, and to intercede with the young Sultan, my late deceafed Lord, for his life, leaving word where I might let him know of the fuccefs of my interceffion. I prefented myfelf before the Sultan with that modeft affurance, which my innocence, my youth, and grief for my father's danger, gave me. I fell down on my knees, and, with a flood of tears, begged my father's life. The Sultan looked at me with fome amazement; and, whatever it was he faw in my face, not only granted my requeft, and confirmed my father in his former poft; but made a profeffion of love to my perfon; and even continued it with more con. ftancy, than I thought a Grand Sultan capable of, having fo many exquifite beauties to divert him, as they generally have. I confented, to fave my father's life; and whether the indifferency I had for all men, made him more eager, I cannot tell; but I found I was the chief in his favour. He had fome other miftreffes now and then, of whom he was very fond. But never teafing him, nor fretting myfelf about it, I eafily found I continued to have the folid part of his friendfhip; and bringing him the firft male child, the prefent emperor, I became the chief Sultanefs: and by his death, and

the

the minority of my fon, am now regent ;
by which I am capable of rendering you
all the fervice the Ottoman empire can perform : which I efteem one of the happieft
events of my life. I returned her the moft
profound bow, and humble thanks a heart
full of the moft lively fenfe of gratitude
could profefs. She offered me the firft
poft of the Ottoman empire, if I would
but become a muffulman, or only fo in appearance. Or if, faid fhe, you had rather
be nigh me, you fhall be the chief officer
of my houfehold. I have had affurance
enough, added fhe, that neither your inclinations nor principles can be forced ;
neither will I endeavour to do it, but leave
you as much at your liberty, as your generous mafter did, when he bought you
of Hamet. I expreffed all the grateful acknowledgments poffible, for fo generous an
offer ; but affured her with an air that
even expreffed forrow for the refufal, that
I lay under religious obligations, which
bound me indifpenfably to return into my,
own country. She was become now as
much miftrefs of her inclinations, as fhe
had acquired prudence and experience by
the long command fhe had over her hufband's heart, and the whole Ottoman empire. So after a month's ftay fhe let me
go, with all the marks of honour her dignity would fuffer her to exprefs. She
would

would have punifhed the perfons that took us, but I interceded for them. Monfieur Godart, who was well rewarded for the lofs of his time and confinement, can teftify the truth of this hiftory. The laft words fhe faid to me, were, to bid me remember, that a Turk and a woman were capable of generous gratitude and honour, as well as Chriftians. So we fet fail for Venice.

[*Secretary.* Here one of the inquifitors came in with a gold medal in his hand, and turning to the examinant, faid, Signor Gaudentio, I believe you have found a relation in Italy, as well as in Africa, and one of the fame nation with your mother. It is the Perfian lady you brought along with you, whom we fecured the fame time we did you ; but would not let you know it, till we could procure intelligence from Venice, and a perfon who could fpeak the Perfian language. We own we find her in the fame ftory with you, and nothing material againft you from Venice. Upon the examining her effects, we found this medal of the fame make with yours by which you knew who your mother was. She fays it was about her neck, when fhe was fold to the Perfian merchant. But fince we fhall give you both your liberties

berties in a fhort time, fhe fhall be brought unto you, and we give you leave to fay what you will to her, with the interpreter by. Upon this the lady was introduced, with her maid and the interpreter. As foon as fhe faw our examinant in good health, feemingly at liberty, a joyful ferenity fpread itfelf over her countenance, fuch as we had not feen before. Our examinant afked her; to be pleafed to give an account of her life, as far as fhe thought proper, and how fhe came by that medal.

Lady. All I know of myfelf, faid fhe, is, that the noble Curd, who bou..ht me of a Perfian merchant for a companion for his only daughter, about my own age, whom he thought I refembled very much, often declared to me, that the merchant bought me of a Turkifh woman, who left that medal about my neck, fuppofing it to be fome charm or prefervative againft diftempers, or becaufe a fifter of mine had the fame faftened about her neck, with a gold chain, which could not be taken off without breaking ; but who, or where the fifter was, I never knew. The noble Curdifh Lord, who bought me, grew prodigious fond of me, and bred me up as another daughter ; and

not

not only fo, but having an only fon,
fomething older than myfelf, he connived at a growing love he perceived
between his fon and myfelf ; which,
after fome difficulties on both fides, at
length came to a marriage ; though it
coft my generous benefactor and father-in-law his life. For another
young Lord of Curdiftan, falling in
love with me, often challenged Prince
Cali (that was my dear hufband's
name) to decide their pretenfions by
the fword, which I had always forbid
him to do ; faying, that man fhould
never be my hafband who expofed my
reputation by a duel ; fince the world
would never believe, that any man
would expofe his life for a woman,
unlefs there had been fome encouragement given on both fides : whereas I
never gave the leaft to any but Prince
Cali. However, the other met him
one day, and attacked him fo furiouf-
ly, that Prince Cali was forced to kill
him in his own defence, making a
thoufand proteftations, that he had
almoft fuffered himfelf to be killed, rather than to difobey my orders. But
the father of the prince who was flain,
with a company of affaffins, laid an
ambufcade for prince Cali and his father, in which this latter was killed,
and

and moſt of his train. But by the valour of his ſon, and two of his companions, the chief aſſaſſins were laid
dead on the ſpot, and the reſt put to
flight. But Prince Cali, after the
death of his father, fearing further
treachery of that nature, preſently after we were married, removed to another part of the kingdom; from
whence being ſent on a commiſſion by
his king, he was inhumanly murdered by the barbarous Hamet. This is
the ſum of my unfortunate life, till I
had the good fortune to ſave yours.

Secretary. We permitted the nephew
and the aunt (for ſo they were found
to be by the medal) to embrace one
another; Signor Gaudentio aſſuring
her, that by all appearance he was
the ſon of her ſiſter and the
mother's ſiſter that was loſt, and both
of them preſerved to ſave each other's
life. The lady then declared, ſhe
would turn Chriſtian, ſince her miſ-
fortunes were come to a period; and
that ſhe was reſolved to leave the
world, and retire into ſome of our
monaſteries. We put her among the
nuns of our order, where ſhe, pro-
miſes to be a ſignal example of virtue
and piety. The inquiſitors ordered
the examinant to give them the re-
B b   remaining

maining part of his life, which, in all appearance, if they found his ſtory to agree with their informations, might purchaſe him his liberty. Upon which Gaudentio proceeded as follows.]

I was telling your Reverences, that at length we ſet ſail from the Porte, and ſteered our courſe directly for Venice, where we happily arrived without any conſiderable accident, the 10th of December 1712. I do not queſtion but your Reverences are already informed, that ſuch perſons did arrive at Venice about that time. Monſieur Godart is well known to ſeveral merchants, and ſome of the ſenators of that famous city, whom he informed of what he ſaw with his own eyes. But there were ſome particular paſſages, unknown to your Reverences, wherein I had like to have made ſhipwreck of my life, after ſo many dangers; as I did here of my liberty; though I do not complain, but only repreſent my hard fortune to your Reverences conſideration, as well as a great many ſtrangers of the firſt rank, to ſee the nature of it. I put on my Mezoranian habit, ſpangled with ſuns of gold, and the fillet-crown on my head, adorned with ſuns of gold, with ſeveral jewels of very great value, which I believe was the moſt remarkable and magnificent dreſs of any where. I went unmaſked being aſſured

my

my face and perfon were unknown to 'all
the world. Every one's eyes were upon
me. Several of the mafque:aders came to
me, and talked to me, particularly the
ladies. They fpoke to me in feveral languages, as Latin, French, Italian, Spanifh,.
High Dutch, &c. I anfwered them all in
the Mezoranian language, which feemed
as ftrange to them, as my drefs. Some of
them fpoke to me in the Turkifh and Perfian language, in Lingua Franca, and fome
in an Indian language I did not underftand. I anfwered them ftill in the Mezoranian, of which no body knew one word.
Two ladies particularly, very richly dreffed, followed me where ever I went. The
one, as it proved afterwards, was Favilla,
the celebrated courtefan, in the richeft
drefs of all the company; the other was
the lady who was with me when I was taken
up, and who was the occafion of my fettling at Bologna; I mean the true occafion, for I will conceal nothing from your
Reverences. Notwithftanding their diligence, I got away unknown at that time.
The next time I came, I appeared in the
fame drefs, but with richer jewels; I had
more eyes upon me now than before. The
courtefan purfued me again in a different,
but richer drefs than the former. At
length fhe got me by myfelf, and pulling
off her mafk, fhewed me a wonderful pretty

ty face, only there was too fierce an affurance in it.   She cried in Italian, O Signor,
you are not fo ignorant of our language,
.as you would feem to be! you can fpeak
Italian and French too : though we don't
know who you are, we have learned you
are a man of honour. If you would not
underftand our words, you may underftand
a face, which very great perfonages have
been glad to look at : and with that put on
one of the moft enfnaring airs I ever faw.
I don't doubt but your Reverences have
heard of that famous courtefan, and how
the greateft man in Venice was once her
flave.   I was juft going to anfwer her,
when the other lady came up, and pulling off her mafk alfo, faid almoft the fame
things, but with a modefty more graceful
than her beauty, which was moft exquifite, and the moft like the incomparable
Ifyphena I ever faw.   I made them both a
moft refpectful bow, and told them, that
it had been much fafer for me, if I had
kept myfeif ftill unknown, and never feen
fuch dangerous charms. I pronounced
thefe words with an air, that fhewed, that
I was more pleafed with the modefty of the
laft lady, thanthe commanding affurance of
the firft. The courtefan, though a little
nettled at the preference fhe thought I gave
the other, put on a more ferious air, and
faid, fhe had been informed, there was
fomething very extraordinary in my character,

racter, and faid fhe would be glad to hear
more of it by herfelf; that her name was
Favilla, and that fhe lived in fuch a ftreet,
where I fhould find her houfe remarkable
enough. The Bolognian lady, whom your
Reverences knew very well, and who was
then at Venice, on account of the death of
her uncle, one of the fenators, who had left
her all his effects, faid modeftly, if I were to
favour her with a vifit, as fhe had been informed that I was a learned man and a vir-
tuofo, being inclined that way herfelf, fhe
fhould be glad of an hour's converfation
with me on that fubject, telling me her
name, and where fhe lived ; adding, if I
would inform myfelf of her character, I
need not be afhamed of her acquaintance ;
nor, I hope of mine, Madam, fays the
other, thinking fhe had been reflected on by
that word.   It was Monfieur Godart, who,
with a levity peculiar to his nation, had
made the difcovery who I was, though he
knew nothing of me but what paffed fince
I came from Grand Cairo.   I was going to
reply to the ladies, when company came
up, and broke off the difcourfe. I was refolved to fee neither of them, and would
go no more to the affembly, though almoft unavoidably I faw both afterwards.
I inquired into Favilla's character, though
I fcarce doubted of it by what I faw and
heard, and was informed that fhe was an
imperious

imperious courtefan, who had enflaved
feveral perfons of the firft rank, of different nations, and enriched herfelf by their
fpoils : this determined me not to fee her.
But, as Monfieur Godart and myfelf were
walking to fee the town, he brought me
either induftrioufly, or accidentally, by
her door ; fhe was fitting at the window
of one of the moft magnificent palaces in
Venice, (fuch fpoils had fhe reaped from
her bewitched lovers.) As foon as fhe
efpied me, fhe fent a fervant to tell
me, that lady Favila would wifh to
fpeak with me : I made fome difficulty, but Monfieur Godart told me, a
man of honour could not refufe fuch a favour as that ; fo I went in, and Monfieur
Godart with me. The lady received me
with a moft charming agreeable air, much
different from her former affurance, and
conducted me into a moft magnificent a-
partment, leaving Monfieur Godart enter-
taining a very pretty lady, her companion.
Not to detain your reverences too long, when
I would not underftand what fhe meant, fhe
offered me marriage, with the inheritance of
all her effects; I was put to the laft nonplus.
I affured her with a moft profound bow,
that though I was not worthy of fuch a
happinefs, I had an obligation never to
marry. All the blood immediately came
into her face : I did not know what fhe was
                                        going

going to do, but finding her in that diforder, I made another bow, faying, I would
confider further on her propofal; and
walked directly out of the houfe, defigning
to leave Venice as foon as my affairs would
give me leave. Some time after Monfieur
Godart came to me, and told me, he was
forced to do as I did; that the lady was
in fuch an outrageous fury he did not
know what might be the confequence.
Three nights after, as Monfieur Godart
and a young kinfman of his, and myfelf,
were going towards the Rialto, in the dufk
of the evening, four ruffians attacked us
unawares; two of them fet upon me, the
other two attacked Monfieur Godart
and his kinfman; the poor young gentleman was run through the body the firft
pufh; I made fhift to difable one of my
adverfaries, but in doing it, the other
run me through the ribs, but the fword
took only part of my body, and miffing
my entrail,, the point went out on the fide
of my back. Monfieur Godart, who, to
give him his due, behaved with a great
deal of courage and bravery, had killed
one of his men, and wounded the other;
and the ruffians, being difappointed in
their nefarious defigns, fled with the greateft precipetancy, and in a place fo diffipat-
ed and corrupt as Venice, it is very eafiy
to elude difcovery, or the hand of juftice;
after this unexpected rencounter, we re-
                                        tired

tired to our lodgings, where we had our wounds dreffed, and as foon as they would admit of travelling, we fet out for Bologna, for probably any longer ftay might have involved us in greater difficulties.

This is a true and full account of my life hitherto ; whatever is blameable in it I hope your Reverences' will pardon, as I fubmit it entirely to your judgments.

[*Secretary.* As I had the honour to inform you before, we inquired into all thofe facts which he faid happened to him in the company of Monfieur Godart ; which finding to be true, we judged the reft might be fo. We afked him, if he would conduct fome of our miffionaries to that ftrange country he mentioned ; he told us he would : but not willing to truft him entirely, as not knowing what he might do with them, when he had them in unknown countries, we thought fit to give him his liberty firft to go where he would, even out of Italy, with affurances, if he came back of his own accord, we would fend miffionaries along with him. He went to Venice and Genoa abought his concerns, and is now come back, with us ; fo that we believe the man to be really what he profeffes himfelf to be.]

www.ingramcontent.com/pod-product-compliance
Lightning Source LLC
Chambersburg PA
CBHW060539030726
47498CB00004B/1254